CHERYL HOLT

Wicked

Copyright © 2014 Cheryl Holt

All rights reserved under International and Pan-American Copyright Conventions

By payment of required fees, you have been granted the *non*-exclusive, *non*-transferable right to access and read the text of this book. No part of this text may be reproduced, transmitted, downloaded, decompiled, reverse engineered, or stored in or introduced into any information storage and retrieval system, in any form or by any means, whether electronic or mechanical, now known or hereinafter invented without the express written permission of copyright owner.

Please Note

The reverse engineering, uploading, and/or distributing of this book via the internet or via any other means without the permission of the copyright owner is illegal and punishable by law. Please purchase only authorized electronic editions, and do not participate in or encourage electronic piracy of copyrighted materials. Your support of the author's rights is appreciated

No part of this book may be reproduced or transmitted in any form or by any electronic or mechanical means, including photocopying, recording or by any information storage and retrieval system, without the written permission of the publisher, except where permitted by law.

Thank you.
Cover Design Angela Waters
Interior format by The Killion Group
http://thekilliongroupinc.com

PRAISE FOR *NEW YORK TIMES* BESTSELLING AUTHOR CHERYL HOLT

"Best storyteller of the year..."
Romantic Times Magazine

"A master writer..."
Fallen Angel Reviews

"The Queen of Erotic Romance..."
Book Cover Reviews

"Cheryl Holt is magnificent..."
Reader to Reader Reviews

"From cover to cover, I was spellbound. Truly outstanding..."
Romance Junkies

"A classic love story with hot, fiery passion dripping from every page. There's nothing better than curling up with a great book and this one totally qualifies."
Fresh Fiction

"This is a masterpiece of storytelling. A sensual delight scattered with rose petals that are divinely arousing. Oh my, yes indeedy!"
Reader to Reader Reviews

Praise for Cheryl Holt's "Lord Trent" trilogy

"A true guilty pleasure!"
Novels Alive TV

"LOVE'S PROMISE can't take the number one spot as my favorite by Ms. Holt—that belongs to her book NICHOLAS—but it's currently running a close second."
Manic Readers

"The book was brilliant...can't wait for Book #2."
Harlie's Book Reviews

"I guarantee you won't want to put this one down. Holt's fast-paced dialogue, paired with the emotional turmoil, will keep you turning the pages all the way to the end."
Susana's Parlour

"...A great love story populated with many flawed characters. Highly recommend it."
Bookworm 2 Bookworm Reviews

BOOKS BY CHERYL HOLT

WICKED
LOVE'S PERIL
LOVE'S PRICE
LOVE'S PROMISE
SWEET SURRENDER
MUD CREEK
MARRY ME
LOVE ME
KISS ME
SEDUCE ME
KNIGHT OF SEDUCTION
NICHOLAS
DREAMS OF DESIRE
TASTE OF TEMPTATION
PROMISE OF PLEASURE
SLEEPING WITH THE DEVIL
DOUBLE FANTASY
FORBIDDEN FANTASY
SECRET FANTASY
TOO WICKED TO WED
TOO TEMPTING TO TOUCH
TOO HOT TO HANDLE
THE WEDDING NIGHT
FURTHER THAN PASSION
DEEPER THAN DESIRE
MORE THAN SEDUCTION
COMPLETE ABANDON
ABSOLUTE PLEASURE
TOTAL SURRENDER
LOVE LESSONS
MOUNTAIN DREAMS
MY TRUE LOVE
MY ONLY LOVE
MEG'S SECRET ADMIRER
WAY OF THE HEART

PROLOGUE

"There is no money for any of you."

At Mr. Thumberton's announcement, Rose Ralston blanched with surprise.

She'd been told to expect a bequest from poor, deceased Miss Peabody. During the woman's final days, as her condition had deteriorated to the point of no return, she'd been very lucid. She'd been possessed of her faculties.

She'd insisted Rose would receive an inheritance.

Rose hadn't wanted to seem like a vulture, circling with avarice as they'd stumbled to the end, but she'd been counting on that inheritance. She'd built up a dozen fantastic scenarios as to how she'd spend it.

Yet it wasn't likely that Mr. Thumberton would be mistaken. He was a renowned solicitor who served only the most prominent families, and for decades he'd been Miss Peabody's attorney and advisor. He'd handled her business affairs, drafted her contracts, and sued the double-dealing fathers who refused to pay tuition they owed for their daughters to attend Miss Peabody's School for Girls.

He'd written Miss Peabody's will for her. He had to be aware of the terms.

"Excuse me," Rose said, "but I could have sworn you just claimed there is no money for us."

"You're correct," Mr. Thumberton somberly replied.

Rose glanced over at her two friends, Amelia Hubbard and Evangeline Etherton.

The three of them had comprised Miss Peabody's faculty, all coming to the school as students and orphans when they were very young. They'd lived in the dormitories, had grown up playing on the beautiful, manicured grounds. As they'd completed their educations, Miss Peabody had had such faith in them that she'd kept them on as teachers.

Now, at age twenty-five, they'd never resided anywhere else, had never had to establish themselves in the outside world. They weren't even sure they *had* the skills to succeed elsewhere.

For months, they'd been worrying over their plights and pondering what Fate held in store. Ultimately, Miss Peabody had assured them that they needn't fret, that she'd provided for them.

Her promise had eased their anxiety and tempered the sorrow they'd suffered over her passing. Though she'd never been much of a maternal figure, she was the closest thing they'd had to a mother. Stern and fair and blunt, she'd doled out guidance as well as criticism and praise when they were due. She'd done her best, and they were grateful for her tutelage.

She'd never married and had no heirs. Her life had been devoted to her school, to the girls she'd taught. If anyone had been her *family*, it was Rose and Amelia and Evangeline. They were as near to relatives as could be found.

They'd thought to pool their bequests, buy the school, and run it themselves. It was a grandiose idea, and they'd had hundreds of conversations about what they would retain, what they would alter, who would be in charge of what duties. The planning had supplied a flare of optimism during a very dark period.

"I don't wish to question your assertion," Rose tentatively ventured, "or to sound greedy, but as Miss Peabody was failing, she told us we would each receive an inheritance."

"She was very clear about it," Amelia agreed. "We were mentioned in her will."

"I understand," Mr. Thumberton commiserated, "and I apologize for any confusion."

"Did she change her mind about us?" Evangeline asked. "Did she decide we didn't deserve her assistance after all?"

"No, it's just that she..." He paused and sighed, shaking his head as if he was vexed and upset. "She provided for you—but not in the way you were anticipating."

The three women scowled, and Rose queried, "What do you mean?"

"She greatly lamented the fact that she never wed or had a family of her own."

"The school was her family," Evangeline loyally declared. "She always said so."

"That's what she *said*," he pompously retorted, "but when people are facing the end, they often have many regrets."

"She regretted the school?" Amelia inquired.

"No. She simply wondered if she should have made other choices. The notion haunted her—especially that she never had any children. She grew to think every woman should have the chance."

"So...where does that leave us?" Rose asked.

"I have some information for each of you."

He reached into his satchel and pulled out three files filled with papers. As he handed them over, he looked abashed.

"I'm sorry," he said. "I tried to talk her out of it, but one of the difficulties of my profession is that clients don't listen."

Evangeline frowned. "What are you sorry about?"

"She bought you husbands."

Amelia gasped. "She...what?"

"She felt you'd be wasting your lives if you remained spinsters. She thought the three of you should marry, that it would be for the best. She used the proceeds from the estate as dowries."

"Dowries?" Rose stupidly mumbled as if she'd never heard the term before.

"Yes, and they've already been paid."

"I don't want to...to...*marry*." Evangeline hurled the word like an epithet.

"She believed you should," was his unruffled response.

Rose gaped at her file, seeing her name—Rose Ralston—printed in big letters. But there was another name too, and it swept through her with incredible unease. Stanley Oswald.

"This man," she said to Mr. Thumberton, "this Mr. Oswald. I'm supposed to wed him?"

"Yes."

"I've never even met him. How could I?"

"Miss Peabody met him for you. She had his background thoroughly checked and decided the two of you would be a perfect match."

Nervously, Rose peered at Amelia and Evangeline, and they were staring at her in return, their expressions demanding she *do* something. Of the three of them, Rose had always been their leader.

"We assumed," Rose said, "that we would receive money. We had planned to pool our resources, to purchase the school and keep it running."

"There was never any chance of that," he said.

"We could have!" Evangeline insisted.

"The property was mortgaged to the hilt," he stated.

"I thought Miss Peabody owned it free and clear," Amelia said.

"She did—in the distant past. But the entire enterprise was very expensive and many families were negligent about paying tuition. It was a constant problem."

"She took out mortgages to stay afloat?" Rose asked.

"Yes."

"We didn't know. She never mentioned it."

"Well, she wouldn't have, would she? She wasn't the type of

person to air her troubles in public."

"No, she wasn't."

There was a fraught, excruciating silence, then Amelia queried, "What now?"

"The property has been sold to square the debts, with the balance used for your dowries. The facility is closing, so you'll have to notify the students. Over the next month, they either have to head home or to another school. They have thirty days to vacate."

"And what about us?" Evangeline inquired. "What are we to do?"

"You'll have this month to deal with the students, then you'll have a month after that to arrive at your new…situations. Your husbands are expecting you." His cheeks flushed bright red, and he turned to Rose. "Except for you, Miss Ralston. I'm told that your fiancé is elderly, and he's requested you leave right away so the wedding can be held at once."

"She's betrothed me to an old man?" Rose bristled.

"Not *old* precisely. Just…older."

"This is insane," Evangeline muttered. "Miss Peabody is dead, and we've been at her beck and call since we were babies. She can't direct our lives from beyond the grave."

Amelia snorted with disgust. "It certainly appears that she has."

"What if we refuse to comply?" Evangeline asked of Mr. Thumberton. "What if we strike out on our own?"

Mr. Thumberton shrugged. "Then I don't know what will become of you. The dowries are your gift from her. There's nothing else."

Rose scowled. "We'd be tossed out on the road?"

"I wouldn't think it will be that drastic. You have two months to apply for other positions."

"It's the middle of the school term, Mr. Thumberton. How could we find another post so quickly? And there are three of us."

"I'm aware of that fact, Miss Ralston. As I previously mentioned, I tried to talk Miss Peabody out of this scheme."

"Why didn't you?" Evangeline harshly chided.

Rose leaned over and patted Evangeline's hand to calm her. Evangeline had always been excitable. Rose and Amelia liked to go along and get along. Evangeline was the one with a temper, with a spark of mischief, the one most likely to land herself in a jam. She'd never been able to accept consequences or blithely obey ridiculous commands. She argued and dissected every circumstance.

"It's not his fault, Evangeline," Rose said.

"He aided and abetted her in her lunacy."

"I did," he admitted, "to my immense regret, but she was very determined. She felt if she simply gave you the money, you'd spend it and then you'd have nothing. She was buying you security. It was her method of protecting you."

"But...*husbands*." Evangeline actually shuddered.

"Yes, husbands." He frowned. "It's not the end of the world, Miss Etherton. You're not the first women in history to be pushed into arranged marriages. There are many worse conclusions for a female. You're not even related to Miss Peabody. She could have kicked you out the door without a penny in your pocket."

"Yet she didn't," Rose mused.

"Lucky us," Evangeline sarcastically retorted.

"These sorts of unions," he contended, "where the parties are carefully selected, can be extremely successful."

"These men are strangers to us!" Evangeline wailed.

"But not to Miss Peabody," he continued. "She went to a great deal of trouble on your behalves. She picked gentlemen who will complement your personalities, who will furnish you with the futures you deserve."

They were quiet again, stunned, shocked beyond measure. Finally, Amelia gazed at Rose and inquired, "What do you think, Rose?"

"I don't know. It's all so sudden."

"It's an even faster—and more difficult—decision for you, Miss Ralston," he reminded her. "Miss Hubbard and Miss Etherton can dither and debate, but your fiancé has asked us to send word today that you're on your way."

Rose paled. "Today?"

"Yes."

She couldn't believe it, couldn't come to grips with the bizarre turn of events.

She'd been expecting money, a bequest that would have allowed her to carry on in the same condition in which she'd muddled through for years. She'd thought they could buy the school, that they could remodel and decorate and make the place their own, but she could see now that it had been a fool's dream, perpetrated by a trio of inexperienced, naïve ninnies.

Hadn't she secretly wished she could wed and have children? Hadn't she secretly hoped that a dowry would magically appear? She'd never had any prospects and had no relatives who would claim her, so she'd assumed her position as a teacher was her only option.

Miss Peabody had given her a different choice, had opened up a whole new opportunity. Should she refuse the gift that had been bestowed? After all, if she didn't take the husband and the change of situation, what would she do?

Mr. Thumberton had insisted she'd have nothing, and the notion of being without funds or alternatives was terrifying.

"Can I ponder this for a bit?" she asked him.

It seemed a reasonable request, but his reply was too, too infuriating.

"You can have a half hour to confer with your friends," he said. "I'll be waiting for your answer."

1February, 1814

My Dearest Rose,

If you are reading this letter, it means I have finally passed on to my Great Reward. You're most likely grieving for me, but please don't. I lived a long and full life.

In my last days, I led you to believe you would receive a bequest from me. I'm sure you expected a monetary inheritance, and I apologize that I misled you. But I was afraid if you knew the truth of my plan, you would try to talk me out of it. And I could not be dissuaded.

As I sit here facing the end, I have come to regret that I did not marry or have any children. I don't want you to make my same mistake.

I'm certain it will come as a great surprise to learn that I have arranged a marriage for you and used your bequest to pay your dowry. Your future husband's name is Mr. Stanley Oswald. Initially, you may be a tad disturbed to learn that he is quite elderly. However, he is very rich, and old men don't live forever. Many brides would say you are entering into a perfect situation, especially for a woman like you who is very firm in her attitudes and opinions.

I know you will be concerned by what I have done, but please know that I acted with only the best of intentions. I hope you will strive at all times to be the bride Mr. Oswald desperately needs. And please also know that—of all the girls who ever boarded at my school—you were always my favorite.

Your very dearest friend.

Miss Peabody

CHAPTER ONE

"I've gone stark raving mad."

It was the only explanation. Rose glanced around the spacious, pretty bedroom suite to which she'd been escorted, and shuddered with dread.

When she'd still been at the school with Amelia and Evangeline, her choice hadn't seemed real. She might have been speaking lines in a staged play. She'd finally shrugged and thought, *Why not?*

What was there to keep her at the school? It was closing, and if she didn't agree to wed, what would become of her?

She'd have had sixty days to find another situation, and as a woman who'd never lived on her own, she hadn't the foggiest idea how to make such a huge change.

Miss Peabody had understood Rose. She'd recognized how Rose regretted her estrangement from her relatives, regretted the fact that she was so alone. Mr. Thumberton had said Miss Peabody interviewed the candidates, that she'd specifically selected Mr. Oswald to be Rose's husband.

Rose had come to Miss Peabody's when she was four. Her parents had died, and her merciless grandfather had declined to bring her to his home and had promptly shipped her off to Miss Peabody.

During all those years when Rose's family had never contacted her, invited her for a visit, or stopped by to check on her condition, Miss Peabody had been Rose's rock and foundation. She'd never steered Rose in the wrong direction, so Rose had no reason to doubt or fear Miss Peabody's plan.

A husband—at long last! A home of her own. Children. They were boons Rose had never dreamed she would receive.

Throughout the journey to Mr. Oswald's Summerfield estate, she'd counted her blessings. She was so lucky that Miss Peabody had been concerned and had arranged Rose's future! But now that she was on the premises...well...

The suite was spacious and grand, complete with sitting room, bedchamber, and dressing room. The sitting room had a small balcony, and she went over and stepped outside. The rolling hills of the estate stretched to the horizon. It was a warm and sunny afternoon in May—the sky so blue, the grass so green—that her eyes ached from trying to take it all in.

Off to her left, she could see the spires from the church in Summerfield village. Off to her right, a lake shimmered, the water lapping on a sandy shore. Cattle grazed in the pasture. A horse kicked up its heels behind the stables. The scene was so picturesque, she felt she'd fallen into a landscape painting of the perfect afternoon in the English countryside.

She'd arrived earlier than expected, so Mr. Oswald hadn't been there to greet her. He was away from the property and wouldn't return until the next morning.

She was desperate to learn more about him. Was he kind? Was he stern? Did he have a sense of humor? Did he enjoy music or art or books? Was he learned? Was he charming?

Before she'd passed away, Miss Peabody had written Rose a letter, urging Rose to accept the match. She'd claimed it would bring Rose happiness and security, and Rose wanted to believe her. There were just two pesky details that rankled: she hadn't met the man and he was seventy. She hated to suppose looks or vigor could matter so much, but she was a romantic at heart.

In her private moments as a spinster and schoolteacher, when she'd pondered the sort of husband she would like to have, she'd never envisioned an elderly fellow. And she refused to remember Miss Peabody's cryptic comment about how an aged spouse wasn't the worst fate for a young bride, that older men didn't live forever. As the remark wormed its way into her mind again, she shoved away from the balcony and proceeded into the bedchamber.

Her portmanteau was on the bed. She opened it and peered down at her pitiful pile of clothes. There were just her three gray and black work dresses, with their white collars and cuffs at the sleeves. Her shoes and undergarments were sturdy and functional.

None of it was fine enough for the opulent surroundings, and she hoped she wouldn't disappoint Mr. Oswald or shame him with her shabby attire.

She walked to the dressing room and peeked into cupboards that were filled with towels. There was a silver bathing tub in the middle of the floor—a luxury Rose hadn't anticipated and couldn't fathom using.

She stared at the tub, trying to imagine it full of hot, steamy water, her hair piled on her head, her naked self immersed up to her shoulders. But the notion was too fantastic to consider.

A wave of exhaustion swept over her. Too many things had happened too quickly, and she still wasn't entirely convinced she'd made the correct choice—especially now that Mr. Oswald hadn't been present to welcome her. It seemed an ill omen, as if they were off to a bad start.

She went to the wardrobe and retrieved her silk robe. It was the only truly elegant item she'd ever possessed, having been her mother's back in the day when she'd been the favored daughter of Rose's much-loathed grandfather, Lord Sidwell.

Her mother had been charmed by Rose's father, an inappropriate preacher with a missionary zeal. She'd run away and married him without Lord Sidwell's permission, so she'd been disowned and disinherited. The breach had never been repaired.

Her parents had travelled to Africa to distribute Bibles to the natives, where they'd contracted a plague and passed away within a week of each other, leaving Rose stranded in Egypt. Somehow, she'd managed to conceal the robe in her bag, and she'd held on to it as she'd been shipped to England, then to Miss Peabody's School for Girls.

Her parents were dead, her grandfather too. Her Uncle George was now the family patriarch. She'd never met him or her cousins, had never so much as corresponded with any of them. All she had to connect her to them was her mother's robe. She had a vague memory of herself when she was tiny, perched on her mother's lap and gliding her hands across the soft fabric, and occasionally, she thought she could smell her mother's perfume in the fabric. But she was never sure.

Feeling reckless and momentarily wild, she stripped off her clothes. At Miss Peabody's, there had been few chances for privacy, and with modesty expected at all times, she'd rarely had the opportunity to be totally alone and do whatever she liked. She couldn't recall when she'd previously shed every stitch, and there was a heady freedom in the act that surprised her.

She slipped into her robe, relishing how the slinky material slithered over her bare skin. She didn't tie the belt and let the lapels flop open so her front was visible.

In the mirror, she studied herself, and it wasn't vanity to acknowledge that she was pretty.

Her eyes were green, merry and arresting, her face heart shaped and inviting, with two pert dimples curving her cheeks. She was five feet five in her shoes, her body shapely and rounded in all the right spots, and she prayed Mr. Oswald would be pleased with the bride he'd found.

Her hair was an unusual shade of auburn, and when she was

younger, she'd fussed and fumed and hid it under scarves and bonnets. Every other girl in her world had seemed to be blond, but she wasn't, and the odd difference had vexed her.

But as she'd grown older, she'd realized the color was striking and remarkable, and she told herself she'd inherited it from her deceased mother whose features she didn't recollect.

There was a brush on the dresser—another of her mother's belongings. She pulled the pins from her chignon, the lengthy tresses swinging down her back, then she grabbed the brush and began tugging the bristles through her hair. As she wandered toward the bedchamber, she quietly mused, "Oh, I hope he likes me."

"I'm sure he will," a male voice replied. "He's never met a female he didn't try to seduce."

She halted, frowned, her mind struggling to register the fact that someone had spoken. Had she imagined it? It was an ancient mansion. Were there ghosts?

She tiptoed to the door that separated the two rooms and peeked out. Her brush fell to the floor with a muted thump. Frantically, she yanked at the lapels of her robe, tied the belt with a tight knot.

She wasn't hallucinating. A man—a very handsome, very roguish man—had made himself at home in her bedchamber. He lounged on the chair by the bed, slouched down, his legs stretched out.

He was about her same age of twenty-five, but there was a hard edge to him, as if he'd seen trouble in his life, as if he'd persevered through adversity. But there was mischief lurking too, as if he would engage in any tomfoolery and enjoy it very much.

His hair was dark, worn too long and in need of a trim, and his eyes were incredibly blue, his gaze curious and bored. He hadn't shaved so his cheeks were shadowed, giving him a reckless, negligent air.

Attired in a flowing white shirt, tan breeches, knee-high black boots, his color was high, as if he'd been out riding.

He appeared lazy and windswept and dangerous, and she probably should be terrified, but she sensed no menace. He was watching her as intently as she was watching him.

"I believe you've wandered into the wrong room," she sputtered.

"I don't think so," he responded. "This has been *my* room since I was a boy. I'm positive I'm not mistaken."

"No, you're wrong," she firmly said. "The maid brought me here directly from the coach. I'm certain *she* wasn't mistaken. She was very clear. This is my room." She made a shooing motion with her fingers. "You have to leave."

"I could say the same to you."

"Listen, Mr.—"

"Talbot. James Talbot."

"I'm only newly arrived at Summerfield, and I'm not dressed. If you were any sort of gentleman, you'd do as I've requested."

"There's the rub for you, darling. I'm not a gentleman, and I've never aspired to gallant tendencies."

"You sound proud of it."

"I guess I am."

"What type of person would boast of low character?"

"My type, I suppose."

"I say it again. Go away!"

"No."

There was a decanter of liquor on the table next to him, and he poured himself a glass and sipped at the amber liquid. He looked vain and imperious and completely in the right, and she had no idea how to proceed.

As an orphan, then a spinster schoolteacher at an all-girls academy, she'd had very restricted interactions with men. It was a rare occasion when a male crossed her path. She'd never been kissed, had never walked down the lane with a sweetheart. She'd never ordered a man to do something and had him do it.

How did a woman make a man behave? Rose had never been told how it was accomplished. In her humble and somewhat limited opinion, men were obstinate, arrogant, and overbearing. They shouted and blustered and acted however they wished. Women had few weapons to fight against their worst conduct.

She should have hurried into the dressing room and put on her clothes, but she was already sufficiently unclad and didn't want to exacerbate the situation. Her other option was to stomp out, to summon help, but she didn't dare inform the servants that there was a stranger in her room.

She hadn't met Mr. Oswald yet. If he learned of the scandalous exchange, what would he think? Her betrothal would end before it began.

She pulled herself up to her full height and mustered her most condemning expression.

"Mr. Talbot, we're at an impasse."

"Yes, we are."

"I'm not in any condition to receive you."

"I see that."

His hot gaze took a slow meander down her body, lingering at several spots where he had no business lingering, and her cheeks flushed bright red. She'd never been ogled, and she scowled and stood even straighter.

"You must depart," she fumed. "I'll repair myself, and then we'll call on the housekeeper to resolve our quarrel. I'm sure she knows to which rooms we've been assigned."

"I wouldn't agree to that."

"Why not?"

"I don't need that old biddy scolding me because I'm sitting in my own room. Nor do I need her to tell me where my bed is located."

"Mr. Talbot! Please!"

"I love it when a woman begs."

He unfolded himself from the chair. He was six feet tall at least, broad shouldered, trim and fit and vigorous, his skin bronzed from the sun, as if he labored strenuously to earn his living. But his clothes were sewn from an expensive fabric, his boots obviously expensive too, so he wasn't a working man.

Who was he? What was he? If the room was actually his as he kept claiming, he had the superior right to occupancy, so he resided in the house and she'd constantly be bumping into him. The thought of him being on the premises, of having to see him day after day, was more than she could abide.

He came toward her, approaching deliberately, like an African lion stalking its prey. She should have shrieked with alarm and fled, but still, she felt no sense of menace. Clearly, he was trying to scare her, to intimidate her, and in some intuitive part of her being, she realized that she shouldn't let him rattle her.

He continued until they were toe-to-toe. He was standing so close that his thigh touched hers, and she was frozen in place, having no clue as to what he intended or what she should do. A more volatile female probably would have slapped his face and accused him of misconduct, but she'd never been keen on theatrics and couldn't imagine she'd pull it off with any aplomb.

He leaned in, forcing her to take a step back so he had her pressed against the doorframe. She'd never been so near to an adult male—certainly never in such a state of dishabille—and there was an odd and unnoted brazenness flowing in her.

It dawned on her that she wasn't concerned about being undressed, didn't care that her hair was down and brushed out, didn't care that he was gazing at her in a way that shouldn't be allowed.

She wasn't afraid of him and refused to be frightened. Men were ridiculous creatures, which his boorish behavior had blatantly demonstrated.

"You must be the blushing bride," he said.

"If you mean that I am here to marry Mr. Oswald, then yes.

I've come to marry him."

He nodded shrewdly, as if assessing her for an ulterior, furtive purpose.

"Are you sure you should?" he asked.

"That I should what? Marry?"

"Yes."

"No, I'm not sure at all," she bluntly admitted. "But I'm a woman who keeps her word. I agreed to the match, and I shall follow through."

"You're awfully pretty." He smiled a lazy, devil's smile. "But you're awfully old to be a bride."

"I'm only twenty-five," she huffed.

"How is it that no other fellow has snatched you up? How did you end up a spinster and having to settle for Stanley Oswald? Are you a secret drunkard? Are you a harpy? Why haven't you wed?"

"As far as I'm aware, I have no bad habits."

"Every female has *some*."

"Not me," she insisted. "I'm boring and ordinary, and I haven't married because no one ever asked me."

"So lucky Stanley swooped in before anyone else had a chance?"

"Yes, and I'm not usually so crass, but I find you to be extremely rude, and I've been more than courteous. Will you please go away?"

His grin widened. "You should be nicer to me."

"I've been plenty nice. In fact, I've been much *too* nice, and you've drained all my kinder impulses."

"Have I?"

"Yes. Now go."

He tarried for the longest while, studying her, his blue, blue eyes digging deep.

She'd never been so thoroughly evaluated, and the sensation was thrilling in a way she didn't understand. She was warm all over, her pulse racing, the throbbing beat pounding in her stomach. Her nipples had tightened into taut, painful buds.

To her astonishment, he reached out and laid a hand on her waist. With her wearing just the thin robe, it felt as if he was touching her, bare skin to bare skin. Her pulse hammered at an even faster clip.

Cunning and intent, he seemed driven to do...something, and for a wild, shocking moment, she thought he might kiss her. There was a strange charge in the air as if any behavior might suddenly be permitted.

Then he stepped away. A spark of energy had flared between

them, and it sizzled out immediately.

"I'll see you at supper." He hurled the remark like a threat.

"I'm having a tray sent up to my room."

"Pity." He extracted a key from his coat and offered it to her. "You'd better keep this and use it. In this ghastly house, if you don't lock your door, there's no telling who might sneak in."

She grabbed the key and flashed her most stern schoolteacher's frown.

"Goodbye, Mr. Talbot."

"Not goodbye," he said. "We'll be together soon—and often." He spun and started out, muttering to himself, "This is going to be so amusing."

The comment aggravated her. *He* aggravated her, and though she should have kept her mouth shut, she couldn't help saying, "Mr. Talbot?"

He glanced over his shoulder. "Yes?"

"Who exactly are you, and what is your position at Summerfield?"

"Me? Why, I'm no one at all. But trust me, we're about to become very closely acquainted."

He left, and she staggered over to the bed, waited a few seconds as she listened to his boots stomping down the hall. Then she rushed to the door and turned the key in the lock, double-checking to make sure it fit and that it worked.

CHAPTER TWO

"Your home is lovely."

"Yes, it is."

"Thank you for inviting me."

Rose forced a smile and tried to look happy.

She'd had the past week to conjure up images of what Mr. Oswald would be like, but none of them came close to the reality.

He appeared hale and hearty, but still, he was seventy, and she was twenty-five. She emphatically scolded herself to stop fretting over the obvious, to stop concentrating on the negative, but it was difficult to ignore the facts.

He was thin and wiry, bald as a ball, and while his eyes had probably once been a striking shade of blue, they'd faded to gray. Most disconcerting to Rose, he was shorter than she was, only by an inch or two, but it was odd to have to glance down whenever she spoke to him.

It just seemed...peculiar. And jarring. Scraped raw were any foolish romantic notions she'd ever possessed about a handsome swain sweeping her away. From the moment Mr. Thumberton had explained the match, she'd understood that Mr. Oswald was older. She had to let it go, had to focus on the truth of her circumstances.

He was wealthy and settled, and he was prepared to marry her and provide for her for the rest of her life. There was some satisfaction to be had in knowing she would finally be allowed to mingle in the social echelon that would have been hers had her mother not run off with the wrong man. That one, rash act had permanently altered Rose's path, and she'd never envisioned that her social position could be regained.

Few women in her situation were ever offered the chance Mr. Oswald was willing to bestow, and she had to remember to be grateful. So far, she hadn't mustered much appreciation, but once she caught her breath, she was positive she'd be delighted.

They were walking in the park behind the mansion, so it was the perfect opportunity to have some questions answered. She was curious as to how their betrothal had come about.

"How were you acquainted with Miss Peabody?" she asked.

"I'd known her for decades."

"I didn't realize that. Did you ever visit the school? Would I have met you there?"

"No. My first wife, Edwina, was friends with Miss Peabody from when they were girls. Edwina was an early patron when Miss Peabody was starting out."

"Really?"

"Yes."

So...he'd known Miss Peabody forever. His wife had been a childhood friend. How long had Miss Peabody planned Rose's engagement? How long had the idea been brewing as a possibility?

Rose had assumed it was a last-minute arrangement, made as Miss Peabody's health was failing, but now, Rose wasn't so sure. Now, she wondered if the marriage hadn't been percolating for years.

"Miss Peabody has been dead for several weeks," he said. "Do you consider yourself to be in mourning for her?"

She was taken aback by his query. It was crudely posed. "I suppose I'll always mourn her. In many ways, she was a mother to me."

"But she wasn't kin."

"No."

He looked impatient and slightly irritated. "I only raise the issue because I'm in a rush to wed. If you're in mourning, there would have to be a delay."

At his blithe mention of a hasty wedding, she grew weak in the knees, and she missed her step and stumbled. He grabbed her arm to steady her.

"Are you all right?" he said.

"Yes. I'm just..."

She halted, wishing she could expound on the myriad of panicked emotions swirling through her, but she was certain it wouldn't be appropriate to tell him she was terrified.

He'd paid for her coach fare, for the inns where she'd stayed along the road, and she'd accepted his proposal. It seemed a tad late to complain.

She peered out at the beautiful park, the rolling hills beyond, the splendid mansion nestled in the trees. It was all too much to absorb.

"You're just...what?" He sounded impatient again. He was brusque and gruff, and it would definitely require some adjustment on her part to grow accustomed to his mannerisms.

"Everything is happening so fast."

"I never dawdle. I reach a decision and move ahead."

"I see that."

"I've never understood why a person would dilly-dally. I'm not getting any younger, and I need to wed as rapidly as possible."

It was such a cold, pragmatic statement about their pending nuptials, and it hurt her. It made her feel superfluous, as if he could have chosen her or any female, which he absolutely could have done.

Stop it, Rose! You've said you'd do it. You agreed. You knew he was in a hurry.

Still, she couldn't help asking, "Aren't you worried about the fact that we're practically strangers?"

"No. Men and women are always strangers when they marry—whether they've been acquainted for a day or a decade. You'll be my fifth wife. There's no mystery on my end."

"Your fifth?" she wanly inquired.

"Yes."

She forced another smile, but couldn't hold it. It was their initial meeting. Couldn't he have tried to charm her? Couldn't he have pretended he was glad he'd picked her?

He studied her face and grimaced. "I've upset you."

"I wasn't aware that you'd been married so many times. It's a shock to me."

"If I'd told you the truth, I wasn't sure you'd have come."

"What became of all your wives?"

"They died. What would you suppose?"

"Well, of course, they died." She was struggling for calm, for levity. "How silly of me to wonder."

"I've been blessed with longevity, Miss Ralston, and I've been cursed with brides who had frail constitutions. I outlived them all, so on this occasion, I'm determined to settle on someone who is healthy and strong. Miss Peabody swore you had the stamina of a plow horse."

"How flattering." There was more aggravation in her tone than she'd intended.

"Don't mock your youth or vigor. They are precisely why I selected you. It's too late for me to fool with weaklings or ninnies. Miss Peabody promised you would surprise me on both counts."

"I hope I can live up to her high opinion."

"I hope you can too." He clasped her hand and patted it. "In all my marriages, I've only ever sired one child, and he passed away years ago."

"I'm sorry to hear that."

"So that is why you've been summoned. I have no time to

waste and need an heir—as quickly as it can be managed. In exchange, I will give you all this." He gestured at the manicured grounds, the grand manor. "It's a fair bargain, don't you think?"

"Yes," she hesitantly concurred, not knowing what else to say.

"Heed me, Miss Ralston. I'm older than you and more experienced in these sorts of affairs. This is the best conclusion for you. After you've reflected on it, you'll see that I'm right."

"I'm sure I will."

They'd arrived at the house, at the steps that led up onto the rear verandah. It was a beautiful day in early summer, and the drawing room windows were open. Male laughter drifted out, and a merry tune was being played on the pianoforte.

Mr. Oswald frowned and muttered, "Those scalawags. They're home from the army and at loose ends. No doubt they're drinking all my liquor and smoking all my cigars."

"Who is visiting?"

"Two of the most disreputable scapegraces who were ever born. You'll meet them soon enough. Unfortunately." He guided her up the stairs. "If you'll excuse me, I'd better chase them off."

Just that abruptly, he walked away, leaving her alone.

He stomped inside. She wanted to tag along, wanted to ascertain who was home from the army, but she'd definitely been dismissed, so she didn't dare follow.

Yet she was dreadfully curious.

She'd spent an hour with Mr. Oswald and hadn't gleaned any information of value. If she'd been a weepy type, tears might have flowed. But she wasn't weepy. Nor was she prone to melancholy.

When she'd agreed to Miss Peabody's scheme, there had been no guarantees of love or affection. There had only been the prospect of marriage and fiscal security, and they were boons that couldn't be discounted.

Eager to wash and rest a bit, she started across the verandah, but she couldn't resist peeking in the window to the drawing room as she passed. There were two men present. Why was she not surprised to discover that one of them was James Talbot?

He slouched on a sofa, drinking hard spirits. A handsome blond man who was probably his same age was seated at the pianoforte. They looked lazy and bored.

Since his unexpected appearance in her bedchamber the prior evening, she'd tried to pretend he hadn't been there. She'd been dying to ask someone about him, but couldn't figure out how to innocently inquire.

He'd studied her as if he knew things about her she didn't know. He'd alluded to Mr. Oswald with a derogatory comment about his being a seducing libertine. Yet she couldn't envision Mr.

Oswald as a roué. He hadn't seemed flirtatious in the least, and Rose had no idea how to find out the truth of the matter.

Was it any of her business? She was quite sure a husband could act however he liked, and she didn't see how she—who was just beginning her official position as fiancée—had any standing to question him as to his personal habits or to complain over conduct of which she didn't approve.

She heard Mr. Oswald inside. "Why are you wastrels in my parlor? Didn't I tell you to keep yourselves busy this afternoon?"

"We are busy," Mr. Talbot replied.

"Doing what?" Mr. Oswald barked. "You've helped yourself to the liquor, and I've learned from past experience that—with Lucas in residence—you'll consume it all before you depart for London."

The blond man's grin was as devilish as Mr. Talbot's. "You're completely right, Mr. Oswald. I'd offer to pay you for it, but you've always been so generous. I wouldn't want to insult you."

"Don't be smart," Mr. Oswald snapped at him.

"I wouldn't dream of it, sir."

Mr. Talbot and the blond man, Lucas, shared a mocking toast, and Mr. Talbot said to Mr. Oswald, "Are you pleased with your bride?"

"She'll do."

"High praise indeed," Mr. Talbot retorted.

He was sitting near the window, and he glanced out to the verandah to the exact spot where Rose was loitering and eavesdropping. He stared directly at her, as if he'd known she was there the entire time.

She blanched and fled.

"Have you managed to scare her off?" James asked Stanley. "I saw you walking with her. Is she staying or has she the good sense to run as fast and far as she can?"

"There are worse places to end up than here at Summerfield," Stanley pompously intoned.

"I can't think of any."

"Ah…family," Lucas chided. "It's so nice to be back in England."

"Shut up, Lucas," Stanley fumed. "I'm in no mood for your mouth today."

Lucas Drake was James's best friend, his school chum and cohort during their decade in the army.

James had joined to escape Stanley. Lucas had been forced to join by his father who viewed him as a useless wretch and who'd felt the army would correct his incorrigible ways. It hadn't. He was even more irredeemable now—if that was possible.

"Will she marry you?" James pressed.

"Why wouldn't she?" Stanley answered. "The dowry has been paid, and I'm not about to give it back."

Stanley was incredibly vain, and in his dealings with women, he was oblivious.

"Did you even bother to propose?"

"Why would I?"

"She's a young woman, Stanley. They're all romantics at heart."

"Romance, bah!" Stanley snapped. "I've had all the romance in my life that one man should have to tolerate."

"A proposal would have made her happy," James insisted.

"She'll be plenty happy at Summerfield. If you'd ever visited that dismal school where she's been locked away all these years, you'd understand that she recognizes how lucky she is."

"A bit of wooing wouldn't have killed you. You could at least act as if you're glad she's here."

"I am bloody glad."

"But is Miss Ralston? She looked fairly miserable to me."

Lucas added, "And terrified."

"I'm doing her an enormous favor," Stanley claimed. "She's realizes that I am."

"Well then," Lucas smirked, "it should work out swimmingly."

Stanley ignored Lucas's sarcasm. "It *will* work out. If I'd had any doubt, I wouldn't have brought her to the estate."

"Was her dowry worth the trouble?" Lucas asked.

"No. It was a pittance, but then, I'm not marrying her for her dowry."

"Why *are* you marrying her?" Lucas inquired. "I still can't wrap my head around it."

"To sire an heir," Stanley fumed. "Try to focus, Lucas. I shouldn't have to explain these rudimentary facts to you over and over again."

"I just can't hold on to the idea, sir. The notion of little ones racing through the halls, with you bouncing them on your knee, is beyond my limited imagination."

"Mine too," James agreed.

"Lucas," Stanley seethed, "I've had about all of your charming company I can abide in a single sitting. Don't you have activities you could pursue this afternoon? Ride to the village and tumble a tavern wench or something."

"I tumbled her last night. She wasn't any fun."

Stanley glowered at Lucas, but of course, his fury had no

effect. Lucas had constantly lived down to his father's low expectations. Stanley's disdain couldn't begin to compare.

Stanley turned his glare to James. "Didn't I ask you not to drag him home with you?"

"Yes, and I specifically told him he wasn't welcome. He's never listened to me."

"No, I never have," Lucas heartily concurred. "Besides, once I heard you were marrying, Mr. Oswald, I was determined to gaze upon your bride with my own two eyes. It was a sight I couldn't miss."

Lucas could push Stanley just so far, then Stanley would have enough of him. The moment arrived swiftly.

"Get out of here, you annoying scoundrel," Stanley raged, "or I'll take a switch to you."

"Do you think you could?" Lucas didn't appear overly worried. "You're quite advanced in age—and I'm quite a bit bigger—since your previous attempt."

In light of Lucas's insouciance, he'd received many, many whippings in his life. Stanley was just one in a long line of people who'd doled out punishment during Lucas's formative years, but the castigations had simply made Lucas even more recalcitrant.

Stanley's glower deepened. "Don't assume—because you're twenty-five and have wasted a decade in the army—that I can't give you the licking you thoroughly deserve."

"It's nice to see you again too, sir." Lucas rose to his feet. "I'll be back for supper."

"Oh, good," Stanley facetiously beamed. "I'll be on pins and needles until then."

"I know you will be. No table is complete without me."

Lucas sauntered out, and James stayed on the sofa, lounged on the arm, listening to Lucas leave. He watched as Stanley went over to the sideboard and poured himself a drink.

"I have never understood your affection for that rude oaf," Stanley said.

James shrugged. "I like him. I always have."

"I have no idea why."

Actually, James was friends with Lucas because Lucas had been kind when James was a boy.

James was an orphan who'd come to live at Summerfield when he was a toddler. Yet as far as he was aware, he wasn't related to Stanley. Though James could never fathom why, Stanley had sent James to the best schools to rub elbows with the sons of the elite. But he hadn't fit in. He'd had no family connection to claim, no exalted name that would have impressed the other students.

In the heated atmosphere of the boarding school, he'd been

bullied and taunted over the obvious fact that he didn't belong. Yet Lucas—who liked to offend and do the unexpected—had glommed on to James, and the harder the other boys had tried to make James an outsider, the closer James and Lucas had grown.

Now, as adult men, they were too attached to be separated. Their experiences in the army had seen to that. James was the stable one, the steady one, and Lucas was a total mess and bungler who needed James's camaraderie just as James had needed Lucas's all those years ago.

James was nothing if not loyal. It was one of the few positive traits he possessed. Not that he'd explain as much to Stanley. Plus, he loved how thoroughly Lucas could aggravate Stanley. It was a joy to behold.

"You've spoken with Miss Ralston?" Stanley plopped into the chair across from James.

"Yes. You gave her my bedchamber, and I barged in without realizing she was there. You might have warned me."

"I wanted you to surprise her. I wanted to find out if she'd react."

"She reacted, all right. I'm lucky I didn't get a slap in the face for my efforts."

"So she's feisty, is she?"

"Definitely."

"What else did you notice about her? I would hear your honest opinion."

"Pretty. Foolish, like all women."

"What else?" Stanley pressed. "You must have observed more than that."

James had observed plenty, but he was hesitant to share his views with Stanley.

When Stanley had lured him home from the army, when he'd made the hilarious announcement that he was marrying again, James had been greatly humored. Now that he'd met Miss Ralston, he was simply confused.

With that wild auburn hair and those expressive green eyes, she was stunning. He felt she deserved much more than a cold, unhappy union with Stanley, but James didn't know her at all. How could he judge what she truly sought from the match?

No matter what her situation, though, he hardly thought Stanley should be the cure. Then again, if she could deliver the desperately needed heir, she'd be set at Summerfield forever. Wasn't such a boon worth it? Any female in the world would likely leap at the chance.

James didn't think Miss Ralston should sacrifice herself, but then, he loathed the estate.

He'd been brought to Summerfield, rescued from an orphanage in London, by Stanley's first wife, Edwina. Supposedly, she'd been lonely and had yearned for a child to keep her company. But why James? Of all the orphans in the kingdom, why had he been chosen?

Stanley had been maddening in his refusal to explain, so James occupied a strange position at Summerfield. He wasn't acknowledged as kin, but everyone assumed him to be.

Rumors abounded that he was Stanley's by-blow from a secret affair, but Stanley had never affirmed or dispelled the gossip, and James couldn't figure out what to believe. He and Stanley didn't look anything alike, not in facial features or stature, so there was no physical resemblance to provide any clues. And there was certainly no similarity of personality.

Stanley had welcomed James into his life, had paid for James's education, had bought his commission in the army. James viewed Summerfield as his home, but what did that mean?

He had no genuine bond with Stanley. Not one that Stanley would admit anyway. He constantly teased James with sly innuendo about James's past, about his parents' identities, about how Stanley knew precisely what James was dying to know.

As a boy, James had been frantic to learn who he was, so Stanley had manipulated him in a thousand small ways, but as the years had sped by, Stanley's power and influence had waned. Especially with James having been in the army for so long.

His ties to Summerfield and to Stanley had worn thin to the point of snapping. The least little incident could sever them. That's what James liked to tell himself. The reality was more complicated than that.

"She's very bright," James ultimately said of Miss Ralston, remembering her refined speech and gracious manners. "You'll never be able to trick her."

"Leave it to me."

"I wish you'd reconsider."

"Well, I'm not going to. What is your answer? Will you help me or not?"

"There has to be some other way."

"You think I haven't reflected? You think I haven't dithered and debated and torn out my hair?"

"Is that where it all went? You tore it out?"

"Don't be smart," Stanley said again as he had to Lucas.

James sighed. "It would be so much easier if she was stupid."

"Stupid! If she was, she'd pass on her insipid traits to my child, and I'd wind up with a dunce for a son. Why would I want that?"

"Why would you want any of this? It can't be worth it to

deceive her as you're planning."

"I can't let Oscar inherit."

Oscar was Stanley's only brother, a pious, cruel, and sanctimonious vicar whom Stanley couldn't abide and whom James detested. There were hundreds of people who relied on Summerfield for their income and employment, and Oscar was pompous and unbending. If he eventually became the owner of Summerfield, it would be a tragedy for all.

"It's too bad you couldn't have been a tad more fertile," James said.

"And it's too bad I've lowered myself to have you as an ally."

James shrugged. "You have to pick your partners where you find them."

"I certainly do." Stanley sipped his drink, watching James with those shrewd, cutting eyes of his. James could barely resist squirming. Finally, Stanley asked, "What is your reply? Are you in or out?"

"Must I decide now?"

"Yes."

"I don't know what's best."

"I told you: If you assist me, I'll give you a thousand pounds. More importantly, I'll give you all the information I have about your parents."

"You liar. You never would. If you came clean, your hold over me would be broken."

"Yes, it would, but you'd have what you crave: your past, your history, your kin. You've always claimed you'd jump any hurdle to discover the details. Will you?"

James stared and stared, eager to get up and walk out, eager to tell Stanley to use some other sap for his dirty work. But the sad fact was that he needed the money, and he was anxious to unravel the secrets only Stanley could provide. Those secrets were the only thing Stanley possessed that could force James to acquiesce. And there was Miss Ralston to consider.

She was remarkable, but naïve and trusting, and she'd journeyed to Summerfield with good intentions. She was extremely brave, traveling so far merely to wed an elderly ingrate. James was amazed by her courage. He wouldn't have dared, but she was ready and willing to proceed.

Stanley was cruel and manipulative and driven to have his own way. If James refused to help, Stanley would bribe someone else. Who might it be?

The notion of what might happen to Miss Ralston, of what Stanley might *let* happen to her, was too disconcerting.

Wasn't it best if James agreed? If he participated, he'd know the outcome. If he didn't, the possibility of a catastrophic conclusion was enormous, and the damage to Miss Ralston would be incalculable.

"All right," he muttered. "I'll do it."

"I knew I could convince you."

"I'll do it for *her*, though. Not for you. For her."

"Aren't you a bloody knight in shining armor?" Stanley snorted. "Persuade yourself in any fashion you wish. We'll start tomorrow."

"I can't wait."

"Neither can I."

Stanley stood and strutted out. He was smug, cocksure, positive that he controlled the whole world and could render any ending that suited his purposes.

"Poor Miss Ralston," James murmured to himself. "The poor, poor woman."

Suddenly, he felt as if he was choking. On Stanley's spite. On Stanley's malice. On his own idiotic complicity.

He leapt up and headed for the stables to saddle a horse. Hopefully, Lucas was in the tavern in the village, and they could drink themselves silly until dawn. Perhaps by then, James would forget the entire sordid, disgusting arrangement.

CHAPTER THREE

"Brandy?"

"You know I don't drink alcoholic beverages. I must set an example for the congregation. Why must you constantly torment me about it?"

Stanley glared at his brother, Oscar, and smirked. "Maybe if you tippled hard spirits now and again, you wouldn't be such a sanctimonious ass."

Oscar pursed his lips, which made his face look like a wrinkled prune. "If you summoned me to the house simply to insult and offend, I'll go."

"Feel free." Stanley waved to the door. "You're not chained to the furniture."

Of course Oscar didn't leave. He was always having a tantrum, threatening to stomp out in a huff, but he never did. Besides his being a pretentious dolt, he was the worst penny-pincher. He was more than happy to dine at someone else's table, to stay late and burn someone else's candles.

They were in Stanley's library, with Stanley seated at his desk and staring at Oscar across the long swath of mahogany. It was a petty vanity, but Stanley couldn't help it. There was no spot at the estate that better underscored their disparate positions than Stanley's large desk and the fact that *he* sat behind it and Oscar didn't.

Supper was over, the guests scattered to talk and mingle. But with Oscar in residence, no one would dare engage in any of the devil's handiwork such as cards or singing. And dancing was out of the question.

Oscar was a stick in the mud, a douser of fun, a complete and utter bore, but he was the vicar at the parish church, so Stanley had to entertain him occasionally—such as when he was introducing his potential bride to the important people in the neighborhood. Oscar couldn't have been excluded.

He was Stanley's only sibling, younger by fifteen years, and from the day of his birth he'd been prickly and unpleasant. They were both bald and shared the same short height, but while Stanley was slender and spry from work and activity, Oscar was lazy and fat as a sow, growing obese from the largesse bestowed on him through his position as vicar.

With Oscar's nasty ways and vindictive character, he was the very last person who should have been a minister, but Stanley refused to pay Oscar's bills. The parish was rich due to Stanley's efforts at Summerfield, so Oscar was well-off financially, and Stanley never had to lay out a farthing of support.

Oscar would like to have more money, but he was too proud to ask for any. For all his pretense and posturing about the saintly state of poverty, he liked his material possessions as much as the next man, and he would have bled the estate dry if Stanley had let him. Oscar was greedy and covetous, always casting his sly gaze around as if assessing worth and trying to decide how wealthy he'd be once Stanley died.

Stanley planned to live forever merely to spite Oscar, merely to ensure that Oscar would never inherit Summerfield.

Their father had been very astute. He'd recognized his sons' strengths and weaknesses and had left the entire place to Stanley, having grasped that Oscar would have been an awful steward. Their father had pushed Oscar into the ministry where he could wallow in the bounty of parishioners rather than earn his own income.

Summerfield had belonged to the Oswalds for two centuries, and Stanley didn't have anyone to whom he could bequeath the property. The whole bloody family had barely procreated. There were no uncles or distant cousins. There was just Stanley and Oscar.

Stanley had had the one son with Edwina—Charles—who'd been a pathetic boy with a pathetic moral constitution. The moment he was old enough, he'd fled to London and taken up with actresses and gambling—so he'd been promptly disowned.

Ultimately, he'd gotten himself shot by an angry husband, killed while pursuing a torrid affair with the man's wife. Since the day that terrible news had arrived, Stanley had never spoken Charles's name again, and despite Stanley's exhaustive efforts with Edwina and all the brides that followed, Charles remained the sole child Stanley had ever sired.

Oscar had performed no better. After having wed three times himself, his only claim to parentage was his eighteen-year-old stepdaughter, Veronica. With Veronica's mother deceased, Oscar was saddled with the girl's care and upbringing.

She was a spoiled, annoying menace, and after listening for decades to Oscar rail over how Stanley had failed in his raising of

Charles, it was delightful to see that Oscar had failed miserably too. Oscar hoped to marry her off and constantly hinted that Stanley should dower her.

But if Veronica had a dowry, she'd be able to convince some hapless fellow to marry her, and Stanley wouldn't play such a cruel trick on any unsuspecting man.

"I suppose you're determined to wed," Oscar said.

"Yes."

"We'll be saddled with Miss Ralston whether we wish it or not."

"Yes."

"Should you pass away, and there is no child from the union—and considering your history, that will likely be the case—what will be done with her?"

"I'll provide for her in my will."

"Out of the estate?"

"Of course out of the estate, you idiot. From where else would the money come?"

Oscar's sour expression grew even more disagreeable. Though he avoided discussions of birthrights and legacies, he viewed himself as the heir apparent and found every expenditure by Stanley to be a squander of his own fortune.

"And if," Oscar seethed, "I feel you shouldn't proceed, I imagine my opinion will be discounted."

"Not only discounted but completely ignored."

"You'll leave me to pick up the pieces."

"As if you could. You're a total incompetent. I'll make sure my affairs are arranged so you won't be in charge. The last thing I need is you mucking up my funeral."

"This is so like you, Stanley, so absolutely typical."

"What's that? That I'm marrying?"

"Yes. You're deliberately cheating me out of my inheritance."

"If I have a son, there will be no cheating involved. He'll be my heir."

Oscar smirked. "Why must we maintain the pretense?"

"What pretense is that?"

"We've all heard the rumors—even at the rectory."

A deadly silence fell, and Stanley let it fester before he asked, "What rumors would those be?"

"Your prior wife was extremely vocal in voicing her complaints about you."

"And they were…?"

"Everyone knows you can't sire a babe, Stanley. It's hardly a secret."

"Are you accusing me of impotence?" Stanley exuded calm and

disinterest, though a wiser man would have noticed the ire in his gaze. A wiser man would have shut the hell up.

Oscar chuckled meanly. "Let's just say that if Miss Ralston suddenly turns up with child, there will be whispers of an immaculate conception."

Stanley leapt up so quickly that his chair toppled over. He was around the desk in an instant, his hand on Oscar's throat. He squeezed, cutting off Oscar's air, and Oscar gasped for breath and pried at Stanley's fingers.

"Listen to me, you pious little shit," Stanley fumed. "I allowed you to remain at Summerfield because Father demanded I be kind to you. I swore I would be, and I take my vow seriously. But I don't think people would care if I decided I've done more than enough and you've overstayed your welcome."

Oscar shoved Stanley away and rose to his feet. They were toe-to-toe, eye to eye, but Oscar had always been a coward and was too gutless to throw a punch.

"I want what's mine," he whined. "You own everything, and you lord it over me like a king. It's only fair that I receive my share, and here at the very end, a stranger is jumping in line ahead of me."

"Well, you irritating gnat, perhaps I'll drop dead planting a babe in Miss Ralston's belly. I'm certain my poor heart won't be able to stand the strain."

"I'm a man of the cloth," Oscar huffed. "How dare you be so crude in my presence?"

"Should I expire while sawing away between her shapely thighs, I'll instruct the butler to send you a note right away so you can be the first to know the method of my passing." He whipped away and went to sit behind the desk. He straightened his coat, his cravat, and flashed a malevolent grin. "Now then, I've extended sufficient courtesy for one evening. Find that annoying tart you call a daughter and get your ass out of my house."

"It will be wonderful to have a woman's touch at Summerfield. I'm so glad Uncle Stanley is marrying again."

As she told the lie, Veronica Oswald smiled at Miss Ralston.

"How long has he been a widower?" Miss Ralston inquired.

"A decade? More? He'd never admit it, but he's been very lonely."

Veronica thought nothing of the sort.

Stanley Oswald was a vindictive cur who never considered anyone but himself. He controlled and nagged and berated, and he'd never had a kind word for Veronica.

Her mother had wed Oscar when Veronica was five, so she'd been living in the vicarage forever. She and Stanley had always loathed each other. She recognized his penchant for malice and manipulation, and he recognized her lack of morals and flair for duplicity. While most people at Summerfield saw her as winsome and remarkable, he saw to her rotten core.

She detested her stepfather, Oscar, even more than she detested Stanley. She hated his pious posturing and fussy manner, and no matter how fervidly he scolded, she would never be the modest, humble daughter he demanded. On the outside, she pretended to be, but deep down, she was very wicked.

Oscar didn't get it, but Stanley did, and that's why she despised him.

Throughout supper, she'd been dying to speak with Miss Ralston alone so she could delve into her past. They were walking in the garden, Veronica feigning friendship, when in reality, the last thing she wanted was a fetching female on the property.

With her black hair, violet-colored eyes, and curvaceous body, Veronica was the prettiest girl in the neighborhood. All the boys doted on her—well, doted as much as they could with Oscar being her father—and she didn't relish any competition.

Veronica was eighteen, and Miss Ralston a very mature twenty-five, but still, the other woman seemed very grand. At the supper table, all the guests kept sneaking glances at her, particularly James and Lucas, and Veronica was determined that neither of them notice Miss Ralston at all.

It had been an eternity since James and Lucas had had a furlough from the army, and she'd been desperately waiting for them to return and enliven the place. Years earlier, she'd decided to marry one of them, and she was finally old enough. She didn't have a dowry, but she'd been whispering with her housemaid and had learned a dozen ways she could force a marriage.

Veronica wasn't averse to trying any of them. In her opinion, any ruse that could extract her from Oscar Oswald's dreary home was worth it.

"Uncle Stanley tells me you were a schoolteacher," Veronica said.

"Yes, I was."

"It must have been exciting to...*work*."

"I wouldn't call it exciting. Most times, it was rather dull."

"But to earn your own salary! How exotic of you."

Miss Ralston chuckled. "I guess it was exotic—especially when we women have such limited choices."

"Where are you from? Who is your family?"

"No one you'd know."

"Are you sure? My stepfather travels a good deal in his ministry."

She was fishing for information that Miss Ralston seemed disinclined to provide, which was infuriating. There'd been no mention of her history, and people were abuzz over where Stanley had found her. Veronica wouldn't be surprised to discover that Miss Ralston had had a scandalous past.

Stanley needed a fertile bride, and Veronica was convinced he'd picked a doxy for the part. In her discussions with her housemaid, the girl had confided that a loose woman was more likely to conceive, a virtuous woman less likely.

From how her stepfather harangued at the pulpit, Veronica would have thought it was the other way around, that a virtuous female would get the baby she deserved, but to Veronica, the world never furnished what a person expected.

She lied and cheated and stole, and she had plenty of fun misbehaving. She couldn't imagine embracing the tedious existence Oscar touted as a goal.

"I'm an orphan," Miss Ralston said. "My parents died when I was small."

"I'm very sorry to hear it."

Miss Ralston shrugged. "It was a long time ago."

They were approaching the manor, and up on the verandah, James stepped outside.

"There's James," Veronica gushed without remembering to hide her interest.

"Are you acquainted with Mr. Talbot?"

"Yes. Have you met him?"

"Briefly, but I didn't catch his connection to the household."

"He doesn't have one, I don't think. Stanley rescued him from an orphanage in London when he was a baby."

"Mr. Oswald did that?" Miss Ralston sounded skeptical.

"Yes."

"Why?"

"To keep his wife company. I guess she was lonely."

"So...he's not kin to Mr. Oswald?"

"No."

They reached the verandah, but James had already come down and sneaked off into the garden, which was so aggravating.

Since he and Lucas had arrived back from Spain, James hadn't spent two seconds with Veronica. During her adolescence, he'd scarcely noticed her, but she was all grown up now and eager for an intimate relationship to commence.

Oscar was sequestered in the library with Stanley, so it was the perfect time to have a few private minutes with James. But first, she had to be shed of Miss Ralston.

"It was lovely to meet you," she falsely said.

"And to meet you."

"I hope we'll be friends," Veronica fibbed.

"As do I. It will be wonderful to have a companion in the neighborhood. I'll look forward to your visits."

Veronica escorted her up the stairs and into the parlor, nearly pushing her through the door in her haste to escape. Then she slipped out and raced into the garden. Off in the shadows she spotted the glowing tip of a cheroot, and she followed the scent of smoke to where James was lurking in the grass.

"Hello, stranger," she cooed as she sashayed up.

"Veronica."

"Where have you been? I've hardly seen you since you returned."

"I've been busy."

"With what?"

He stared at her, moonlight gleaming off his hair, making his blue eyes sparkle like diamonds.

He didn't answer her question, but asked instead, "Why are you out here by yourself? Oscar would have a fit if he knew you were with me."

"He won't find out. Besides, I'm eighteen. It's not his business if I talk to you."

The summer would be thrilling. She and James would flirt and tease, and ultimately, he would propose. Yet if she couldn't get him to agree to be alone with her, how would they ever take matters to the next level?

"I have a lot on my mind, Veronica," he said. "I don't want any trouble with you."

"Who's stirring trouble? We're just chatting."

"In the garden, in the dark. I'm not in the mood to tangle with Oscar."

"Let me have a puff of your cheroot."

"No."

"I can smoke. I'm not a child anymore."

"No, you're not, and that is precisely the problem."

She beamed with mischief. "You've noticed that I've grown up, have you?"

"Oh, I've definitely noticed."

Up on the verandah, a door opened, and suddenly, her stepfather called, "Veronica! Where are you? We're leaving."

James motioned toward the stairs and mouthed, "Go."

She hesitated, pretending she might not, pretending she might linger and be caught with him, but his steely frown informed her that she'd pushed too far.

"Goodbye," she whispered. She flashed her most enticing grin, then flounced off, giving her hips an extra sway to emphasize her shapely backside.

"I'm sorry no one bothered to introduce us."

"So am I."

Rose smiled at the handsome blond man she knew only as Lucas. He smiled in return, appearing much too charming, much too amiable.

"You won't swoon because I'm being forward, will you?"

Rose chuckled. "I'll try not to."

"A fellow can never be sure with females. I've spent enough time in London ballrooms to have learned many of the absurd rules of etiquette."

"And what are they?" Rose asked.

"A man should never brazenly introduce himself. He must have someone else intervene—someone who knows the lady and can vouch for his stellar character."

"I'm told that's important."

"It's a great breach to forge ahead, but I figured you could stagger through."

"I would hope so."

"In this house, if I waited for people to remember their manners, I'd be ninety years old before it was accomplished." He took her hand and made a very polite, very proper bow over it. "Lucas Drake, at your service, Miss Ralston."

Her heart literally skipped a beat. "Lucas...Drake?"

"Yes. Of the very lofty, very pretentious, very patronizing Sidwell Drakes. No doubt you know of us. Please say you do. If I have to tell my father, George, Lord Sidwell, that you haven't heard of his exalted self, I can't predict how he'll bear up."

"No," she lied. "I'm not acquainted with your family."

"How awful of you not to pretend."

"I guess I need to develop some guile."

"You certainly do—if you expect to swim in this ocean of sharks. You're much too nice. You'll be eaten alive."

A young lady hailed him from across the room, and he smiled at Rose again. He was such a charismatic rogue, but he was fully aware of his allure. She imagined he'd broken hearts all over the kingdom. What girl could resist such a devil?

"The vicar has departed." He murmured the news to Rose as if they were conspirators. "With him having left, we can start dancing."

"He doesn't approve of dancing?"

"He doesn't approve of any frivolity, so we have to behave until he's gone. Then the fun can begin." He stepped away. "I promised to help move the furniture in the parlor to clear the floor. When there's dancing, I usually play the pianoforte—I know all the bawdy songs—but you must drag me away at least once so I can be your partner."

"I will," she lied again.

His smile became even more beguiling, and he swept off. She stood, frozen in place until he vanished around the corner, then she slipped out the French windows onto the verandah and fled to the garden.

She wasn't sure where she was headed. Reeling with emotion, she couldn't decide whether to be furious or humored. But why would she feel anything at all? What was Lucas Drake to her?

Her cousin, that's what.

The old Lord Sidwell had been her grandfather, the man who'd disowned her mother and dumped Rose on Miss Peabody when she was four. The current Lord Sidwell was her uncle, the man who'd never contacted her, who'd never visited, who'd never invited her for a single holiday.

Lucas Drake was so oblivious and self-centered that he didn't note their close relation. It was outrageous. It was humiliating. It was galling.

Had Lucas never been told about Rose's mother who was his aunt? Had he never been told he had a cousin? If he'd been informed, had he never been apprised of Rose's name? Did he know her name—Rose Ralston—but was so maddeningly dense that he didn't grasp their connection?

She was in a blind temper, marching along in the dark and angrier than she could ever recollect being. What with her having agreed to wed Mr. Oswald, she had enough on her plate. Must she deal with Lucas Drake too?

When he'd provided his surname, she should have curtly and succinctly notified him of precisely who she was, but she'd been too stunned to speak up.

Having discovered his identity, she would find it excruciating to socialize, and she wasn't certain she could be civil. Rumor had it that he and Mr. Talbot were to leave shortly for London. How soon would that be?

She rounded a corner and, to her horror, crashed into a man who was approaching from the opposite direction. She hit him so hard that she nearly knocked him down.

"Oh, oh, pardon me," she gasped. "I'm sorry. I'm so sorry. Are you all right?"

"You're in quite a hurry, aren't you?"

"I wasn't watching where I was going. I'm sorry," she repeated.

The man straightened, and he was rubbing his chest where her forehead had smacked into him. As she peered up into his face, she was vexed to see that it was James Talbot.

He'd attended the supper, and they had studiously avoided each other through the entire ordeal, a boon for which she'd be eternally grateful. Now he'd turned up—like a bad penny—to plague her.

"Miss Ralston"—he was grinning—"what's the rush? Are you running away?"

"No, I'm not running away. Don't be ridiculous."

"You're just out for a leisurely stroll?"

"Well...yes."

"For a moment there, you looked ready to commit murder."

"I was a bit...undone by a comment I heard inside." Instantly, she realized it was a stupid admission.

He scowled. "What comment was that?"

"It was nothing."

"You can tell me. Were you insulted?"

"No, no, don't be silly, and don't worry about me." She forced a smile, struggling to appear a tad less deranged. "I'm merely a little distressed over the changes I've endured the past few weeks. I'm not handling all of this with much aplomb. No one could, I dare say. But...I'm fine. Really. I'm fine."

She was babbling, and he was staring at her with a concerned expression that was unnerving. She could barely keep from flinging herself into his arms and weeping.

She was sad and disheartened and weary. Why was life so difficult? Why was there never any reward for effort and toil? She was a good person, with high moral standards who always tried her best.

She'd had no part in her parents' folly, yet she'd been punished for it every day. She'd been an unloved orphan, then a spinster schoolteacher, with Miss Peabody being the only one kind enough to offer assistance.

A daughter of the exalted Drake family, she'd had her fortunes descend to the point where she had to wed an elderly stranger to gain some security. It was so unfair, so unjust.

Frivolous, lazy Lucas Drake could wallow in iniquity without consequence. He could behave in any disgusting manner he pleased, then he could go home to his despised father and be welcomed back. *He* could do those things, but Rose had to marry Mr. Oswald.

Suddenly, tears surged into her eyes and dripped down her cheeks. She swiped at them, but there were too many, and she couldn't hide them.

He was aghast. "Are you crying?"

"No."

"You are! You're crying."

"I told you I was distressed."

"You also told me you were fine. You don't look fine."

"I am, though. I am."

She took several deep breaths, wishing the horrid encounter was over, wishing the ground would open and swallow her whole.

"Would you excuse me?" she mumbled, and tried to skirt by him, but he put his hands on her waist, steadying her, stopping her.

"What's wrong?" His voice was low and seductively compassionate.

"I'm just…unhappy," she blurted out.

Oh, why couldn't she be silent? She simply needed to shut her mouth and hurry to her room where she could compose herself, then return to the party without Mr. Oswald being aware she'd been absent.

Yet for some reason, she didn't want to leave Mr. Talbot. When he stood so close, there was no word to describe the sensations that were stirred. She felt better with him near. She felt less alone and afraid.

He snuggled her to his chest, and though it was recklessly inappropriate, she let him. She didn't push him away or attempt to maintain any space between them. She wrapped her arms around his waist and held on tight.

She might have been on a ship, riding high waves that were about to crash her onto a rocky shore. At the moment, he was the only stable port, the only safe harbor.

It dawned on her that she couldn't remember ever being comforted. She supposed it had happened when she was tiny, when her mother had still been alive, but it certainly hadn't happened at Miss Peabody's school.

She hadn't realized that comfort could be so appealing. He had broad shoulders, the type a troubled woman could lean on for support. But they were in an isolated section of the garden, and her emotions were at a dangerous ebb. She gave herself a few weepy seconds to enjoy the embrace, then she eased away.

She peeked up at him, and he was frowning, his brash, egotistical character tucked out of sight.

"You don't have to marry Stanley," he vehemently whispered.

"I want to," she half-heartedly insisted.

"But you don't have to. Truly you don't."

"I think I should. I think I must."

"I can take you into the village in the morning. The mail coach stops around ten. I'll buy you a ticket to whatever destination you request. You don't even have to tell him. You can just leave."

"Where would I go, Mr. Talbot? That's the problem. Where would I go?"

They stared and stared, a thousand messages swirling, and it occurred to her that she was incredibly attracted to him. She'd had such limited interactions with men, so it was difficult to recognize it for what it was, but once recognized, it was impossible to ignore.

Was he feeling the same? Was he attracted to her as well?

She grew wearier. It was another calamity heaped on top of meeting her cousin, of having him on the premises and reminding her of the inequities of life.

James Talbot was handsome and virile, the sort of fellow any girl would die to marry, but Rose was marrying Mr. Oswald. Mr. Talbot would be another encumbrance to make her question her choices, to make her rue and regret. How did a woman move forward in the midst of such turmoil? How did a woman thrive under such burdens?

"Don't let him coerce you, Miss Ralston," he said.

"I'm not being coerced."

"Aren't you? Just say the word, and I'll send you away from here."

"There's nowhere for me to go, Mr. Talbot. There's nowhere for me at all."

She spun and ran, a foolish, wild part of her wishing he'd call her name or chase after her, but he had the good sense not to. As she slipped in a rear door, she breathed a sigh of relief that he hadn't followed.

CHAPTER FOUR

"May I be frank with you, Miss Ralston?"

"I hope you always will be."

Rose smiled hesitantly at Mr. Oswald.

She never quite knew how to carry on with him. His demeanor reminded her very much of Miss Peabody who'd been abrupt and blunt. She'd had little patience for folly and had been extremely quick to dish out criticism.

The notion of being wed to a male version of Miss Peabody was dreary and depressing. Rose saw a long, miserable slog ahead.

At least at the school, she'd had the chatter and energy of the students to break up the monotony. Here, she would have lengthy quiet interludes, interrupted by an occasional supper party or a sound scolding when she upset her husband. She'd endured plenty of them under Miss Peabody's caustic eye, and the realization that she hadn't escaped that tedious existence, that she might have simply substituted one for the other, was distressing and sad.

Shouldn't marriage be a time of new beginnings? Summerfield was so beautiful. Why couldn't she be happy? She was such a foolish romantic and was focusing on small details when she had to focus on the bigger ones, on the magnificent estate she would be able to call her own.

They were walking in the garden again, another day having passed where she was supposed to have toured the neighborhood. Instead, she'd hidden in her room, not having had the stomach to socialize with her cousin. And after her encounter the previous evening under the verandah with Mr. Talbot, she hadn't known what to do.

She still didn't understand his relationship to Mr. Oswald, and she was terrified he might mention their meeting and confess that Rose was having second thoughts. If Mr. Talbot could engage in mischief, he seemed the type who probably would, and it would definitely be to her detriment.

"I need to discuss an important issue with you," Mr. Oswald

was saying.

"What is that?"

"Before we start, you must assure me that you'll be completely discreet. Can you be discreet? Can you promise me?"

She didn't like having her character questioned, but she swallowed down any comment to that effect and replied. "Of course you can count on my discretion. I view myself as a very loyal person. I would never speak out of turn."

"I assumed that about you, but this is such a delicate matter I had to be certain."

They were near a garden bench, the pretty pond stretching in front of them. He gestured for her to sit, then he stood, gazing out at the water, his posture very straight, his fingers linked behind his back.

Clearly, he was about to reveal a very difficult topic, and she could barely keep from begging him not to. She recognized that a wife was lucky if her husband shared his concerns, but still, they were scarcely acquainted, and she was so conflicted about their arrangement.

She needed more time to settle her mind and accept her future. If he told her a horrid secret, it would only make her path rockier.

Finally, he spun around, and if he'd been a cheery sort of fellow, his expression might have been a smile, but she didn't imagine he ever smiled.

"I'm pleased with you," he said.

"Well...good."

"You're every bit as sensible and refined as Miss Peabody claimed."

"I'm glad to hear it."

"You possess all the stellar traits that must be passed from mother to child."

"I like to think so."

"But here's the rub."

He looked flummoxed, which was a surprise. She didn't suppose he was ever out of his element.

"What is it?" she urged after an agonizing pause.

"I've brought you here under false pretenses."

Her spirits flagged. He didn't like her? He didn't want her? What?

"You don't wish to marry me?" she asked.

"No, no, it's not that. I'd be delighted to wed you. *Any* man would be, but I'm in a desperate situation."

"What situation is that?"

"I'm old, Miss Ralston." She was about to stroke his ego, to politely state that he wasn't *that* old, but he held up a hand to stop her. "I'm seventy. There's no need to deny it, and I have to have an heir."

"I realize that fact."

"I've tried for decades with too many brides—to no avail. I've no son to show for my intense efforts." More grumpily, he muttered, "I couldn't even sire a piddling daughter."

She scowled. "I wouldn't consider a daughter to be piddling. I'd welcome a boy *or* a girl."

"Yes, yes, but you're a woman. You're expected to have a tender heart, but I'm a man, and *I* must have a son. I don't have time for daughters. I don't have time at all."

They struggled through another severe silence, and she said, "So what are you telling me?"

"Are you aware of how a babe is conceived, Miss Ralston?"

Her cheeks flushed bright crimson. "No."

"It's a...physical act that's quite simple. I'll teach you how it's done, and I have no doubt you'll take to it in a thrice."

She'd like to ask him what the act entailed, what—precisely—would be required of her, but she had no idea how to raise the embarrassing subject. Apparently, it involved nudity and caressing of private parts, and she couldn't envision stripping off her clothes and letting him touch her all over. The prospect left her dizzy with dismay.

The mere mention of the topic was so disturbing that if he didn't immediately move on, she would jump up and run back to the house. Alone.

"Will there be anything else, sir?" she haughtily inquired.

"Yes, actually. My point is that I can't risk you being barren." He shook his head. "I simply can't."

"I see," she mumbled.

"No, you don't, but here is what I propose as our solution."

Our solution, she caustically thought. She'd traveled to Summerfield to wed him. As far as she was concerned, naught had changed on her end of the bargain.

"What is it, Mr. Oswald?"

"I should like you to stay for three months."

At his long hesitation, she pressed, "And...?"

"We shall do our best to get you with child, but if we can't, I'll return your dowry to you. We'll claim we weren't compatible, and you can be on your way."

She pondered the statement, but couldn't make sense of it. "I'm confused."

"I understand." He nodded in commiseration. "We would marry only *after* I plant a babe. If no impregnation occurs, you'll be free to leave—with your dowry money in your purse."

"We wouldn't marry?" She frowned. "But...we'd be having marital relations, and I'd be ruined."

"I would come to your bedchamber using a rear stairwell. No one would know I'd visited, so your reputation would remain spotless."

"*I* would know what we'd done."

He shrugged. "Yes, and I'd know too, but I'd never tell."

"How would we explain the delay in the wedding?"

"We'd say we were taking our time to become better acquainted."

"People would wonder and gossip."

"Let them."

"It's a sin—what you're asking. It's wrong. It's morally and ethically wrong."

"Yes, it is, but I'm asking anyway." He pointed to the hills in the north. "If you ride up the road, very soon, you arrive at the Scottish border. Have you ever heard of a handfasting?"

"No."

"It's an ancient Scottish custom. A couple would share their bed, usually for a year and a day. They'd try to procreate, and if they couldn't, they'd separate."

"That sounds scandalous," she scoffed, "and demeaning."

"The country folks still do it, so it's not unprecedented in these parts. If you require a moral license in order to proceed, we'd merely be following local custom. What I'm suggesting has always been practiced here."

She studied him, assessing his stern countenance, his erect posture. He was such a cold man, so lacking in emotion and determined to have his way, and she couldn't begin to calculate how deeply he'd just hurt her.

Though she'd had misgivings about the match, she'd suffered a secret joy at knowing she'd been wanted, at knowing she'd been picked. From the moment her parents had died when she was four, she'd never been wanted. Even her own family hadn't cared about her.

Marriage would have supplied a home of her own, a place where she belonged, but he'd snatched it away. He expected her to perform like a brood mare, like a slave birthing a baby for her master. If her womb could catch a child, she'd get what he'd promised to Miss Peabody in their furtive negotiations, but if Rose was barren, she'd slink away, having failed at her essential task.

It was galling to have the burden dumped on her shoulders. Everyone insisted that—if a union generated no offspring—it was the wife's fault. Why was that? Why was the woman to blame? It certainly seemed as if Mr. Oswald should be questioned on his ability.

He'd either been extremely unlucky in selecting his brides or he carried some of the responsibility. Which was it? And why was it Rose's duty to fix his problem? How was it fair for her to be cast aside?

"I don't know what to think, Mr. Oswald," she murmured.

He increased the pressure, raised the stakes. "If you'll agree, and we're not successful, I'll add five hundred pounds to your dowry. You'll be able to establish yourself elsewhere and start over. I'll help you to relocate. If you'd like to teach again, I'll find you a position—and you'll have a fat nest egg too."

She leaned forward, her elbows on her knees, and she stared at the grass. She was buying time, delaying as she struggled to dissect his sordid proposal.

She didn't understand what marital behavior entailed, and she wished there was someone in whom she could confide. But there was no one, and the very idea of discussing such a squalid plan was too humiliating to consider.

"Could I have the dowry money now?" She peeked up at him. "Could I leave?"

"No. I fully intend to marry you if you conceive." He gestured to the house, the park. "If you prove fertile, Miss Ralston, all this will be yours for the rest of your life, and it will be your son's for the rest of his. Wouldn't such an outcome be worth any price?"

"I don't know," she murmured again. "I truly do not know."

"Come to church with me."

"What?" The abrupt change of subject was disconcerting.

"Come to church."

"When?"

"This evening."

"Why?"

"My brother is the vicar, and he holds a Wednesday night service I want you to witness. You've met him, haven't you?"

"Yes."

"You must hear him preach, must listen to his brand of piety as he rails about sin and damnation. Rumor has it that he will shame a young girl who's gotten herself in trouble with a local boy. Rumor has it that she will be publically whipped by him. I'd like you to see it."

"To what end, Mr. Oswald?"

"If you can't birth me a son, Miss Ralston, then my brother is my heir, and I can't imagine a more horrid conclusion for the people of Summerfield. Can you?"

"I don't believe it's for me to say."

"Well, it's definitely for *me* to say. He can't inherit. He will *not* inherit. It will not happen, Miss Ralston. My family has owned Summerfield for two centuries, so I can hardly bequeath the place to strangers. Watch my brother's service, then give me your answer in the morning."

They stared and stared, his expression intractable, his stubbornness crushing her.

Then, without another word, he spun and walked away, and she was left to fret and stew by herself.

"Hello, Miss Ralston."

"Ah!" she shrieked and leapt with fright.

James couldn't help but be humored by her reaction.

He'd sneaked into her bedchamber again and was seated in the chair in the corner. He hadn't seen her all day and was worried about her condition. She wasn't any of his business, but he'd felt the strongest urge to check on her anyway.

After decades of living under Stanley's thumb, James knew what it was like to deal with the man. Stanley was adept at artifice and tricks, at putting a person in an untenable position.

Poor Miss Ralston was a quick learner. She was beginning to realize that Stanley might not have her best interests at heart. She could never win against him and would most likely never attain any of what she'd sought through matrimony.

James was involved in his own scheme with Stanley and desperately craved the money and information he'd been promised. James would only receive both if he used Miss Ralston in the worst way. So what was he doing? Why stop by to chat?

"We're becoming so intimately acquainted," he said. "I should probably call you Rose. *Miss Ralston* sounds ridiculously formal."

"We're not on familiar terms, Mr. Talbot."

"We could be. Call me James."

"Absolutely not. Why are you in here again?"

"I was nostalgic for my old room, so I decided to visit."

"While I am occupying this suite, you are not to barge in. I'm afraid I have to insist."

"Feel free to order me about, but it's pointless to boss me. I never listen—particularly to women."

"Marvelous," she fumed. "Pray tell, how am I to be shed of you?"

"I'll go when I'm good and ready."

"That's what I figured you'd say."

As if he were invisible, she marched by him to the dressing

room. He pushed himself to his feet and tagged after her. He dawdled in the doorway, observing as she took off her cloak and hat, as she hung them on the hook on the wall.

She went to the dresser, tugged the combs from her chignon and let the auburn mass fall down her back. She ran her fingers through it, shook it a few times, then tied it into a ponytail with a length of ribbon.

"I love your hair," he said.

"Leave me alone," she grumbled.

She came toward him, planning to return to the outer chambers, but he was blocking her path. She approached until they were toe-to-toe, and she stopped, expecting him to move. When he didn't, she snapped, "Do you mind?"

"No, not at all." He seized a curly strand of her hair and wrapped it around his finger. "This shade of auburn is such an intriguing color. I've never seen the likes."

"I'm delighted to hear it, but I'd appreciate it if you'd keep your hands to yourself."

She slapped his hand away and shoved him aside so she could proceed to the sitting room. He followed again, finding her leaned against the windowsill and staring out into the park. It was after ten, the lingering summer twilight having faded, so it was dark with just the stars for scenery.

She was so forlorn, and he hated his visceral response to her woe. He yearned to take her in his arms and tell her everything would be all right, but he doubted it would be. He had to maintain an emotional distance, which was extremely difficult.

There was a composure about her that tempted him in a manner he didn't like or comprehend. He felt as if he were a moth, and she a flame, and she exerted an irresistible pull that would—if he weren't careful—lure him too close and burn him to ashes.

"Were you hiding today?" he asked.

"Yes."

"From what? Or should I say *who*?"

"I don't like you—"

"Me? What's not to like?"

"—or your friend Mr. Drake. I'd rather avoid both of you, but him in particular."

The comment surprised him. "Lucas is harmless."

"I still don't like him."

"Was he rude to you?"

"No."

"Then why the ill will?"

She glanced at him over her shoulder. "Must I state a reason?"

"Yes. Men are never too keen on him, but women usually love him. If he knew you weren't charmed, he'd be flabbergasted."

"The poor boy," she sarcastically oozed. "Not adored by quiet, boring Miss Ralston. How will his enormous ego stand the strain?"

He scowled. "You're in an awfully feisty mood."

"If you don't like it, you don't have to stay."

"I didn't say I didn't like it. Actually, I'm fascinated. I didn't realize you had a temper or were capable of such strong opinions."

She snorted with disgust. "Oh, you're being ridiculous. Why is it odd that I would have a temper or strong opinions? I'm not a dressmaker's mannequin. I'm an adult who's been on this Earth for twenty-five years. Of course I have opinions."

"Of course you do."

"And why is it necessary that I like Mr. Drake? Just because you're his great chum, doesn't mean I have to be."

"Too true."

She whirled away to stare outside again, and he wandered over until he was near enough to touch her. He didn't, though. With the snit she was in, there was no predicting how she might react.

He assessed her profile while she studiously ignored him, but she wouldn't be able to persist for long. He simply took up too much space in any room he entered.

"You didn't come to supper," he said.

"No, I didn't."

"Where have you been? You seem upset."

"If you must know, Mr. Oswald and I went to church."

"Ah," James mused.

He'd heard there was to be some sort of brouhaha at Oscar's prayer service.

James had sat through a few of those services. In his younger days, when he'd still felt he had to obey his elders, he'd been the central topic at some of them. There was nothing quite so humiliating as being summoned down to the front of the congregation and having Oscar rant over a minor infraction.

James had received his share of admonishments and even some whippings from the annoying preacher, but the punishments had only lasted until James had grown taller than Oscar. Oscar liked to pick on people who were weaker and smaller.

How dreadful that Stanley would drag her there. Oscar was unpleasant enough in a dining room where he was constrained by societal norms and etiquette. Behind a pulpit, in full religious regalia, he was nauseating. What was Stanley thinking?

"I take it you weren't pleased with what you witnessed," he tentatively said.

"That's putting it mildly."

"Oscar is a bully and fiend. Don't let him bother you. He's not worth it."

She looked sad and weary and so alone. There was an air about her that rattled his masculine instincts, urging him to protect her, to shelter her from harm. But her situation was beyond him, and he had to remember that it was.

"May I ask you a question?" she said.

"I can't guarantee I'll answer, but you can certainly ask."

"If you were pressed to commit a moral wrong, but by doing it you'd be serving the greater good, would you proceed?"

"That sounds like the sort of unsolvable philosophical puzzles my professors posed when I was in school."

She held out her palms, as if weighing two heavy objects. "Would you risk sin and damnation or would you cast caution to the wind?"

"I have no idea."

"What if you had no other option but to agree? What then?"

"Then...I suppose I've never viewed a bit of *sin* as being all that horrid. And the *damnation* I'll leave to pious idiots like Oscar Oswald."

"You're hopeless," she scoffed. "Do you ever wish you could snap your fingers and suddenly become someone new and different?"

"I used to—when I was younger."

"But not anymore?"

"No. My life's all right. It wasn't so grand when I was a boy, but then I grew up and went off to the army. Things were better for me there."

"I heard you were brought to Summerfield from an orphanage."

"Why, Miss Ralston!" he mocked. "Have you been gossiping about me?"

"Yes. Quite flagrantly."

"Shame on you."

"I expect you'll survive it."

"I expect I will too, and I must confide that I'm positively ecstatic to discover you were interested in learning more about me."

"Be silent, you vain oaf." She peeked up at him and inquired, "Why are you pestering me? There are dozens of women on the estate and hundreds in the village. Why not harass one of them? Why me?"

"I don't know," he honestly told her, and he truly didn't. She intrigued him, and he hadn't a clue as to why. He couldn't stay away.

And wasn't it best if he wooed her? It would make the ending so much simpler.

"You *know* why you're doing it," she chided. "Are you trying to get me in trouble with Mr. Oswald? Are you trying to jeopardize my betrothal?"

"No."

"If you don't want me to marry him, admit it. Don't play these games with me."

"It doesn't matter to me if he marries you. I'm serious. His business isn't any of mine."

"How can you say that? You live here! You've always lived here, and while I don't for a second understand your relationship with Mr. Oswald, everything he does affects you."

"It affected me when I was a child. I'm an adult now, and he can go hang for all I care."

"Then why are you in my room? Tell me the real reason so we can deal with it and I can convince you to depart before we're caught together."

She turned from the window so she was facing him. He gazed down at her, riveted by the green of her eyes. She was smart and fetching, and she deserved so much more than Stanley and the plans he had for her.

It would be wonderful if James could steal her away from Stanley, if he could sneak off with her and wed her himself. Yet he didn't have the money or the desire to ever wed. Many of his friends had let themselves be leg-shackled, and none of them were happy.

If James was eager for feminine company, he fraternized with trollops who made no demands on him. They were content to frolic without any extended commitment. A gently bred female like Rose Ralston would bring a host of responsibilities he prayed he'd never have the misfortune to assume.

"You fascinate me," he confessed.

"You barely know me. I couldn't possibly."

"You're so brave."

"Me? Brave?"

"Yes. You picked up and traveled to Summerfield, and you're ready to proceed with Stanley. I'm fascinated and charmed."

"You shouldn't be."

"I am."

When he stood so near to her, he could feel a current of energy flowing between them. He'd never experienced such a stirring sensation and couldn't seem to tamp it down. He didn't *want* to tamp it down. He wanted to fan the flames, wanted to let it grow and grow until it spiraled into an inferno that couldn't be controlled.

Where would it lead? Where would it end? The answers to those questions were alarming.

She was Stanley's. She'd always be Stanley's, and James couldn't forget that fact. Still, he was a cad and scapegrace. Stanley would be the first to complain about it. If James took liberties, if he misbehaved, wasn't it expected? Who would ever know? It wasn't as if he'd shout the news to the servants.

"Close your eyes," he murmured.

She frowned. "Why?"

"Just close them."

To his surprise, she obeyed.

The woman was a trusting ninny! She claimed to have heard rumors about him, but clearly, they weren't the worst ones. He was an avowed libertine, and they were alone in an isolated wing of the house. He might perpetrate any wickedness, and she wouldn't be able to stop him.

Not that he would harm her, but still...

Before he could change his mind, before *she* could change hers, he dipped down and kissed her.

In the entire history of kisses, it wasn't much about which to brag. He didn't grab her and crush her to his chest. He didn't yank the ribbon from her hair and run his fingers through the auburn tresses. He simply rested his palm on her waist and touched his lips to hers.

As he drew away, he was shocked to find that his pulse was racing, his blood pounding in his veins. He was awash with lust, his body crying out for him to ravish her, and the strength of the urge frightened him.

Her eyes fluttered open, and as she peered up at him, she looked young and confused and very, very pretty.

"You shouldn't have done that," she quietly scolded.

He shrugged. "I'm renowned for doing what I shouldn't. I've always been that way."

"It's so wrong. Everything about this place is wrong. Mr. Oswald. You. Vicar Oswald. Summerfield. The betrothal."

"It's why I think you're so brave to have come."

"Would you take me away from here and marry me yourself?" she stunned him by asking.

"See what I mean? You're so courageous." He smiled and shook his head. "I don't have the resources to rescue you. I don't have the funds or a home of my own, and I'm so aggravatingly vain.

You wouldn't want me as a husband."

She nodded, her cheeks flushing with shame. "I shouldn't have asked that. I'm sorry."

"It's all right. I'd help you if I could."

"You don't have to humor me."

"It's not foolish to hope for a better conclusion."

"Well, I've made my bed, and it appears it's time to lie in it." She stepped away and straightened, and she seemed different somehow, as if she'd erected a barrier she wouldn't let him breach again.

"You have to go now," she insisted.

"Yes, I suppose."

"Are you and Mr. Drake leaving for London?"

"That's the plan."

"When will it be?"

"Maybe tomorrow or maybe in a few weeks."

"I can't keep bumping into you, Mr. Talbot. We have to avoid each other."

"I don't want to avoid you."

"We *have* to, and we most assuredly can't be together like this. Please stay away."

"Call me James." He was absurdly eager for her to speak his name. "Call me James and perhaps I'll comply with your request."

"No, you won't, and you must depart at once. I believe I've betrayed Mr. Oswald sufficiently for one evening, don't you?"

She slid away and went to the door. She peeked into the hall and gestured for him to hurry out.

He hesitated, debating whether he should argue, debating whether he should remain, but she didn't realize she had no control over what was about to happen. In the future, she would have plenty of reasons to hate him, and he didn't need to supply any extra ones so early in their relationship. It would only make matters harder between them down the road.

He went to the door too, and as he passed her, she reached into her pocket and withdrew the key.

"Don't come back," she warned. "You won't be able to get in."

He might have told her there was another entrance, a secret staircase that he'd used often as an adolescent when he'd been anxious to sneak out unseen.

But he didn't tell her. She'd learn about it later on.

"Good night," he said.

She didn't offer the same goodbye, and he walked out, dawdling until she spun the key in the lock. Just to be sure, he tried the knob.

"Go!" she hissed on the other side of the wood.

He strolled away, feeling disconcerted and more alone than he'd been in a very long time.

CHAPTER FIVE

"You'll remain by my side all evening."
"I don't know why I should have to."
"Because I said so."

Veronica peered over at her stepfather. Usually, she could manipulate him—within reason—but he was being abnormally recalcitrant.

She was an inch away from letting loose with vitriol, but it was pointless to fight with him. She had to sweet-talk and flatter and cajole, had to plant an idea in his head, then hammer away until he presumed it was his own.

He was a self-important twit who believed people were impressed by his cleric's collar. In reality, he was widely recognized as a belligerent incompetent. It never occurred to him that she might have views that differed from his own or that she might not care two figs for his opinion.

They were at Summerfield Manor again, Stanley hosting another supper party with neighbors invited to meet Miss Ralston. For a horrifying interval after their invitation arrived, Oscar had claimed they wouldn't attend, but of course, he couldn't bear to refuse.

He loved to be observed as he strolled through the house, loved to remind others that he was Stanley's only brother.

"I like Miss Ralston very much," Veronica said. "I hope she and I will be great friends."

"If you wish to befriend her, it will be while you are beside me so I can keep an eye on you."

"Why are you so upset? Have you been quarreling with Uncle Stanley?"

"Yes. That is why I nearly didn't come, but it's important for my parishioners to see me out and about. And that I extend my forgiveness to Stanley. I must shower him with Christian kindness."

Veronica wanted to gag. Oscar was the least Christian-behaving man in the world, and he and Stanley were always at odds. Stanley constantly taunted Oscar over how he might not inherit Summerfield, and Veronica thought it was terrific fun.

"There's Miss Ralston now." Veronica gestured to where the woman was standing in the corner, and she flashed her prettiest smile. "Please, Papa Oscar. Just for a few minutes? You can watch me the whole time."

"Oh, all right," he ultimately grumbled, "but stay where I can see you. I'd better not have to chase you out in the garden ever again."

"I wouldn't dream of going anywhere without your permission," she lied.

She slipped away, and as she felt his stern gaze following her, she sighed with exasperation. She was eighteen and lived in a bloody preacher's rectory. Her stepfather was hated by all. They were disliked, isolated from society, with Stanley their sole relative. Despite how Oscar nagged, Veronica intended to enjoy herself.

At the prior party, he'd left early, so he'd made her leave too. She'd missed the dancing, and it couldn't happen again. She had to find more ways to sneak away—especially with James and Lucas visiting.

James was her rescue plan, her escape route to the exciting life she deserved. Previously, she'd been too little to attract his attention, but she'd grown up. He was too smart to tarry in a boring place like Summerfield. With his having quit the army, he would move to London where he and Lucas would wallow in adventures she couldn't begin to imagine.

It seemed fitting that they take her along. She was determined to marry James, so she needed opportunities to flirt. A friendship with Miss Ralston was an innocent ploy to spend more time at the manor with him.

Plus, Veronica wouldn't let Miss Ralston have James all to herself. She might get ideas. She might look at handsome, virile James, then at elderly, decrepit Stanley, and decide she'd rather have the younger man. But he wasn't available to Miss Ralston or any other female.

Miss Ralston had to understand that she could only have what Veronica was willing to give her. And it certainly wasn't James Talbot.

"Will she agree?"

"Yes."

"Has she told you she will?"

"No, but I expect to have her affirmative answer in the morning."

Stanley glared at James, visually warning him to be silent. Stanley was in no mood to have another inane discussion about Miss Ralston. The bargain was struck. Why hash it out all over again?

James had resided at Summerfield most of his life, and as a boy, Edwina had spoiled him, so he occasionally assumed his position to be higher than it was. He occasionally assumed he had the right to question Stanley, but no one was allowed to do that.

Stanley was king of his domain, but in light of his current predicament, he'd had to confide in James, and he loathed that fact. He didn't like James to know his business, didn't like to be beholden to James on any level, but he'd finally been confronted by a situation he couldn't manage on his own.

"She might surprise you," James said.

"No woman ever has."

"She has a stronger constitution than you envisioned and an ingrained sense of right and wrong. She might refuse just on general principles."

"She won't."

James scoffed. "One blasted time, I'd like you to be mistaken. It would humor me immensely to see you thwarted."

"I won't be. I specifically chose her because she's all alone. If she doesn't behave as I'm demanding, she has nowhere to go, and I've always found a female's need for fiscal security to compel her into any circumstance that will provide it. How do you think whores end up flat on their backs?"

"You're such an ass," James snorted. "She doesn't want to marry you."

"Who would?"

"She's having second thoughts. She might renege. It could happen."

"It won't. I took her to church with me, and Oscar was in fine form."

"Yes, I spoke with her afterward. She was extremely distressed."

"Marvelous," Stanley mused. "She realizes why I require an heir. She'll view it as her duty to protect the people at Summerfield. She won't disappoint me."

The house was filled with guests. He and James were huddled together in the main parlor, observing the crowd.

Miss Ralston was across the room, chatting with Veronica, and Stanley made a mental note to talk to her about the girl. Veronica spread trouble wherever she went. Unfortunately, there were few young ladies in the neighborhood who were close in age to Miss Ralston, so it was natural that a bond might bubble up. Stanley was determined it wouldn't.

"I wish," James said, "you'd picked someone who wasn't quite so nice."

"What an idiotic comment."

"I just hate to have her hurt. It would be easier to bear if she was less likeable."

"How am I *hurting* her?" Stanley gestured around the ornate parlor. "If a child catches in her womb, she'll spend the rest of her life—in luxury, I might add—in this grand mansion. Her son will be lord and master after I'm gone. That's hardly a detriment."

"But until you pass away, she'll be wed to you. I wouldn't exactly cite it as a benefit."

"There are worse things than marrying a rich, landed gentleman such as myself."

"Yes," James caustically concurred. "She could fail to conceive, and you'll ship her off to parts unknown, ruined and with coach fare and a few pennies in her purse. You won't think twice about her after that."

"No, I won't." Stanley scowled. "And why would you? Don't tell me you're becoming a romantic at the ripe old age of twenty-five."

James shrugged. "I like her."

"Bully for you. Like her. Don't like her. As far as my bargain with you, it changes nothing. Now if you'll excuse me"—he nodded to where Veronica was still chatting with Miss Ralston—"I can't have that little tart getting too cozy with my fiancée. I'd better run her off."

"Yes, heaven forbid that Miss Ralston have any friends at Summerfield."

It was an old complaint that harkened back to James's own childhood. There had been scarcely any children on the estate, which was the reason Stanley had sent James to boarding school against Edwina's vehement wish that he not.

James never thought Stanley proceeded with James's interest in mind, but every blasted choice had bestowed boons on James that he'd never deserved.

"Well," Stanley said, "heaven forbid that it be Veronica anyway. She is not—and never will be—a suitable companion for Miss Ralston. You should watch out for her too. I hear she has the morals of an alley cat."

"This is not news to me," James replied.

"I didn't suppose it was. Be careful she doesn't lure you into a jam."

"She couldn't."

"I'm never surprised by the mischief a pretty girl can instigate. Don't let yourself be snared in her net."

"She's not smart enough to trap me."
"If that's what you believe, then you're a fool."

"What are you doing out here by yourself?"
"Moping. What does it look like?"

James was on the verandah, leaned on the balustrade and peering out into the dark garden. He stared over his shoulder at Lucas.

"You, moping?" Lucas said. "You never mope."
"I'm trying new things."
"The vicar finally left. We're going to dance again. Come inside and help me move the furniture."
"I don't want to move furniture *or* dance."
"So? Come inside anyway. We have too many women and not enough men."
"Have you become Stanley's social secretary?"
"Yes. It appears I've found my calling." Facetiously, Lucas added, "My father will be so proud."

James chuckled and spun around as Lucas joined him, and they studied the house. The rooms were bright and gay, the light from dozens of candles wafting out, giving the mansion a festive glow. Guests were mingling, laughing, and drinking Stanley's liquor, which James liked to see.

"You're actually sulking," Lucas said after a protracted silence.
"I told you I was."
"What's wrong? Is it being back at Summerfield?"
"You know I always hated it here."
"No, you didn't. You hated Stanley. You didn't hate the estate."
James considered, then nodded. "I suppose not."
"If he's harassing you, we don't have to stay. It's not as if we're children who must blindly obey. Let's head to London. I can't figure out why we've tarried as long as we have."
"You were opposed to going right away," James reminded him. "You're broke, and there will be creditors chasing you who still haven't been paid from the last time you were on furlough."
"There is that."
"Why don't you write to your father? You could ask him to square your debts."
"I'm not ready."

Lucas had no shame. He overspent and overindulged in every conceivable way. Yet when push came to shove, he'd slink home to Lord Sidwell and beg for rescue. Lord Sidwell would huff and bellow and scold, then he'd relent and bail Lucas out—literally on occasion—but Lucas had to be in very dire straits before he'd seek the man's assistance. With their dawdling at Summerfield, his situation was hardly ominous. There was no reason for a fast departure.

"Seriously," Lucas said, "let's ride out in the morning. Bugger Stanley. If he's upsetting you, I'm happy to take my chances in London."

"I can't leave now."

"Why not?"

"I agreed to help him resolve a problem he's having."

"What is it?"

"It's nothing. It's just...I swore I would."

"Well, I must point out that if you're letting yourself be sucked into one of Stanley's schemes, you have only yourself to blame when it crashes down."

"You're correct."

"Whatever he's asked of you, you shouldn't proceed. It can't be to your advantage."

"He told me if I aid him, he'll give me the information about my parents. And a thousand pounds to boot."

"You believed him?"

James hemmed and hawed, not sure how to answer. He and Stanley had such a strange relationship. Stanley insisted he'd been kind to James because Edwina had insisted, but Edwina had been dead for almost two decades. So what was Stanley's motive? Why persist? It made no sense and never had.

Stanley had never liked James and claimed he didn't like to support James or have him on the premises. But the instant James got fed up and tried to sever ties, Stanley would lure him back, and James was unable to evade Stanley's incessant pull.

Where Stanley and Summerfield were concerned, James had no spine whatsoever.

Did he trust Stanley? Did he assume Stanley would follow through on a promise?

"I don't *not* believe him," he ultimately said.

"What does that mean?" Lucas asked.

"Don't listen to me. I'm morose and miserable."

"You certainly are, so we'll have to start the dancing without you. What with Vicar Oswald finally leaving, we barely have the energy for amusement. Your glum attitude would ruin what's left."

Suddenly, Miss Ralston appeared in one of the windows. She was wearing her schoolteacher's dress—gray fabric, white collar and cuffs, every inch of skin covered from chin to toe—and it occurred to James that she must not have a garment that was more fetching. Not a single gown suitable for a party. It was the saddest notion ever.

Yet even attired in the drab, conservative outfit, she was shockingly pretty. On seeing her, his pulse raced.

Stanley might be expecting to marry her, but that act had no bearing on how James behaved. He'd be more than happy to show her things that Stanley never could.

Would she hate James in the end? He prayed that she wouldn't.

"There's Miss Ralston," Lucas said.

"What do you think of her?"

"She's much too fine for the likes of Stanley Oswald."

"My opinion exactly."

"Let's bet on whether I can seduce her," Lucas eagerly suggested, and on hearing the ridiculous remark, a wave of jealousy swept through James.

"You never could," James told him. "She doesn't like you."

"Not *like* me? Don't be absurd. Women love me."

"Not her. She finds you vain and annoying."

Lucas's jaw dropped in astonishment. "She didn't say that."

"She did."

"Then I'll just have to spend the evening changing her mind, won't I?"

He waltzed away, and James snickered to his retreating back, "Good luck."

"Luck has nothing to do with it," Lucas scoffed. "It's skill and charm and cleverness. She doesn't stand a chance against me."

Lucas flitted inside, and James observed until Lucas sidled up to Miss Ralston. His flirtatious charisma was visible even from James's removed vantage point.

The entire charade was too ludicrous to watch. He spun and fled into the garden.

Rose hurried down the garden path. She wasn't sure where she was headed, and thankfully, there were lanterns lighting the route so she wouldn't barrel into anyone as she had when she'd nearly knocked down James Talbot.

The party was still in progress in the house behind her, and she'd begun to feel as if she couldn't breathe. With Lucas Drake fawning over her, Veronica Oswald pretending friendship, and Mr. Oswald glowering, she'd had to escape.

As she went farther and farther, the laughter and voices dimmed. Finally, she was away from the festivities, away from the lanterns. It was dark and quiet, the moon gleaming off the water in the pond.

She saw the bench where Mr. Oswald had seated her when he'd unveiled his sordid proposition, when he'd talked about Scotland and local custom and handfasting. His proposal was an insult to Rose, as if she was nonessential in even the most elemental fashion.

She was desperate to discuss the situation with someone, to get advice. She'd struggled for hours to compose a letter to Amelia or Evangeline but, in the end, she hadn't put pen to paper. What could she possibly say to her two old friends?

Both women would be shocked beyond belief, and they had no more experience with men and matrimony than Rose had. The only effect a pleading missive would render would be to alarm Amelia and Evangeline about their own pending marriages.

If Miss Peabody would throw Rose into such a horrid quandary, what might she have done to Amelia and Evangeline? There was no way she could explain to Amelia and Evangeline. And even if she'd dared, they hadn't the means to help her.

She had to help herself, the problem being that she had no idea what to do. She didn't have any power or influence over Mr. Oswald, and she certainly didn't have any funds to leave. Mr. Oswald had them, and he would provide them to her *after* she'd participated in his squalid scheme.

She had staggered to a stop, when suddenly, a man stepped from the shadows.

"Miss Ralston, Rose," James Talbot said. "Why are you out here? Has something happened? You look upset."

"Don't call me by my given name."

"Why shouldn't I?"

"Because it's wrong. Because it confuses me."

"Good. I want you confused."

He came to her, quickly covering the ground that separated them. The moment she'd recognized him, she should have fled. But she hadn't, and now, she couldn't move. She was frozen in place, watching him approach.

"Why are *you* out here?" she asked, anxious to break the tension festering.

"I was thinking about you."

"No, you weren't."

"I was. I was thinking about you with Stanley. I was thinking about you marrying him."

"Don't say that. Don't pretend you care about me."

"Why shouldn't I?"

"Because I want someone to care! I'm so alone, and I need a friend, but it can't be you."

"No, I never have female friends, and friendship isn't what I'd like from you. Where you're concerned, I have more despicable ideas."

"I have to go back inside." Still, she didn't move.

He leaned in, standing so close his boots slipped under the hem of her skirt, his legs tangled with hers. He drew her to him, her entire front—breasts, stomach, thighs—crushed to his.

Sparks ignited, and she felt thrillingly alive in a manner she never previously had. Sounds were clearer. Colors more vibrant. The night air pressed down, and a sense of expectation arose, as if any wild, heady conduct would be allowed.

Before she realized what he planned, he dipped down and captured her lips in a torrid kiss, stirring a desire she hadn't understood herself to possess. She yearned to do things and try things she didn't comprehend. Her body seemed to reach out with longing, as if it instinctively knew there was a way to connect with him on a deeper, more potent level.

His hands were in her hair, and he was plucking out the combs that kept the weighty mass anchored in its tidy chignon. Fleetingly, it dawned on her that she didn't have any others, that she'd have to sneak out in the morning and hope she found them before a gardener stumbled on them and wondered what loose woman had been misbehaving in the dark.

She'd never carried on so brazenly, and she truly intended to pull away, to stop him, but she couldn't bring herself to make him halt.

She couldn't predict what might have occurred, what she might have permitted, but his naughty, crafty fingers had drifted to her chest and were unbuttoning her dress. Every inch of her being, down to the tiniest pore, shouted for her to encourage the reckless liberty, but she knew better, and she yanked away.

They were breathing hard, as if they'd run a long race. He was staring at her, looking angry, looking as confused as she always was in his presence.

She lurched away, and he grabbed for her. Her mind screamed for her to let him hold her, to begin again, but she simply couldn't.

"I can't do this," she murmured.

"Yes, you can."

"No. This isn't the way. This could never be the way. You said so yourself. You don't want me."

"I *do* want you," he vehemently replied, and he certainly appeared to mean it.

"Yes, here in the garden where no one can see, where no one will know, but nowhere beyond that."

"No," he coldly said. "There's no room for you in my life."

"And there is no room for you in mine."

She turned and dashed away as she should have from the very first.

"Rose!" he called, his daring to loudly speak her name only underscoring how matters were escalating.

But she ignored him and kept on.

CHAPTER SIX

Rose heard a noise, and she tensed, but it was only the floorboards creaking. She breathed a sigh of relief that it wasn't Mr. Oswald sneaking into her bedchamber so they could march down the road to perdition.

She'd agreed to his scheme. She shouldn't have, but she'd struggled and fretted and couldn't think of a viable alternative.

She'd humiliated herself by asking James Talbot to rescue her, but he'd had the sense to refuse. Then, she'd briefly flirted with the notion of revealing her identity to Lucas Drake, throwing herself on his mercy and begging for assistance, but he was even more of a reprobate than Mr. Talbot—if that was possible.

Her final choice would have been to borrow coach fare from someone and travel back to Miss Peabody's school. But to do what? She didn't know if Amelia and Evangeline were still in residence, and even if they were, how—precisely—could they help Rose?

If they hadn't already left, they would shortly be on their way to meet their new husbands, and Rose couldn't tag along on that journey. She had to hope that both women had a better conclusion than Rose had had. She would hate to suppose it would be awful for all three of them.

She was twenty-five and had no family to claim and no place to call her own. If she could furnish Mr. Oswald with an heir, she would belong at Summerfield. The solution was that simple. She was an optimist, and she *would* bear him a child. She *would* give him what he wanted and get what she wanted in return.

Then, for the rest of her life, she'd pursue ethical causes, praying that a plethora of good deeds would erase whatever sins she committed with Mr. Oswald at the very beginning.

Another noise echoed, and she braced, positive he was arriving. But again, the house settled, and she relaxed on the pillow.

It was late, and she was in her bed, wearing her nightgown and naught else. Her hair was down and brushed out, a blanket over her lap. She hadn't a clue what was about to transpire, but it couldn't be too horrid. Women throughout history had experienced it and survived.

Mr. Oswald insisted it was simple to accomplish, and she took him at his word. He was much older than she was and would be able to quickly and deftly show her how it was done.

If she'd once had romantic notions of wedding a dashing swain—someone like Mr. Talbot for instance—she shoved the thought aside. She wasn't a naïve girl, wasn't a foolish dreamer.

This was reality. This was Rose taking charge of her future, and the reward for her efforts would be motherhood.

Suddenly, a door opened and closed, and her pulse raced with alarm. The sound had come from her dressing room so, apparently, there was a secret door she hadn't noticed. Footsteps tiptoed across the floor, and momentarily, Mr. Oswald appeared. She'd been expecting to see him in his nightclothes, but he was attired as he'd been earlier at supper, coat, cravat, trousers, shoes.

"Miss Ralston." He gave a slight bow.

"Mr. Oswald."

"You look very pretty," he said.

"Thank you."

"Are you nervous?"

"Yes."

"Don't be. It will be over in a thrice, and the first time at any endeavor is always the most difficult, isn't it?"

"Yes."

"Once you learn the ropes, you'll think back on tonight and wonder why you were ever afraid."

"I'm not afraid," she claimed, though she was. "I'm just anxious over what I don't know."

"Every bride is. It's the nature of the beast, I suppose."

She blushed. "I hope I please you."

"I'm very pleased. You suit my purposes."

High praise indeed!

He walked to the bed and eased a hip onto the mattress, but he didn't touch her. He simply stared, then stared some more.

The strain was too onerous to be believed. She'd assumed he'd grab her and push her onto her back, or...some such behavior. Yet nothing happened.

He laid a palm on the top of her head and stroked it down her hair, his fingers riffling the auburn tresses. To her shame, she jumped.

"Sorry, sorry," she hastily said, struggling to calm herself sufficiently that she didn't slap him away and leap off the mattress.

"It's all right," he soothed.

"I guess I'm a tad more distraught than I realized."

He nodded. "That's perfectly normal."

Still, he didn't proceed.

"Should I...*do* something?" she finally asked. "I must remind you that I'm quite ignorant as to what's required of me."

"No, no, there's nothing you need do." He clasped her hand in his. "There is another detail I have to confide."

"I see," she slowly responded, but she didn't *see* at all.

"Initially, it may seem odd to you, but you must trust me. You trust me, don't you?"

She absolutely didn't, but could hardly say so. "Yes, I trust you."

"You can't ever tell anyone about what occurs in this room."

"I won't. I already gave you my word."

"Yes, but there's a second part to it I didn't share."

"What is it?"

"Give me your promise again. Swear that I have your complete discretion."

"Of course you have it."

"This won't go in the exact direction you're envisioning, but I'm sure—once you're cognizant of the facts—it will be much more enjoyable for you this way."

"I have no idea what you mean."

Motion in the doorway caught her eye, and she glanced over to discover that James Talbot had entered. He was silent, leaned on the doorframe and watching her as Mr. Oswald had been watching her. He appeared bored, as if he'd rather be anywhere else in the world but in her bedchamber.

Rose blanched with surprise, her thoughts chaotic as she tried to unravel the sudden turn of events. What was happening? What scheme were they hatching?

"Why is Mr. Talbot here?" she hotly inquired.

"Remember when I told you," Mr. Oswald replied, "that the marital act is very physical?"

"Yes, yes, I remember."

"I am an old man, Miss Ralston, and it is not possible for me to perform as I must in order to sire a child."

"I don't understand."

"There is a...situation that must arise for me to accommodate you, but my body can no longer achieve it. I haven't been able to in years."

"So...what are you saying?"

Mr. Talbot answered for him. "He's saying that *I* will do it for him. My body is working just fine."

Rose peered at Mr. Talbot, then Mr. Oswald, then Mr. Talbot again. Their expressions were unreadable, enigmatic, revealing no detail, and she was perplexed over what her response should be. There were a thousand questions she should ask, but she was so unschooled in amour that she couldn't imagine what they should be.

From the very first, she'd been uneasy about the betrothal. Yet she'd agreed to the terms—despite her misgivings. Then Mr. Oswald had changed the terms, refusing to marry her unless she proved fertile. She'd agreed again.

She'd been stupidly accommodating throughout, and this—*this!*—was what he proposed? That she engage in marital relations with Mr. Talbot?

It was sordid and immoral and despicable. How dare he demand it of her!

Mr. Oswald was the one who couldn't procreate, but he'd put the burden on her shoulders, pretending it would be her fault if no babe was conceived. He was contemptible and shameless. He was wicked and disgraceful and dishonorable and...and...and...

She couldn't count the derogatory adjectives needed to describe him. And as to Mr. Talbot...well...

"No," she firmly said. Mr. Oswald was still holding her hand, and she yanked it away and repeated, "No."

"Now Miss Ralston," Mr. Oswald simpered, "if you'll just—"

"No!"

"You must listen to me."

"Get out of my bedchamber. Both of you get out."

"If you'll let me explain."

"You couldn't—not if you had a hundred years to try."

"Our bargain will be exactly the same, except you'll proceed with James."

"Get out!"

"He's young and handsome, and I'm old and decrepit. You're a smart girl. Think how it would be with me—and how much better with him! I'm doing this for you."

With each idiotic comment, Rose's temper spiked. If she'd been clutching a pistol, she'd have shot him in the center of his cold, black heart.

She glared at Mr. Talbot. "Did he put you up to this or did you conjure it up on your own?"

Mr. Talbot shrugged. "He asked me, and I owe him many favors."

"You'd do this for him as a...*favor?* You have the gall to say such an offensive thing to my face?"

He shrugged again. "It's for the best if it's me."

"The best for whom?" she spat. "You? Him? For I certainly cannot imagine where there is any benefit for me!"

She slithered to the other side of the mattress and leapt to the floor.

"Get out of here! Or I will start screaming, and I will continue screaming until the footmen arrive to learn what is wrong."

"Miss Ralston, honestly!" Mr. Oswald fumed. "I detest female hysterics and won't tolerate them in my home."

"Hysterics?" she hissed. "I'll show you hysterics!"

She went to the wardrobe and jerked it open. She grabbed her shoes and threw them at the two men. Her winter boots were next. She raced to the fireplace, seized the poker and tossed it too. There were logs in a basket, and she pitched them in a wild volley, finally managing to hit Mr. Oswald in the arm.

"Obviously," Mr. Talbot told Mr. Oswald, "she's in no condition for rational discussion. Let's go. We'll talk about it tomorrow."

Mr. Oswald frowned at Rose, exhibiting what appeared to be a huge amount of malice, as if she'd turned out to have every bad feminine trait after all.

"Come on," Mr. Talbot urged, and Mr. Oswald huffed over to him.

"We're not finished," Mr. Oswald hurled at Rose like a threat.

"Oh, yes we are," Rose replied.

"We'll see," he seethed.

They stomped out, and she listened as they departed through the hidden door.

She rushed to her dresser and snatched up the key Mr. Talbot had given her. She ran to the dressing room and searched the walls, locating the door behind a hanging tapestry. She stuck the key in the lock, delighted to find that it fit and it worked.

For good measure, she dragged the bathing tub over to block the entrance, providing herself with even more security.

Then she staggered to the bedroom and sank down on the bed. As the quiet settled, she stared at the wreckage from her tantrum. Footwear and logs were strewn everywhere, and she should have straightened the mess, but she was too astonished to move.

What now? What now?

There was only one answer to that question.

She retrieved her battered portmanteau and began packing her clothes.

Her situation was no different than it had been when she'd first agreed to Mr. Oswald's absurd proposition. She had no money and no relatives or friends to offer shelter, so she had no idea where she'd go—or how she'd get there—but one thing was certain: She would not remain where she was for another second.

"Hello, Miss Ralston." She ignored James, marching on as if he were invisible, so he tried again. "Fancy meeting you here."

"Sod off, you despicable cur."

"Miss Ralston! Such language! I'm shocked, shocked I tell you."

He bit down a chuckle, recognizing that levity would make her even more furious. The angrier she became, the more difficult it would be to mend the muddle Stanley had caused.

Stanley thought he knew best, that his age and maturity conveyed insight into the human condition. But Stanley was a fool.

After she'd chased them from her bedchamber, James had told Stanley she'd leave, even though it was the middle of the night, but Stanley had insisted she wouldn't. James's current location—out on the road and almost to the village—proved who had been correct.

He jumped down from his horse, reins in hand, and walked beside her, matching her stride for irate stride. It was dark, but the moon was up, so it was easy to see their route.

In the festering silence, her rage was palpable. He deserved her wrath, he supposed. He'd warned Stanley that there were better ways to win her acquiescence, but Stanley's greatest deficiency was that—when he set himself on an path—he couldn't be dissuaded.

"If I call you Rose, you'll probably bite my head off."

She halted and whipped around to face him.

"Sod off!" she fumed. "What part of that crude insult don't you understand?"

"Where did you learn such a derogatory phrase?"

"I grew up in a boarding school, Mr. Talbot. I was a teacher there for the past eight years. Do you think boys are the only ones who have a lock on foul speech? Well, I can promise you they're not. I am fully fluent in epithets and cursing. Should I demonstrate?"

"I wish you'd call me James."

"In your dreams."

"Yes, in my very vivid dreams where we aren't fighting and where you have the chance to discover that I'm actually wonderful."

"I repeat: You are a despicable cur, now slink back to your master like the wretched dog you are. Leave me be!"

She started off again, her pace more determined, and he remained with her, his mind racing to find words that would calm her, but there weren't any.

"May I carry your bag for you?" he asked.

"No."

"I'll bet it's heavy. Let me tie it to my saddle."

"No!" she said more firmly.

She peeked up at him, missed her step, and nearly fell. Her portmanteau tumbled out of her hand and skidded across the dirt.

"Look what you made me do!" she seethed.

"Me? You tripped. I hardly see how it's my fault."

She moved to pick up the bag, but he was faster. He hoisted it onto his horse and latched it with the strap. She tried to skirt by him, to pull it down, but he blocked her.

Her fury spiked. "Give me that!"

"No."

"It contains everything I own. You shall not have it!"

"I'm not keeping it. I'm helping you. Where are you headed? Into the village?"

"My destination is none of your business. My plans are none of your business. My future is none of your business."

"Let's return to the estate."

"Are you mad?" She sputtered with affront. "I wouldn't go back there if hornets were chasing me."

"Your situation won't seem quite so grim after a good night's sleep."

"A good night's sleep? In Mr. Oswald's house? You are deranged."

"What is your other option? You don't have any money. You told me so yourself. Will you continue on to the village? And then what?"

"Apparently, you're having trouble concentrating, so I must be a bit clearer with you: I am none of your business."

"I'm not about to let you go off half-cocked."

"Half-cocked? I can assure you that I have never been more lucid."

"It's the middle of the night, you're marching down a dark road without a penny in your pocket, and you deem yourself to be lucid?"

"I have no idea of what I will do when I arrive in the village, but whatever I choose—to camp in a ditch, to sell myself into slavery, to starve to death in a cave—I swear it will be better than what I've just endured."

She glared at him, appearing aggrieved and magnificent and very, very young. His masculine instincts stirred again, and he wanted to guide and protect her, to shelter and keep her from harm. In his pitiful life, he'd never pined for much more than what he'd had. He'd been a lucky orphan, raised by a rich man, and he'd always assumed he had more than enough.

Yet right that moment, he'd love to sweep her away and make her his own. It was a few miles to the border, and it would have been hilarious to ride off with her, to elope to Gretna Green and return to Summerfield with the riotous news that James had wed her himself.

It would be the ultimate double cross, the ultimate betrayal. But he couldn't do it to her or to Stanley. While Stanley had no scruples, James had some.

He had no funds to support a wife, and Stanley—for all his treachery and spite—had provided for James in incalculable ways. So while it was amusing to consider perfidy, he simply couldn't behave so badly.

"He won't let you escape," James murmured.

"Who won't? Mr. Oswald? He doesn't own me! He can't force me to stay. I *won't* stay."

"It's pointless to fight him. Trust me. You might as well come home, and we'll figure it out in the morning."

"No."

"I'll talk to him for you. I'll try to persuade him to give you some money to compensate you for the mess he's made."

"No," she said again, but her shoulders slumped, her rage waning.

Tears flooded her eyes and dripped down her cheeks. She swiped at them as he reached out and rested a palm on her waist, being delighted when she didn't slap him away.

"Don't cry," he said. "Stanley isn't worth it."

"Before I moved here, I had a fine life. I wasn't wealthy or renowned, but I was at a spot where people liked me. I was relevant. I was happy there."

"I'm sorry for you. Truly."

"Then one day out of the blue, an attorney showed up to inform me that it had ended. Just like that." She snapped her fingers at the starry sky. "I had to pack my bag and leave—for Summerfield."

"I'm sorry." What else could he tell her?

"I was nervous, but excited too. I assumed I'd have my own home and a chance to be a mother—when I'd never dreamed that could be my path."

"You could still have them."

"How? How could I have them?" She clutched a fist over her heart. "Should I shame myself? Should I engage in sin and immorality? Should I imperil my soul and be damned for eternity—merely so Mr. Oswald can thwart his brother?"

"I don't know a lot, Rose, but I know some things that you don't. You wouldn't be damned for this. Neither would I."

"How can you say that? Are you God now?"

"No, but I've traveled the world, and I've seen much more of it than you. Nothing is ever black and white, and our choices are never clear cut. Sometimes you must skirt the edge of what is proper to arrive at the correct place. Sometimes you can't get there any other way."

"I thought you liked me," she suddenly hurled.

"I did like you. I *do* like you."

"When you were sneaking into my bedchamber and kissing me in the garden, I thought you were thrilled to be with me. I thought we shared an affinity."

"Yes, it's very strong."

"Don't lie to me!" she bellowed.

"I'm not lying." He clasped her waist and gave her a slight shake.

"You were buttering me up—for Mr. Oswald. You were ingratiating yourself, so I'd let you seduce me, so I wouldn't protest your arrangement with him."

"That's not true," he insisted, and it wasn't.

He was fascinated by her. Stanley and his sordid scheme were totally separate from James's interest, and he was cursing his deal with Stanley, but he wouldn't apologize for it.

He owed Stanley for all the boons in his life, boons that Stanley had extended without expecting or demanding repayment. Stanley's request regarding Rose was the only time he'd asked James for a favor in return, and James hadn't been able to refuse. He hadn't *wanted* to refuse, and despite what Rose presumed, a physical relationship between them would be wonderful.

He was an experienced lover who could arouse a woman, who could please a woman, and he could please Rose—if she would allow him to. The trick was to convince her that Stanley's plan was for the best.

James had a male opinion of sexual conduct. He was pragmatic and saw it as a means to an end. In the past, he'd exchanged plenty of money in order to engage in carnal acts, and he didn't view Rose's situation as being any different from that of other females with whom he'd consorted over the years.

Stanley was proposing a sensible business agreement. She would offer up her chastity, and if James could plant a babe in her womb, she would be handsomely rewarded. Why should it matter if it was James or Stanley who did the planting?

No one outside the three of them would ever know what had

happened, and the final result would be the same: marriage and a home and family for Rose, the inheritance secured for Stanley's child.

And for James? He'd have the private satisfaction of his son growing up to be lord and master at Summerfield. James didn't intend to ever wed or have sons of his own, so his child with Rose would attain a position in the world that James could never have hoped to provide.

"I believed I could belong here," she woefully mumbled.

"You can belong. You will belong."

"I don't know what to do."

She started to cry in earnest, and he couldn't bear to see her so sad. He pulled her into his arms and held her as she wept. He'd never previously comforted a distraught woman and hadn't understood that it would be so pleasurable. While he stroked a soothing hand up and down her back, she gripped his coat as if— should he release her—she might float off into the sky.

Eventually, the tempest was spent, and she collapsed against him.

"Let's go home," he whispered.

"I can't."

"You *can*," he advised. "A bit ago, you told me that you don't know what to do. I'll decide for you."

"It's wrong," she moaned. "It's all wrong."

"But we'll make it right."

He lifted her, in a quick move seating her on the saddle. He wrapped her fingers in the horse's mane.

"Hold on," he said. "We'll have you snuggled in your bed in no time at all."

She stared down from her high perch, and she was such a lonely sight, silhouetted by the silvery moon.

His heart lurched in his chest, an enormous ache of yearning bubbling up from somewhere deep inside. He tamped it down, grabbed the reins, and headed for the estate.

CHAPTER SEVEN

"Let's walk in the garden."

"I don't think so."

Veronica peeked up at James, aggravated that he'd scarcely noticed her.

They were in the main parlor at Summerfield, with her popping in unannounced. Stanley was nowhere to be found, so Veronica had James all to herself. When she'd arrived, she'd told the servants to bring tea and cakes, acting as if *she* was mistress of the manor. James had stumbled in shortly after, so now she was entertaining him.

Life could be so wonderful!

"How about a ride then?" she suggested. "It's beautiful outside."

"I'd rather not."

"Spoilsport. We used to ride together all the time."

"We did not," he scoffed.

"We did! Our trips are some of my favorite memories. You can't have forgotten. I'll be crushed if you have."

He was telling the truth, and she wasn't. There had been a tiny handful of occasions—when she was ten and eleven—where James had humored her by trotting down the lane at her side. A groomsman was always a few yards behind, watching her every move and reporting back to Oscar, so there'd never been a chance to engage in any misbehavior.

At that early age, she wouldn't have known misbehavior if she'd tripped over it, but it was during those chance meetings that her path had become clear: She would marry James Talbot when she grew up.

Whenever he was home on furlough, he'd still been in the army, so he'd pranced around the estate in his red soldier's coat. When he wore it, she was quite sure there couldn't have been a more attractive man in the entire kingdom.

She'd spent long hours imagining their wedding to the point where she'd decided who would be on the guest list, what gown she'd don for the ceremony, and what food would be served at the breakfast. But if she couldn't ever convince him to be alone with her, how would she achieve her ultimate goal?

"Then let's play cards," she said.

"No."

"Oh, you are such a maddening grump today."

"Tell me again: Why are you here?"

"I've come to visit Miss Ralston."

"I don't believe she's having callers."

"That can't be right," Veronica baldly lied. "She specifically asked me to stop by at two o'clock."

"It appears she changed her mind."

Veronica smirked. "Does she seem like a fusspot to you?"

"No. Why would you pose such a ridiculous question?"

"She's slated to wed Stanley, but she's not very happy about it."

"She seems plenty happy to me."

"You must be joking. Stanley has had to order her to attend every party he's hosted, and she looks so miserable she could be sucking on sour pickles. Then she sneaks out the instant no one is watching."

He glared at her. "It occurs to me that you're much too worried about Miss Ralston. She's none of your business."

"Not my business!" Veronica huffed. "You're joking again. If she marries Stanley, she'll be my aunt. She'll live in the house and direct the activities. She'll have all sorts of influence over me."

"Good," he muttered. "Your mother passed away years ago. You could use some feminine guidance."

"I'm ready to wed," she boldly announced. "I'm eighteen, and I'm weary of Papa Oscar lording himself over me."

"I was raised under Stanley's thumb, so I can understand the feeling."

"I merely have to find someone who tickles my fancy."

"You'd trust Oscar to pick a husband for you?"

"No. I'll pick him myself."

"Really? Would you elope?"

She straightened on the sofa, eager for him to note how pretty she was in her lavender dress. It highlighted the violet color of her eyes, making her appear exotic and unusual. He might have traveled the world in the army, but he'd not have seen any female as fetching as she was.

"I'm not a child anymore."

"No, you're not."

"Who can predict how I'll behave?"

"Not me."

"I might do any wild thing—if the right person asked me."

"I'm sure that's true."

She frowned, trying to decide if she'd just been insulted, and she was irked by the notion. Why was it that men could act outrageously? Why was it that girls' conduct was circumscribed by morals and convention? It was so unfair.

"I'd like to live in London," she said.

"Wouldn't we all?"

"I'd like to be a grand hostess with a thousand friends. I'd hold thrilling parties and surround myself with interesting people."

She'd tossed out a few of her private dreams, anxious to give him a hint of the spectacular path she envisioned for them, but he simply said, "Yes, Veronica, I'm certain you'll have a thousand friends in London someday." He stood and motioned to the door. "Shouldn't you be going? Oscar has to be wondering where you are."

"I'm waiting for Miss Ralston. If she comes down, and I'm not here, she'll be disappointed."

"She'll get over it."

"Yes, well, that's easy for you to say. You're not the one who just moved to a new place and is learning her way. She *needs* me."

"I'll tell her you called."

He walked over to the sofa, took her arm, and lifted her to her feet as if he might drag her out. She wasn't about to embarrass herself by wrestling with him.

"Yes, please tell her I was here," she agreed, mustering her aplomb, "and that I'll visit tomorrow at the same time."

"She'll be delighted."

He gestured to the door again, his implacable glower urging her out. While she could typically coerce men to dote on her, he seemed immune.

"It was lovely," she told him, "having this opportunity to chat with you."

"Goodbye," he said, refusing to bestow the flirtatious response she'd been dying to receive.

She hesitated another second, struggling to figure out an excuse to linger, but she couldn't devise a suitable scenario.

She flashed her most winsome smile, then flounced out. She yearned to glance around to see if he was watching, but she didn't dare.

The butler was in the foyer with her cloak and bonnet—as if he'd been eavesdropping and had known she'd been thrown out. She offered more smiles, then left.

As the door was closed behind her, she dawdled on the front

steps, enjoying the prominent view of the bricked drive and wishing the house was hers. Eventually, she stomped down the stairs and proceeded to the stables, but she wasn't in any hurry to have her horse saddled or to start for home.

To her surprise, Lucas Drake was headed to the stables too, and her smile widened to a grin. James had been rude and irritable, but Mr. Drake never was. Perhaps he'd like to go for the ride that James had declined. Perhaps *he* would like to pass the afternoon with a very pretty, very popular girl.

If they spent a few hours together, who could guess what might transpire?

※ ※ ※ ※

"There's a secluded spot by the pond. Shall we stop?"

"We probably shouldn't."

"I declare, you're as stuffy as James."

"Me! Stuffy?"

Lucas feigned indignation and laughed at Veronica. As he was leaving for the village, she'd magically appeared. She'd asked him to escort her to the vicarage, but James had warned him to be wary.

Not that a bit of danger had ever prevented him from engaging in folly. But still, he'd rather not tussle with Vicar Oswald. And if Lucas *did* misbehave and was caught, Stanley would ban him from Summerfield, which Lucas would hate to have happen.

Over the years, he'd been at the estate constantly—when he was at odds with his own father. In many ways, Summerfield was more his home than his family's seat at Sidwell. Stanley had always been more welcoming too, and that was really saying something.

Plus, now that he and James had mustered out of the army, Lucas didn't know what would become of them. They were both at loose ends. Who could predict where they'd be in another month? In another year?

If James stayed on at Summerfield, Lucas wanted to be able to stay on too, so he couldn't risk getting tossed out. Especially not over a slattern like Veronica.

Yet it was humorous to envision the mischief he could instigate. He'd never been interested in morals or decency, and when a female was begging for trouble, he was happy to oblige.

"When do you have to be back?" he inquired.

"Not for hours."

"You won't be missed if you tarry?"

"No. Papa Oscar believes I'm visiting Miss Ralston."

Her pronunciation of *Papa* reminded him of how young she was. Then again, plenty of girls her age were wed already and had several babes in the nursery. Wise parents usually married off the wild ones before they could commit too many sins.

Veronica was on the verge of a major scandal. If her mother had still been alive, there'd have been a responsible adult to guide her. But there was only the vicar, and he was blind to anyone but himself.

"I suppose we could stop by the pond for a bit," he said.

"Truly?" She beamed with pleasure.

"Yes. Show me your secret spot."

She kicked her horse into a trot, went up the road, then reined in and turned off. He followed, ecstatic to note that they were instantly swallowed by the forest, the thick foliage rendering them invisible and hiding them from passersby.

They emerged to a flat, shady bower. A narrow beach beckoned for him to remove his boots and wade in the cool water. Through the trees, he could see the chimneys of Summerfield Manor.

"How did you discover this place?" he asked, surprised he'd never stumbled on it himself.

"Oh, everyone in the village comes here eventually. If a girl has a beau, it's practically expected that she sneak away at least once."

"Vicar Oswald must not have heard about it."

She chuckled. "Definitely not."

"What's it been like for you, being raised by him?"

"About as horrid as you can imagine. But you know what they say."

"No, what?"

"The preacher's daughter is always the worst."

"That's the rumor, but I've never found it to be true."

"It is," she claimed, and he wondered if she was lying or bragging.

He'd seduced every sort of female—highborn, lowborn, rich, poor, young, old, fat, thin, pretty, ugly—and numerous ones had been vicar's daughters. They'd all sat through too many of their fathers' sermons and were finicky, naïve, and absurdly worried about their chastity.

As to himself, he ignored church teachings and was proudly hedonistic in his disrepute. While previously, he'd enjoyed the flirtation and chase, he now deemed virtuous girls to be incredibly tiresome. He'd choose a doxy any day of the week.

Which would Veronica prove herself to be? Innocent or trollop?

They dismounted, and he seated himself on a boulder, watching as she pranced in front of him, letting him get a good look.

"How many times have you been out here with village boys?"

he asked.

"A half-dozen," she boasted, "but usually, I come with grown men. Boys are so immature."

"Yes, they can be annoying," he mockingly said, "especially when you're so mature yourself."

She missed his sarcasm. "Exactly. I love it when adult men pay attention to me."

"If we're caught, I won't marry you."

"Marry me!" she huffed.

"Yes. I won't care how your reputation has been shredded or how loudly your stepfather rants. So if that's what you're hoping, that you'll end up compromised and rescued from him by a fast wedding, we should be very clear at the start."

"Is that why you think I brought you? To wind up as your wife?"

"It occasionally happens to fellows like me."

She snorted. "I'd never have you for a husband."

"Smart girl."

"Yes, I'm very smart. Besides, I'm marrying James."

"James Talbot?"

"Yes. Does he like me? Has he ever said?"

Lucas could barely bite down a guffaw, aggravated to recognize what a juvenile person she actually was.

"Oh, James is mad for you," he lied, relishing the chance to play a nasty trick on his friend. "He's mentioned it often."

"I knew it!" A sly gleam flared in her eye. "He pretends to be so disinterested. Is he toying with my affections?"

"That must be it. Men are mysterious creatures. They frequently say one thing but mean another."

"Marvelous." She walked toward her horse, suddenly telling him, "Let's go."

"What's the rush? I thought you were eager to dabble with me in the forest."

"Well, there's no need for it now, is there? Not when you've assured me that James will come up to snuff after all."

"Why should we let James ruin our fun?"

"Are you insane? I have to save myself for him."

"Save yourself? I could have sworn you said you've been out here with numerous men. Grown ones at that."

"I was trifling with them," she hastily insisted. "I didn't do anything I shouldn't."

"You little tease," he scolded. "I should get some amusement for my trouble, don't you think?"

"I'm not a tease," she seethed.

"From where I'm sitting, it certainly seems like you are. You begged me to sneak in here with you."

"You didn't have to."

"No, but I participated in anticipation of a reward. I still want it. What should it be? What should I demand?"

"What are you talking about?"

"You're awfully innocent for a girl who regularly trifles with boys."

"I'm *not* innocent!"

"Prove it," he said.

"How?"

He was being an ass. There was no doubt about it, and if he was a gentleman—which he'd never been—he would have taken pity on her and let her slink away. But the longer he dawdled in her company, the less he liked her, and for some reason, he was determined to make a point.

The rash child! By luring him to the private, secluded area, what did she imagine would occur? She was lucky she hadn't been ravished a thousand times over.

"Come here," he said.

"Why?"

"You have to learn what happens when you're not careful. And with you being such an irritating trollop, you'll probably like it."

"I'm not a trollop! How dare you call me names!"

"Come here," he stated more firmly, and he gestured impatiently.

For all her impudence and attitude, it was impossible for her to ignore his command. She took a hesitant step, then another, approaching tentatively until they were toe-to-toe.

He pushed himself to his feet, and with his being six feet tall, he towered over her. He'd expected her to lurch away, but she didn't. Perhaps she was too stupid to realize she could flee. If she ran off, he was too lazy to chase her down.

"What?" she snapped, her expression mulish.

"I want to see your breasts."

She gasped. "Absolutely not."

"It's the price I'm charging for you wasting my time."

She dithered and debated, finally declaring, "I won't do it. You can't make me."

"I can't? You idiot. You're out in the woods with a dissolute, older man, and you don't believe I can force you into any conduct I wish?"

"I'm not scared of you," she asserted, but she was trembling.

"Fine. Loose your bodice." Her expression became more defiant, and he coaxed, "You claim you misbehave with other fellows all the time. Why not with me?"

"I don't like you. I thought I did, but I've changed my mind."

"Would you like to know what I think? I think you've never been out here with a boy. I think you envision yourself as being reckless and naughty, but in reality, you're just a prudish vicar's daughter."

"Bastard!" she hissed.

"You've learned some curse words. How nice."

He waited, then waited some more, wearing her down with his greater age, size, and male authority.

Her cheeks reddened, then she reached for the top button on her dress and flicked open the top one. She was bound up from chin to toe, every inch of skin concealed as a proper English girl should be, and he saw only a flash of chest.

He grabbed her and undid a few more buttons, then tugged down fabric to bare her upper arms. He yanked at corset and chemise, and two very plump, very delectable breasts popped into view.

He studied them, deeming them to be perfectly delightful. Too bad they were attached to such an unpleasant shrew.

"You're embarrassing me," she mumbled.

"You embarrassed yourself. I had nothing to do with it."

He clasped her by her waist and drew her to him, holding her close so she couldn't escape. With his free hand, he stroked one mound, then the other. He pinched a nipple, liking how it tightened, liking how she frowned at him.

"This is what a man wants," he told her. "This is what a man likes."

"I knew that," she said.

"Liar," he chuckled. "He'll touch you here. He'll kiss you here. And other places too."

"I'm not afraid of a bit of kissing."

"I'm sure you're not. In fact, I'm positive—in the future—you'll get all kinds of fools to lust after you. But I won't be one of them."

He shoved her, and she stumbled away.

"Are you finished?" she spat. "May I cover myself?"

"Yes, you may."

He watched her, his expression stony, as she strutted around, straightening herself. She marched to her horse and let him help her mount without protest.

Once she was seated, she fumed, "You're despicable."

"Yes, I always have been." He grinned. "Good luck with your pursuit of James. I'll be happy to inform him that your teats are very pretty."

She growled with offense, jerked on the reins, and kicked her horse into a gallop. As she hurtled through the trees, she called another slur over her shoulder, but she was too far away for him to hear.

"Stupid chit," he muttered.

He climbed onto his own horse and rode away at a much slower clip.

<hr>

"Please, Miss Ralston."

Stanley stared at her, waiting for her to reply. When she didn't, he tried again. "Please. It's all I can say."

Still, she was silent as a tomb. Women typically drove him batty with their incessant chatter. Now, when he wished one of them would speak, she couldn't be bothered.

He recognized she was in a snit, but they had to move forward, the difficulty being that—with all his cards on the table and his hand rebuffed—he had no idea how to win her agreement.

James appeared to understand her better than Stanley ever could. He'd caught her out on the road, headed for the village in the middle of the night. To do *what* when she arrived, Stanley couldn't guess. The little fool had no money or place to go. The ridiculousness, the irrationality of females never ceased to amaze him.

They were in his library, with her ordered down to attend him. He was seated at his desk, and she was in the chair across. He probably should have brought James in to join the discussion, but he'd decided James's presence would make matters worse, so Stanley and Miss Ralston were alone.

It was late afternoon, and she'd been cowering in her room all day. He'd had enough.

"How can we end this idiotic quarrel?" he said.

"We're not quarreling," she finally responded.

"Yes, we are. How can I mend the situation?"

"You can't."

"Nonsense. Every problem has a solution. Let's find ours."

He hated to grovel, never attempted it, wasn't proficient at it, and loathed that he had to plead with her. He had no aptitude for begging.

"What precisely is the nature of your complaint about James?" he asked.

"I have no complaint about Mr. Talbot."

"Then it's some moral question vexing you?"

"Yes, it's a moral question," she mocked.

"I suppose we could invite the vicar to counsel you," he sarcastically retorted.

She shot a glare so virulent that he was taken aback. After

hearing Miss Peabody's description of her, he hadn't presumed Miss Ralston to be strongwilled. The notion that she was tougher than he'd assumed made him more determined to have his way.

"I have to know something," she said.

"What is it?"

"And tell me the truth."

"As much of it as I'm able."

"What is Mr. Talbot's relationship to you?"

"There is no relationship," he scoffed.

"So…you've resolved to have a son at all costs, to pass him off as your own, and you'll have him sired by a virtual stranger. You expect me to believe that?"

"James is hardly a stranger at Summerfield, Miss Ralston. He grew up here, under my tutelage, and you have two eyes in your head, so you've seen the facts for yourself. There is no finer male specimen in the kingdom, and any child he fathered would be remarkable." He nodded, considering the subject clarified and settled. "It's what I want: a remarkable, extraordinary heir to be in charge after I'm dead."

"With *me* as the mother," she jeered.

"Yes. Should I apologize for thinking you're remarkable too? Well, I won't. I can't have some trembling ninny for this role. I need a woman who can give me the son of whom I've always dreamed. Why are you so convinced that it can't be you?"

"You're mad," she insisted.

"You're not the first person who's thought so."

"Let me go away. Return my dowry and I'll leave. I'll take your secret to the grave. I promise. Just let me go."

"No."

"Please?"

He'd started the conversation with begging, and she'd ended it with begging.

He sighed with exasperation.

As far as he was concerned, her predicament was exactly the same except that she'd suffered a fit of pique over Stanley's arrangement with James. She still had no money or kin, and—if her womb proved fertile—she could marry Stanley and be mistress of Summerfield. He merely had to persuade her that his plan was best.

"You're distressed today," he said.

"Who wouldn't be?"

"You shouldn't make decisions when you're angry."

"I won't feel any differently tomorrow."

"Perhaps not. But how about in a week? You'd be surprised how the passage of time can alter one's opinion."

"I won't change my mind."

"I want you to stay for a month. Meet more of the neighbors and become better acquainted with James. You should be absolutely certain you wish to leave."

"I'm certain now."

"A month, Miss Ralston," he cajoled. "How can it hurt? It's not as if you have an offer of shelter or employment. Remain here—as my honored guest. Grow comfortable. Learn to love my home as I have always loved it."

"I repeat: You're mad."

"No, not mad. Not in this." He softened his expression so he'd seem wise and kind—when he was neither. "I'm an old man, Miss Ralston. I've spent my entire life chasing this magnificent but elusive goal. I can't give up without a fight. Tell me you'll stay. Tell me you'll help an old man in his hour of need."

For an eternity, she stared at him, then—when she broke away and peered down at her hands—he knew he'd won.

"Just one month," she grumbled, "and when the thirty days are up and I ask to go, you won't prevent me."

"Of course I won't."

"No arguments. No wheedling discussions. No playing on my sympathies or trying to dissuade me. You'll let me go."

"Yes, I will," he lied. "In the meantime, as an insurance policy for you, I'll write to some of the schools where I am a patron. If you ultimately choose to depart, you'll have a teaching position waiting for you."

"Swear it," she demanded.

"I swear," he lied again.

"All right." There was a lengthy, fraught silence, then she pushed herself to her feet. "May I be excused?"

"Yes, and I hope you'll join me at supper."

"I will."

"In the morning, I have a seamstress coming to speak with you."

"A seamstress? Why?"

"You're very pretty, and you should have some pretty clothes."

"You mustn't trouble yourself on my behalf."

He forced a smile. "If you're to be my bride, Miss Ralston—and I'm an optimist who's fully expecting it to happen—you must look the part."

"If I'm leaving shortly, it will be a waste of money."

"I don't think so. I'm betting it will be the best investment I've ever made."

"No, trust me. It will be a great waste."

She spun and left.

The door shut behind her, and he smirked with satisfaction. She'd never escape him, and she was a fool to assume she could.

He rang for the butler to summon James. The boy had to get to work on wooing her. She hardly required new gowns to incite James's attention, but they couldn't hurt.

CHAPTER EIGHT

"Hello, Mr. Talbot."

"Hello."

It was very late, the whole house abed, and he was in her suite again, in the sitting room and seated in a chair by the fire. She'd just returned from a neighbor's supper party. James could have gone, but hadn't, and he'd found himself regretting the decision, because he'd missed the chance to socialize with her.

To his great relief, she hadn't tried to sneak away again. Not that she could have. After James informed Stanley that he'd caught her out on the road and brought her back, Stanley had assigned footmen to furtively spy on her so she couldn't make a second attempt.

He grinned. "Aren't you surprised to see me?"

"No."

"We've only been acquainted a few days. Have I become predictable already?"

"Very predictable." She frowned. "I don't suppose it would do any good to tell you to leave."

"A waste of breath."

"That's what I thought."

She marched by him and proceeded through the bedchamber and into the dressing room. He followed, tagging after her as if he had every right.

Though he was pretending the previous evening hadn't happened, he hadn't succeeded in forgetting it. He kept thinking of how angry she'd been at Stanley, but mostly, he kept thinking about the quiet moment they'd shared on the dark road.

There was something so tenderly touching about how she'd snuggled herself to his chest and wept as if her heart was breaking. It had rattled him in ways he didn't like and hadn't intended. Apparently, he'd developed fond feelings for her, when he couldn't have any feelings at all.

He had to get their relationship back on track, had to reestablish himself as the cad and libertine he'd always been. Yes, he'd spent some intriguing minutes comforting her, but he wasn't a sympathetic person, and the encounter was over. He had to stop reflecting and move on.

She was standing at the mirror, taking down her hair and completely unconcerned that he was watching.

"I love your hair," he told her. "It's very beautiful."

"So you've said."

"Am I so miserly in my compliments that I'm repeating them?"

"Yes."

He hated that she was ignoring him, and he was determined to get a rise out of her.

"Aren't you incensed that I'm here? Aren't you going to shoo me out?"

"As you mentioned, Mr. Talbot, it would be a waste of breath."

"When we're alone, you must call me James."

"No."

"Since I was bribed to bed you as quickly as I could manage it, it seems ridiculously pointless to be so formal."

She whipped around, shooting him a glare so lethal that, if her eyes had been bullets, he'd have been dead on the floor.

"There won't be any *bedding* or anything else between us, so if that's why you're lurking, you can leave."

"Stanley tells me he's convinced you to stay for a month—so I can charm you."

"Mr. Oswald is an idiot."

"Too true." His grin widened. "I'm delighted to learn that you are such an excellent judge of character. It was years before I figured out his genuine nature. Of course, I was a boy when I arrived, so I can't be castigated for failing to notice what he was like until much later on."

She picked up her brush and started pulling it through her hair. She rubbed her temples, shifted her neck and shoulders.

"Do you have a headache?" he asked.

"Yes, my hair is very heavy. I always take it down the minute I can."

"You can wear it down whenever you're with me. I won't be shocked. In fact, I prefer it down."

"I'm sure you would. Isn't it the accepted style for trollops? I'm guessing you'd be intimately familiar with such a thing."

"Yes, my favorite doxies all wear it down."

She snorted and muttered a remark he couldn't hear, and he leaned against the doorframe, holding onto the wood to keep himself in place. He wanted to saunter over and brush her hair for her, but she was still furious. If he approached, she might whack him with the ivory handle.

"Your brush is very fine," he pointed out.

"Too fine for a mere schoolteacher? Is that what you're hinting?"

"No, just...commenting."

"Lest you accuse me of theft, it was my mother's. It's one of the few items I have that belonged to her."

"Who was your mother? Who was her family? Would I know them?"

She scowled over her shoulder. "No, you wouldn't know them."

"You're an orphan, so I'm assuming she's passed on."

"You're assuming correctly."

"What happened to her?"

"She and my father perished from a plague in Egypt when I was four."

"Really? You were living in Egypt? How very exotic."

"Yes, I'm a veritable bubbling cauldron of unusual traits."

"Why were they in Egypt?"

She sighed as if his questions were a burden, but he couldn't stop asking them. He was much too fascinated by her, and despite what she believed, Stanley was insisting the seduction proceed.

James hadn't decided how he felt about it. It was only proper to back out, yet she was still on the premises and would remain for thirty more days. James was aware of how Stanley could grind people down and coerce them into doing his bidding. Before it was finished, any ending might occur.

"My father was a missionary," she said.

"Your mother too?"

"No. My mother married *down* and was disowned for it. She was trailing after my father because she loved him madly and foolishly. She'd perished for her folly."

"I'm sorry," he murmured.

"It was a long time ago."

She laid down the brush and came toward him. He was blocking the door, and at her sudden proximity, sparks ignited.

"I like it that you're brazen enough to take your hair down in front of me."

"Well, James, if I waited for you to depart so I could do it without you watching, I'd have a headache the rest of my life."

"You called me James! We're making progress."

"You're right for once. With how forward you've been, there's no reason to pretend formality."

She shoved him, and he obliged her, stepping back to let her by.

"I'd like to put on my nightgown and robe," she said as she walked on, "but I suppose it's too much to hope that you'd go away so I can get ready for bed."

"You can change your clothes. Don't mind me."

"You are a rude, impertinent beast," she growled.

"Yes. I was raised without parents. By the time I arrived at Summerfield, Edwina tried to temper my worst habits, but they were too ingrained."

"Poor woman."

"Yes, she was a very poor woman indeed."

Rose continued on to the sitting room, and he followed. She was over by the table in the corner. The maids had delivered a tray with a decanter of wine and slices of bread and cheese. She poured herself a glass of wine and nibbled on the cheese.

"Drinking, Rose?"

"Yes, drinking, James."

"I'm shocked."

"I didn't enjoy many pleasures at Miss Peabody's school. She was a stickler for proprieties and her teachers had to set an example."

"So no alcohol?"

"Actually, I think she was just miserly and didn't wish to buy any for us. She kept wine in her room, but she never shared." She gulped down the contents of her glass, then poured herself another. "I've agreed to tarry for a month, and I've decided to view my sojourn as an overdue holiday. I plan to indulge myself."

"Good for you."

"Mr. Oswald told you I'm staying."

"Yes."

"Is there anything you two don't discuss?"

"There's plenty, but where you're concerned, it appears I'm his only confidante."

"Wonderful. When you're gossiping about me, you may inform him that—while I'm in residence—I intend to pamper myself. I never had a chance to imbibe at Miss Peabody's, so now, I shall. The situation seems to call for it."

"Aren't you worried you'll become a lush?"

"Who cares? Not me, I assure you."

The maids hadn't realized she'd have a guest, so there was just the one glass. He took it from her, expecting to relish his own long swallow, but she let him have only a taste, then yanked it away.

"In many respects, I'm very much like Miss Peabody," she said. "I hate to share. Next time, bring your own glass."

"I'm delighted to hear there will be a *next* time."

"You're like a bad rash, James. I haven't a clue how to be rid of you."

"Why would you want to be rid of me? The more frequently we

socialize, the more I promise you'll grow to like me."

"Yes, I'm certain I will," she facetiously chided.

She poured more wine, then went to the window and stared out across the park. He came up behind her and stepped close, the front of his body touching hers all the way down. She could have moved away, could have jabbed him with her elbow and forced him back, but she didn't.

They stood quietly, and he was curious as to what she was thinking. As for himself, he was overwhelmed by her smell. It was a fresh, flowery scent that rattled his masculine sensibilities.

Unable to resist, he reached out and stroked his hand down her hair, riffling his fingers through the soft strands. Again, she didn't protest or push him away. She seemed to have lost the energy to fight. Or maybe he was so insignificant to her that she simply didn't notice.

"Your hair is such an unusual shade. Did you inherit it from your mother?"

"I have no idea. I don't remember much about her."

"We have that in common."

"You don't remember your mother, either?"

"No, not at all. I don't even know her name. Or my father's."

"How sad for you."

"Yes, it is sad. It's always bothered me."

"I can imagine it would," she said. "I have fleeting visions of me being very tiny, sitting on her lap."

"If you look like her, she must have been very pretty."

"I'd like to think she was."

She turned so she was facing him, and still, she didn't shove him away, which was an encouraging sign. Then again, she was on her third glass of wine and that was just the ones he'd seen her drink. She'd probably had more at the supper party, and he was tantalized by the notion that she might be intoxicated.

He thought liquor worked wonders on a woman's disposition, and he was more than happy to take advantage when inhibitions were lowered.

She gazed up at him, her green eyes probing, digging deep.

"Tell me something," she said.

"Anything."

"Why did you agree to Stanley's scheme?"

He shrugged, trying to be flip. "Why not?"

"Don't act like that," she scolded, frowning.

"Like what?"

"Like it's a game, like the entire affair doesn't disturb you."

"All right," he nodded. "Let's be candid."

"Let's be."

He pressed himself to her, pushing her against the wall. He could feel every inch of her, her firm breasts, her flat belly, her shapely thighs. His cock sprang to attention, turning hard as stone.

"He asked me," James admitted, "when he's never asked me for any favor before. I said yes. I shouldn't have, but I did."

"Why couldn't you refuse? What is his hold over you?"

"He has no *hold*. Despite his gruff exterior, he's showered my life with blessings. I'm grateful for them."

"Why did he do all this for you? It can't be because his wife demanded it."

"The rumor is that I'm his natural-born son."

"Are you?"

"How could I be? Can you picture Edwina—or any wife—welcoming a bastard child into her home? She was kind to me. She didn't live long after I arrived—her health was failing when I got here—but for the period when I knew her, she was very kind."

"You don't resemble him in even the slightest way."

"No. That's why I've never given much credence to the gossip."

"And Mr. Oswald? What does he say? Have you asked him?"

"A thousand times."

"What is his explanation? It can't be that you were the one lucky street urchin, selected from all the street urchins in London."

"He claims it was exactly that. He claims he wrote to the orphanage and requested a healthy, smart boy to entertain Edwina in her last days. I was the one who was sent."

"You believe him?"

"Of course not. It's how he manipulates me. He realizes that I'd love to know, so he hides the truth. If I learned it, he'd have no further means of influencing my behavior."

Suddenly, his heart was pounding. He never discussed the situation with others. Lucas had been apprised, but mostly, people assumed he was a poor relative or that he was Stanley's ward and reared at Summerfield out of legal duty.

James never clarified any misconceptions, and he most definitely never expounded on his place in the household. Yet with no effort at all, she'd drawn out the whole story, and he didn't like that she had such an ability to delve and pry.

Needing a moment to compose himself, he took her glass of wine, downed the contents, then spun away to refill it. He sipped at it, watching her as she watched him in return.

He set the glass on a nearby table, then he came back and rested his palms on her waist, pulling her to him. She studied him, wary and a tad aggrieved, but she didn't tell him to stop.

"Why would you sire a child for him?" she inquired. "I don't understand it."

"I told you: He asked it of me."

"How could you blithely lie down and commit marital acts with impunity? We're not even remotely acquainted. How could you consider it?"

"Physical lust is different for a man than it is for a woman. It's simply that: physical conduct. A man can do it with any female. There doesn't have to be an emotional attachment."

She scoffed. "You make it sound sordid and unpleasant."

"I'm just stating the facts." On explaining it aloud, he seemed so cold and callous. What had he been thinking? He hadn't been thinking; that was the problem.

When Stanley had first broached the subject, James hadn't viewed her as a real person, and he'd figured he wouldn't like her very much. After all, if she was the type who'd agree to Stanley's proposal, she had to be a ninny. It had been easy to scheme against her.

"But if I'd been amenable," she said, pressing the issue, "if I'd let you try, I would have birthed your son, and Stanley would have been hailed as his father. Wouldn't that have bothered you? Wouldn't it have galled you to keep silent and pretend the boy wasn't yours?"

"I hadn't thought it through that far. It was extremely difficult for Stanley to confide in me, and I felt I could repay my many debts to him by giving him the one thing he'd always craved most in the world." He laughed miserably. "I thought we'd finally be even."

"And you'd be free of him," she mused, absolutely getting it.

"Yes, and my son would have been heir to Summerfield. It was enough for me, and I'm very vain. I liked the notion of having a secret to hold over Stanley for a change. It intrigued me."

She raised a brow. "You've furnished some very pretty excuses, James. Perhaps I don't hate you quite as much now."

"See? We *are* making progress."

"It appears we are," she concurred.

He was tired of chatting, tired of stirring a pot of old memories. What was the point? It simply left him morose.

They couldn't alter the past, couldn't forget that James had plotted with Stanley to her disadvantage. They could only move forward in some sort of rational way.

He'd probably forsaken his vow to Stanley, had probably abandoned his intention to deflower her. But nevertheless, a relationship was blossoming between them. Should he ignore it? Should he pursue it?

If he jumped into a liaison, what was his goal? Would he be doing it for Stanley? For himself? What was the benefit to himself? What was the benefit to her?

He was positive there was no benefit for her. There was just detriment, but he was randy and unprincipled. If she was offering herself, he would take much more than she'd meant to give him, and he wouldn't hang around through any wretched ending. Yet she didn't know that, and he wasn't about to apprise her.

She likely presumed him possessed of the honor that Stanley lacked. If so, she'd assumed wrongly.

He was desperately attracted to her. What man wouldn't be? She was smart and pithy and beautiful. He'd have to be blind and stupid not to desire her, and suddenly, she seemed much more amenable to an affair, when he had no idea why she'd have changed her mind.

He was certain it was the wine talking. She'd had too much of it, when she wasn't a regular drinker. It was late and they were alone. She'd brushed her hair while he'd watched. The act was intimate in a manner he couldn't describe, more intimate than if she'd removed her clothes.

In their world, it was a tantalizing gift, and if he lingered long enough, what others might she bestow?

He dipped down and nibbled at her nape, taking small bites that made her squirm and chuckle.

"I want you to kiss me again," she stunned him by saying.

"I plan on it." He licked her skin with his tongue. "What brought this on?"

"When I decided to pamper myself this month, it dawned on me that there are many things I've never tried."

"Kissing is one of them?"

"Yes."

"So...I'm in the perfect position to show you how it's supposed to be done."

"That's what I was thinking."

"You've had an enormous amount of wine. You know that alcohol lowers inhibitions, don't you?"

"Yes, I know that."

"It's entirely possible that you'll allow liberties tonight that you'll regret in the morning."

"Yes, it is." She grinned. "But I'm on holiday, remember?"

"Yes, I definitely remember."

"I'm in the mood for a little excitement."

"And I am just the man to provide it."

CHAPTER NINE

"Would you call me Rose?"

"Absolutely."

"And just for a bit, would you pretend I'm the most wonderful woman you've ever met?"

James chuckled. "I'd be happy to."

Rose sighed with pleasure.

She was pressed to the wall, his long, muscular body crushed to her own, and she'd never endured anything quite so marvelous. He was nibbling at her nape, goose bumps cascading down her arms. Her skin was tingling, her pulse racing.

She was trying to figure out what she was doing, where they were headed, but she had no idea.

She didn't know him, didn't particularly like him, and he'd thrust himself into her path with the worst of intentions, but their encounter on the road the previous night had altered her. She felt attached to him in ways she shouldn't be, felt that he understood and cared about her, which was nonsense. Where he was concerned, her emotions were now a jumble of confused yearning and regret.

He was a cad and a bounder, the exact sort of man she should have avoided like the plague, and normally would have. But she'd attended a supper with Stanley, and as they'd returned home, her cheeks had ached from all her fake smiling.

During the lengthy evening of socializing, she'd had an enormous amount of time to ponder her situation.

She'd agreed to remain at Summerfield for one month, and gradually, it had dawned on her that she could use the interval to rest and regroup. She'd told James that she considered herself to be on holiday, and she'd meant it.

She'd never gone on holiday before. As a girl, she'd been a year-round boarder at school, and as an adult, she'd never earned enough money to frivolously travel. After drinking more and more wine, an ember of excitement had begun to burn.

There was no need to cower in her room, moping and

bemoaning her fate. Mr. Oswald had insisted she was his honored guest, so why not act like it? She'd never stayed in such a fine house, had never been fawned over or spoiled. Why not indulge? Why not treat herself? Why not?

In a month, when she packed her bag and trotted down the road, she was sure—wherever her destination—it would never be a place so grand as Summerfield.

So...she planned to enjoy herself. She would eat and dance and revel at every party that was hosted. And she was going to misbehave with a very handsome, very remarkable libertine.

It was a reckless decision, and—as he'd mentioned—she'd had too much wine and was likely making bad choices, but she'd proceed anyway.

Once she departed Summerfield, her life would return to the drudgery of work, and there would be no opportunity for flirtation. If she resumed teaching, she wouldn't be allowed to marry. She'd have to remain a spinster. So if she stole some kisses, in the dark of night, in the privacy of her own bedchamber, where was the harm? Who would ever know?

He abandoned her nape to finally capture her lips in a torrid kiss that was wild and exhilarating and much too thrilling to be refused.

She wrapped her arms around his waist and pulled him nearer, and he appeared to relish her boldness. He groaned low in his throat and leaned into her, his firm torso crushed to hers in a way that was invigorating and arousing.

"You have too many clothes on," he murmured.

"Well, I'm not taking any of them off."

"How about just a few of them?"

"How about I leave them right where they are?"

"What fun would that be?"

He started kissing her again, his tongue sliding in and out of her mouth in a stirring rhythm that made her nipples throb and her womb clench. He was touching her all over, his busy hands gliding across her shoulders, her waist and hips.

He stroked in broader and broader circles until he was caressing her buttocks, holding her loins to his, and the feeling was indescribable, like nothing she could have imagined or anticipated.

Her limbs were rubbery, her knees weak. She could barely keep her balance, and if he hadn't been gripping her so tightly, she'd have collapsed to the floor in a stunned heap.

It occurred to her that—in her drive to engage in a dalliance—she might not have fully grasped the significance of what she'd set in motion. She'd viewed herself as worldly and mature, that she could use him to learn the secret details of amour, but she wasn't prepared for the unrelenting onslaught. She was about to beg him to do whatever he wished to her—and damn the consequences.

There was a sofa next to them, and he drew away from her and lie down. He tugged her down too, so in a thrice she was stretched out on top of him.

He was still kissing her and hadn't stopped for a single second. As the embrace went on and on, the temperature of the encounter spiraled out of control. His hands were on her bottom again, and he was flexing into her, the fabric of her skirt the only barrier separating them. Each brush of his loins sent shocks of delight coursing through her entire being.

"Why are you moving like that?" she managed to ask.

"Because it feels wonderful."

"Yes, it does."

"It's a preliminary step toward mating."

She froze. "We're not mating."

"No," he hastily said. "We're simply enjoying ourselves."

"We're sinning, aren't we?"

"Yes, but I never thought a bit of sin was such a bad thing. Not when it feels this good."

She definitely agreed. The reason ministers complained so vociferously about carnal conduct had to be that they hated to have people discover the pleasure it elicited.

If maidens and spinsters had any idea of the ecstasy to be had, they'd ruin themselves with impunity. If females knew the truth, who could ever convince them to behave?

"If Vicar Oswald could see us now," she mused, "he'd have an apoplexy."

"He'd have us dragged to church and whipped."

"And guess what?"

"What?"

"I wouldn't be sorry!"

They giggled like unruly children, and she couldn't remember the last time she'd been so free or happy. The insight disturbed her. It made her think that perhaps she'd been *un*happy but hadn't realized it. It made her think she liked James Talbot more than she should, when she hadn't planned to like him at all.

As their chortling waned, the kissing commenced again. He rolled them so she was on her side and wedged to the back of the sofa. Without her noticing, he'd unbuttoned the front of her dress. Cool air swept over her chest and was the first indication that skin was exposed, but she didn't protest or order him to desist.

His sly fingers slipped inside her gown, slithered under corset and chemise to touch her breasts. The sensation was so arresting that she gasped aloud.

"Oh, my," she murmured against his questing lips.

"Oh, my indeed. You have a knack for this, Rose."

"Are my reactions natural then?"

"They're very natural."

"I like this so much. It's not…abnormal?"

"No. It's very, very normal. Why do you suppose it's so soundly condemned? It's so much fun, we might never leave this sofa."

"A marvelous notion."

"It certainly is."

He pinched her nipple, rubbing it, squeezing it, as he deepened their kiss, as he held her even closer.

They'd finally crossed a boundary she shouldn't have allowed, and she meant to call a halt. She really did, but then he undid the remainder of the buttons on her dress and tugged down the sleeves so her upper arms were bared.

To her astonishment, he nuzzled a trail to her cleavage and sucked a nipple into his mouth. He nursed at it as a babe would have, but there was nothing innocent about the conduct. It felt wicked and delectable, and she pulled him even nearer to urge him on. For an eternity, he suckled and played, and she let him proceed, being too overwhelmed to resist.

Eventually, he slowed and ceased his torment, and she could hardly keep from begging him to continue on until…until…

She couldn't describe the end she sought.

He smiled, and there was warmth and affection in his gaze. She was shocked by how it washed over her, by how she reveled in it. She suffered a huge wave of her own affection, and clearly, there was a fondness developing between them that she hadn't expected to arise.

"Why did we stop?" she asked.

"We shouldn't go any farther."

"There's more to it?"

"Yes, quite a bit more."

"Show me."

"I don't think you actually want that."

"Maybe I do," she brazenly said. "Maybe it's exactly what I want."

"It just might be, but I'm not about to give it to you."

"You're too cruel, James, to toy with me like this."

"Yes," he laughed, "cruelty is my middle name."

"I thought this was merely a trifle, but it seems like it was more profound than that."

"It was—because we share a heightened attraction."

"Why would we?"

"It's an unanswerable question."

"A mystery of the universe?"

"Yes."

They were silent, staring. He was studying her as if she'd disturbed him, as if she'd turned out to be entirely different from what he'd imagined.

"What now?" she inquired.

"I should probably go." But he didn't move.

"I feel strange—as if I've been scraped raw on the inside."

"It's desire rattling you."

"Desire?"

"Yes. A woman can experience very potent desire. It's a secret that's supposed to keep you females from misbehaving."

"And I've definitely misbehaved." She pondered for a moment, then asked, "Am I still...?"

"Chaste? Yes, you're still a maiden."

"How would I change the situation? Mr. Oswald said it was a physical act and that he couldn't perform it anymore."

"It is very physical," he agreed, but didn't expound.

"What does it entail?"

"I might demonstrate sometime," he cockily retorted, "if you're very, very nice to me."

"Vain oaf," she scoffed.

"Yes, I am much too vain and much too dissolute to be with you like this."

She shrugged. "I told you I'm on holiday. I'm trying every new thing I can."

"Yes, but what you don't realize is that an innocent frolic can swiftly lead to trouble you never intended."

"I *intended* all that just happened. I practically begged you to proceed, remember?"

"Oh, yes, I remember."

He kissed her very sweetly, very tenderly, and when he pulled away, he was smiling even more affectionately.

He sat up and stood, and she should have stood too, but she couldn't. The room seemed off balance, as if the floor was crooked and she couldn't find a straight spot.

"Promise me something," he said.

"What?"

"If you discover you're in the mood to try new *things* again, try them with me. I can't have you pestering the stable boys."

She laughed. "You are the worst."

"I want you all to myself."

"You talk as if I roll around with strange men everyday. This was a once in a lifetime occurrence, I assure you. Otherwise, I might begin to like it too much."

"I've created a wanton! How marvelous." He tapped a finger on the tip of her nose. "Let me explain about desire."

"What?"

"It has to be assuaged. If it's not, you'll drive yourself batty."

"You're expecting me to be discomfited?"

"Yes, and it's a dreadful bother." He went to the door. "If you get too miserable, I'll be happy to come back and alleviate your...problem."

"I'll keep that in mind."

He grinned, and she did too, and they stared like two halfwits. A thousand comments swirled, and she was desperate to say the right parting remark, but she couldn't figure out what it should be.

Finally, she murmured, "Thank you."

"For what?"

"For being kind. For showing me this. I didn't know how it could be."

"Now you do."

"I feel like you opened a hidden door, and I peeked in at a different world."

"We can walk through if you want. I can teach you more and more."

"I can't."

"It was worth a shot to ask."

"It was."

"We're a terrific match, you and I."

"Yes, we are."

"I hate to have all this unbridled passion go to waste."

"It won't be wasted. It will sizzle whenever I see you in the halls."

"Then I'll make it a point to bump into you often."

He tarried, as if he couldn't bear to leave, then he nodded.

"Goodnight, Rose."

"Goodnight, James."

"We're a pair, aren't we?"

"We definitely are."

He slipped out, vanishing so quickly that he might never have been there at all. She couldn't even hear his footsteps fading down the hall.

"You spent time with her."

"Yes."

"You spoke at length."

"Yes."

Stanley glared at James, waiting for him to provide details, but he was maddeningly silent.

"And...?"

"And what?"

"Were you able to make any progress?"

"Are you asking if she's been deflowered?"

"Yes. Don't pretend to be surprised by my interest."

"Trust me, I'm not surprised."

"Have you pressed the issue?"

"No."

"Then why were you with her?"

"I like her," James said. "I like her very much. We had an enjoyable time together."

"In her room."

"Yes."

"Alone."

"Yes."

"Yet you expect me to believe nothing happened?"

"I don't care what you believe."

"Ah," Stanley mused. "So you *did* make some progress."

"We chatted. That's all."

"Was any clothing removed?"

"No."

"Buttons unbuttoned?"

"No."

"You were in there for over an hour. Were you drinking tea?"

"Wine."

"She had plenty at supper."

"She had more with me."

"It didn't render her amorous? It didn't lower inhibitions? Why couldn't you take advantage?"

"I didn't try," James claimed, which was an outright lie.

They were in Stanley's library, having a late night brandy. A bit earlier, Stanley had been astonished to see James sneak into her room, and he was irked by the discovery. He liked to know what went on under his roof.

The fact that James could dabble with Rose, that he had the youth and physical stamina to do so, made Stanley sick with envy. He hated being old and having his manly parts fail. He'd always been a masculine, virile fellow, and he couldn't abide that he'd lost his ability and couldn't fix the problem.

"Where are we in our bargain?" he asked.

"There is no bargain. We're calling it off."

"We are not."

"We are."

"If you refuse to proceed, where does that leave me?"

"Where you were before you ever spoke to Miss Peabody about her. You have to find another girl."

"I have no desire to find another girl. Have you any idea how difficult it was to find Miss Ralston? I need someone who's all alone, who has no family she can run to. I need someone who will do what I say."

"I guess you picked wrong with her."

"I doubt it. I have thirty days to get my way."

"Only if *I* help you, and I've changed my mind."

"Have you suddenly grown noble and decent?"

"No. I simply don't want to participate. It was a stupid plan. I never should have agreed."

"Will you give up your chance to learn about your parents?"

"Yes. I'm sure you wouldn't have turned over any true information anyway."

"What about the thousand pounds I promised you? That kind of money could take a man a far distance."

James shrugged. "I have many contacts from my years in the army. I'll stumble on an opportunity. I don't have to rely on you."

Stanley hid his reaction to the comment. It was his greatest fear that James might not need him any longer. Stanley was accustomed to having James on the premises and under his thumb. Though he'd initially fought Edwina's demand to bring James to the estate, Stanley was glad he had.

James was smart and shrewd and interesting, loyal and faithful, the sort of boy any father would love to claim. Other men were fools by comparison. Just consider Lucas Drake.

"You're not leaving for London, are you?" he said.

"I probably will. With our bargain cancelled, there's no reason to remain."

"What about Miss Ralston?"

"What about her?"

"You have a budding relationship with her. Wouldn't you like to discover where it will lead?"

"There is no relationship."

James pushed himself to his feet and headed for the door, and Stanley called to his retreating back, "What will Miss Ralston think when she hears you've departed?"

"She won't think anything. We're scarcely acquainted."

But Stanley knew it was another lie.

Although James didn't realize it, there was a peephole that looked directly into her bedchamber. Stanley could lurk in the dark in the rear stairwell and watch her.

He'd drilled the hole years earlier, during his third marriage, when his impotency had first begun to flare. He'd always enjoyed observing women as they undressed and pranced about, and he received an extra thrill from furtive surveillance.

At the start, it had seemed the perfect cure for what ailed him. It hadn't worked, though, and the clandestine viewing left Stanley even more disgusted by his lack, because he came away with powerful desires he couldn't slake. Yet despite how raw the experience, he was addicted to the activity and couldn't stop.

He'd witnessed the entire encounter between James and Miss Ralston.

James could protest all he wanted, but he and Miss Ralston shared a hot, searing attraction. With a bit of maneuvering, it would blossom into a full-blown romance. James was too fascinated by her, and Stanley had to keep him at Summerfield, had to prevent him from going to London.

It was only a matter of time before James behaved precisely as Stanley was hoping. Deal or no deal, Miss Ralston would be ruined, and Stanley would get his child and his bride.

And...he'd get to see the affair unfold, right before his perverted, spying eyes.

Oscar tugged on the reins of his gig and pulled his horse to a halt.

He was outside the gates to Summerfield, and down the long lane, the manor house glimmered in the moonlight. There was a lone candle glowing in an upstairs window, but other than that, the residence was shut down for the night.

He'd had supper with the neighbors, but he'd departed shortly after the meal was finished. His hosts had planned to let their daughter play the harpsichord, and Oscar didn't feel—as vicar—that he should participate in such a frivolous endeavor. He'd slipped out as quickly as he could, leaving the other guests to the devil's mischief.

Stanley had been present, Miss Ralston perched at his side like a faithful dog. She was very pretty, very pleasant, and Oscar had quietly studied her and seethed over how much people seemed to like her.

In Oscar's opinion, she was a thief and interloper, sneaking in at the last minute to seize what should be Oscar's. He had suffered through Stanley's other marriages, the death of Stanley's only son, the sad reality that no others had been birthed.

Oscar had begun to believe that Summerfield would

eventually be his. He could practically see himself seated in the big chair at the desk in the library.

According to Stanley's prior wife—who'd been crude and spoiled and very, very vocal about her unhappiness with Stanley—he was incapable of performing the marital act. Stanley was too proud to admit it, but Oscar knew the truth.

There was no way Stanley could sire a babe on Miss Ralston, and regardless of how he paraded her around, regardless of how he boasted their wedding was pending, no date had been set.

What did that mean?

Supposedly, Stanley was impatient to marry immediately, but one of Stanley's cooks was extremely devout, and she regularly reported to Oscar on the goings-on in the manor. There had been no talk of Stanley's wedding among the servants, no orders from Stanley to prepare for the celebration.

Why not? Why the delay? Wasn't he in a hurry?

Oscar had once taunted Stanley that Miss Ralston would have to conceive by immaculate conception, and he hadn't been joking. If Miss Ralston turned up with child, Stanley couldn't have planted it. Oscar was sure of his facts and determined to prove Stanley's deficiency. Oscar just had to figure out how.

He wouldn't be cheated out of his inheritance. Not by Stanley. And most definitely not by Miss Ralston.

"I'll find out what's happening," he muttered to the cold, dark night. "If I hear you're increasing, Miss Ralston, I'll dig and dig until I uncover the truth. You have my word on it."

He clicked the reins and drove off.

CHAPTER TEN

"Egypt, really?"

"Yes."

James glanced over at Lucas. They were discussing Rose who'd suddenly become his favorite topic. He couldn't get her out of his head.

"That's an exotic personal tidbit," Lucas said. "Why were her parents in Egypt?"

"They were missionaries."

"I had a cousin whose parents died in Egypt when she was little. Or maybe it was India. I don't remember."

James frowned. "How could you not remember something like that?"

"There was some trouble—with my relatives there always is—so they'd been disowned or disliked or some such. We never mentioned them." Lucas brightened. "You don't suppose she's my cousin, do you? It would be hilarious to find out we were kin but hadn't recognized the connection."

"She's an orphan," James told him. "When her parents passed, she didn't have any other family."

"Poor girl. No one to claim her, and now, only Stanley to wed her." Lucas gave a mock shudder. "Do you imagine he will?"

"He insists he wants to."

"What about her? She doesn't appear to have many options."

"No. Her plight makes me glad I'm a man. You and I can just pick up and leave. It's so much more difficult to be a female."

They were in the main parlor, having a lazy afternoon whiskey and gazing across the park. Out on a groomed path, Rose and Veronica were walking and chatting. He should have leapt up and joined them, should have rescued Rose from Veronica's adolescent prattle, but he couldn't stir himself.

In their bonnets and shawls, they were very fetching, especially Rose who was wearing a green gown that was the exact color of her eyes.

Since she'd arrived, she'd worn only her drab schoolteacher's dresses, and he couldn't stop watching her. He couldn't guess where the money had come from for the purchase, but it fit perfectly and flattered her in every way.

From the first, he'd thought she was very striking, but in the new garment she was even more stunning. The realization disturbed him, and he couldn't discern why. He wasn't blind. He knew she was attractive, so why obsess?

"I had the strangest conversation with Stanley this morning," Lucas said.

"What about?"

"He practically begged me to stay at Summerfield for awhile. Is he ill?"

"No, why?"

"I've been trying to make sense of his request. He loathes me. Why would he ask it of me?"

"He wants *me* to stay," James explained. "He's figuring if you don't leave, I won't, either."

"Why would he want you to stay? He doesn't like you much more than he likes me. Originally, he seemed eager to be shed of both of us."

"You talk as if I have a unique insight into the man's thinking processes. He's always been unfathomable."

"Yes, he has, so what's his game? Is he scheming on you for some reason?"

"If he is, I'm not aware of it."

James chuckled and sipped his drink, his attention focused outside on Rose and Veronica. He couldn't let Lucas notice his expression.

For all Lucas's sloth and ineptitude, he was actually very astute, and he'd known James forever. If he had any idea of the conflict roiling within James, he'd have jumped on James in an instant and forced him to spill all.

Although James had informed Stanley that their bargain was off, it was obvious Stanley was hoping to keep it percolating. No doubt in his convoluted mind, he expected proximity to ignite a romance between James and Rose.

The great problem with the scenario was that it skirted very close to the truth of the situation. Where Rose Ralston was concerned, James was just as despicable as Stanley. He constantly ruminated over the fact that she was all alone in the world, that there was no father or brother to protest any ill treatment.

She was lonely and looking for an amorous adventure before life dealt her more painful blows. It would be easy to convince her she should engage in some naughty flirtation.

He should have left for London at dawn, but he hadn't, because he felt something wonderful could happen to them. Absurd as it sounded, it seemed Fate had thrown her into his path, and he shouldn't walk away without getting to know her in a more intimate fashion.

It was madness. It was lunacy. It was all rolled up in his peculiar, disturbing relationship with Stanley. Privately, James couldn't help preening over the notion that he could have her in ways that Stanley would never be able to manage.

In a sick, twisted manner, James wanted to take Rose from Stanley—even though seduction would hardly be *taking* her. He simply couldn't abide the prospect of Stanley ending up married to her. It galled. It infuriated, when James couldn't comprehend why.

He had no intention of marrying her himself, so why would it matter if she wed Stanley or anyone?

"I saw Veronica's breasts," Lucas suddenly said.

"You what?"

"I made her show them to me."

"You did not."

"I did."

"Bared?"

"Yes, and I can merrily attest that they're quite fine."

James rippled with irritation. "Didn't I tell you to be careful? I wasn't joking. She's a tart."

"She definitely is."

"She could get you in all kinds of trouble."

"I warned her right up front that it was futile to try."

"Well, her stepfather might decide it was worth it to ensnare you. If he caught you fooling with her, there'd be hell to pay."

"It wasn't my fault. *She* asked me to go into the woods with her."

"And you just went? What are you, a dunce? You're twenty-five and she's eighteen. Have some sense. You couldn't say no?"

"Why would I have?"

They were sitting side by side in their chairs, and James reached over and whacked Lucas on the arm as hard as he could. The blow jostled Lucas's drink, and he nearly dropped the glass on the floor.

"What was that for?" Lucas grouched.

"For being an idiot," James chided.

"I may be an idiot, but I saw her partially unclad. The virginal little vicar's daughter is chaste as a nun, so I consider it a huge victory. Besides"—he flashed a sly grin—"she's not interested in me any longer."

"Why is that? Did she figure out you're a horse's ass?"

"No. I set her sights on someone else."

James frowned. "Who?"

"You."

"Me! Are you mad?"

"She was desperate to know if you were sweet on her, so I told her you were."

James snorted with disgust. "You are too annoying to be believed."

"Is that supposed to be an insult?"

"Just stay away from her. Please?"

"I will. The first encounter was thoroughly disagreeable."

"So there's no reason for a second one."

"Gad," Lucas groused, "you sound just like my father."

"With how you're acting, I'm beginning to have some sympathy for him."

"If I wanted to be scolded like a disobedient boy, I'd trot home to Sidwell."

"Maybe you should."

"I can't go now. Stanley needs me to remain at Summerfield. I couldn't bear to disappoint the old fellow."

James rolled his eyes. "I'm sure he'll be eternally grateful."

"I'm sure he will be too."

Lucas stood and started out, and James said, "Where are you off to?"

"I thought I'd say hello to Veronica."

"Absolutely not."

"Well, then, I'll flirt with Miss Ralston. She's crazy about me."

"She is not. I told you she doesn't like you."

"Yes, but since then I've ingratiated myself. She's wild about me."

The notion of Lucas flirting with Rose was enormously vexing. James stood too, and they walked into the hall together.

"Why don't you leave both women alone and find a trollop in the village?"

"I've met all the trollops in the village. They don't amuse me in the least."

"Then ride to the next village and look for some over there."

"I might."

"And let's depart for London in the morning." James felt overwhelmed by temptation and crushed by the need to be away. "It was our initial plan. We never intended to tarry here."

Lucas considered, then shrugged. "As you wish. We can go or not. It makes no difference to me."

"Good."

They went to the foyer, and when Lucas turned toward the rear verandah so he could step outside and chat with Rose, James steered him in the other direction.

"I'm so glad you're at Summerfield," Veronica gushed.

"I am too," Rose replied.

She kept her smile firmly in place, not certain if the comment was a lie. She'd thought she hated the estate, that she was angry and ashamed, but maybe she wasn't. Maybe the fling in her room with James Talbot had changed her mind.

She'd assumed she was too smart to involve herself in a romantic entanglement, but maybe she wasn't. It was highly likely that she had no sense at all.

They were strolling in the garden. She hadn't actually wanted to socialize with Veronica, but when Veronica had stopped by it would have been rude to decline.

The more time she spent with Veronica, the clearer it was that they didn't have much in common. Rose was seven years older, and Veronica was nearly the age of Rose's prior students. When Veronica prattled on and on, Rose felt ancient, as if she was back at Miss Peabody's school and listening to a pupil.

"My mother died many years ago," Veronica said.

"Yes, I had heard that."

"There's never anybody to talk to about my concerns or difficulties."

"It must be hard, living with your stepfather."

"It is! It is! Mostly, if I have questions about an important subject, our housemaid is quite brilliant in her advice."

"It's a bit tricky, though, gossiping with the hired help. I'm certain you know to be careful."

"Usually, she's the only one in the house."

"That would present problems."

"But now, you'll be marrying Stanley, so I can come to you instead."

Rose simply nodded, neither confirming nor denying any pending nuptials. She'd promised Mr. Oswald her discretion, and whatever else might transpire between them, she wouldn't betray his secrets.

"I hope I can be as brilliant as your housemaid," Rose facetiously said.

"I'm positive you will be."

Rose peeked over at Veronica, and there was a slyness in Veronica's eye, as if she didn't like Rose or expect she'd be brilliant at all. Rose ignored Veronica's pettiness and continued walking.

They were headed back to the manor, and shortly they'd be inside. Rose would make an excuse about having an appointment and send Veronica on her way.

"What is it you'd like to discuss with me?" Rose inquired.

"You have to swear," Veronica warned, "that you won't tell a single soul."

"I won't. You have my word."

"This conversation must be private."

"I understand."

With each passing second, Rose was reminded more and more of her students. At Veronica's age, every incident that occurred was grand or tragic. There wasn't any middle ground in their swings of emotion.

"It's about a boy," Veronica explained.

"A boy...well!"

"Not really a boy. A man."

"What man? Is it anyone I've met?"

Veronica leaned nearer and whispered, "James Talbot."

"Mr. Talbot..." Rose kept her expression blank. "I see."

"He's wild about me."

"Is he? Are you sure?"

"Yes."

"How do you know? Has he confessed his feelings?"

"Not directly to me. No."

"Then what makes you think he's smitten?"

"I talked to Mr. Drake. I asked him if I had a chance with James."

"What did he tell you?"

"He said yes, absolutely."

Suddenly, there were so many issues swirling that Rose couldn't decide where to start.

Veronica was much too young and naïve to fraternize with a bounder like Lucas Drake, and she was out of her league with James Talbot too. And there was the problem with Rose and her budding attraction to James.

Rose was closer in maturity and temperament to James, *and* he'd been completely eager to misbehave with Rose. She hadn't doubted that he was beginning to like her as much as she liked him.

A wave of jealousy swept through her, which was ridiculously misplaced.

She was scarcely acquainted with James, had no claim on his affection, and didn't *want* to have a claim. She'd frolicked with him in order to learn what the amorous fuss was about. It had been like a scientist conducting an experiment. She'd tested the waters, found them pleasant, but didn't intend to try again. Still, she had to bite down the comment, *He's mine. You can't have him, you fool!*

She took a deep breath and let it out. Took another and let it out too.

"So…what are you asking me?" she cautiously ventured.

"I've known him since I was tiny, when he'd come home for visits from the army. He's always treated me as if I was a bothersome little sister."

"I can see how that would happen."

"But I'm all grown up now. Mr. Drake says James has noticed."

"Has he?" Rose tightly said.

"Yes." Veronica seized Rose's hands and squeezed them. "Do you suppose he'll speak to Papa Oscar about me? Is there a way to find out? That's what I'm dying to discover. How should I proceed under these circumstances?"

"All right." Rose forced herself to seem calm and wise. "I have many pieces of advice for you."

"I figured you would!"

"First, I don't believe you should spend any time with Mr. Drake."

Veronica frowned. "Why not? He's like a big brother to me."

"Yes, but you mentioned how you've grown. You're not a child anymore."

"I'm so glad I'm not!"

"You need to be more careful. You need to guard your reputation."

"Well, that's silly. How could I harm my reputation by chatting with a man I've known for most of my life?"

"It's just"—Rose paused, struggling to locate the proper words—"different once you're older. You can't carry on as you did when you were younger."

"And what about James? How can I learn what he's thinking?"

If Rose had had a thousand years to ponder, she couldn't picture Veronica and James together, and she hated to crush the girl's romantic fantasy. But honestly!

"You probably shouldn't count on Mr. Talbot."

"Why not? Mr. Drake was very clear."

"Yes, but has Mr. Talbot shown any inclination toward you that's changed?"

Veronica thought and thought, then admitted, "No."

"Then you must be patient. If his fondness blossoms, you'll know immediately."

"I can't bear any delay! I want it to occur very fast, so I can marry and move to London with him."

"My! What a grand plan."

"I don't belong in this stupid town. Neither does James. He's the perfect husband for me."

"It's fun to dream, isn't it?"

"It's no dream," Veronica firmly stated. "It's meant to be. It's simply a matter of time before it all works out."

"I hope you're right," Rose lied.

Up on the verandah, the door opened, and James stepped outside.

Veronica gasped and murmured, "He saw I was here! He came out to speak with me!"

Rose bit down another caustic reply. *He came to see me. Me! Not you!*

Yet she couldn't say so aloud, and after her conversation with Veronica, she wasn't sure of anything.

Was James smitten with Veronica? Could he be announcing his affection for Veronica to his friend, while dabbling with Rose in the dark of night? Was he that crass? That cold-hearted?

Rose hadn't a clue how to judge his true feelings.

Veronica grinned and patted her hair. "How do I look?"

"Very fetching," Rose said.

"I'm certain he'll notice. Don't you think he'll notice?"

Veronica drew away from Rose and raced up the stairs to where James was waiting for one of them, but *which* one, Rose wouldn't try to guess.

James sneaked down the hall to Rose's bedchamber. It was late, and he'd hardly seen her all day. There'd been just the brief encounter out on the verandah when she'd finished her walk with Veronica.

He'd told himself to leave her be, to ride off and find his own amusement with Lucas, but in the end, he'd hurried out. But of course, Veronica had blustered up first, had filled the moment with her inane chatter.

Rose had offered a quick hello, then disappeared before he could be shed of Veronica. He hadn't been able to stumble on Rose after that, and for supper, she and Stanley had gone visiting. So he'd eaten with Lucas, and much as he enjoyed Lucas's company, he'd kept glancing out the window, watching for Rose to return.

When they'd finally rolled in, he'd been in a rear parlor playing cards, so he'd missed her arrival, and she'd headed straight to her room.

He'd headed to bed too, but as he planned to depart in the

morning, the notion of going without spending a few private minutes with her was extremely disconcerting.

He tiptoed to her door, the glow of the moon lighting his way. He spun the knob, expecting to slip inside as he had in the past. To his consternation, it was locked.

He knocked very quietly and whispered, "Rose?"

With bated breath, he listened for a reply, for the sound of a footstep, but her room was completely silent.

"Rose?" he whispered again to no avail.

Forlorn and hideously disappointed, he dawdled, wishing she'd answer. Fleetingly, he considered climbing the secret stairs to her dressing room, but he swiftly discounted the idea.

Obviously, she was sending a clear message that she wasn't interested in a meeting, and he wasn't such a boor that he'd continue to thrust himself on her. He'd believed their flirtation the prior night had been wonderful, that it had shifted their relationship to a thrilling level, but evidently, she had a different opinion.

He wasn't an idiot that would tilt at windmills.

Let her have her month at Summerfield. Let her socialize and mingle with Stanley and his neighbors. Let her have some pleasant days on her own—before life dragged her away on a new and likely dreary path.

What was it to him if they didn't have a last evening together? What was it to him if he left without a goodbye?

Still, as he whirled and crept away, he felt as if his heart was breaking.

CHAPTER ELEVEN

"This is much better than what you originally planned."

"What plan was that?"

James glared at Lucas, struggling to focus on his friend, but he was too distracted by Rose. They were in the main parlor, the furniture shoved back for dancing. A neighbor girl was playing the harpsichord, her sister the violin.

Couples were promenading down the floor, Rose included. Every man in the county seemed to have partnered with her—except for James—and he was disgusted to find himself feeling extremely jealous.

"We were riding to London this morning," Lucas said. "You insisted we were leaving."

"Yes, well, Stanley practically chained me to the fence so I couldn't go."

"Last night, I asked if Stanley was ill. Now I'm wondering if it isn't you who's sick."

"Why?"

"Ever since we arrived at Summerfield, you've been leashed to him like a trained puppy. It's so unlike you."

"I know."

"When you get along with him, it spoils all my fun."

"I'll try harder to aggravate him."

"Please do. I don't like it when things change. If you and Stanley became chums, I'd worry that the world was ending."

"Trust me: Stanley and I will never be chums."

"I certainly hope not. My poor heart couldn't stand the strain."

The music stopped, the couples rearranging as the violinist called out the next tune.

"It's my turn with Miss Ralston." Lucas grinned and hurried off to claim his dance.

James was forced to observe as Rose was whirled across the room. She was in fine spirits, laughing as Lucas chattered away. Even though she'd declared she didn't like Lucas, she definitely appeared to, and James couldn't figure out why he hadn't marched over and claimed his own dance.

Pride was preventing him. Nerves too.

If he danced with her, he wouldn't be able to hide his fascination. Summerfield was a small community, where people gossiped constantly. They would detect his budding attraction—and would be curious as to what it portended. She was supposed to be at Summerfield to marry Stanley, so they'd speculate, and James liked her too much to damage her reputation.

Since she'd come downstairs for the party, he'd barely spoken to her, and it was growing more and more difficult to stay away.

That morning, he'd risen early and had been eating breakfast, intent on having a filling meal, then packing his bags. But Stanley had rushed into the dining room and announced that he'd been summoned to London on emergency business.

He'd already organized several suppers for Rose, and he hadn't wanted to cancel them. He'd all but begged James to host the events while he was in the city.

Like the fool he clearly was, James had immediately relented, which meant he was trapped at Summerfield—with Rose available and Stanley gone—for at least a week.

With James and Lucas on the premises, Rose had needed a chaperone, so Stanley had asked an elderly, mostly deaf neighbor to play the part. She was dozing in the corner and no barrier at all to any misbehavior.

James and Rose would be in frequent contact, thrust together over and over with too many chances to learn how much they liked each other outside the private confines of her bedchamber.

Stanley's ploy was easy to decipher. He was hoping to lure James back into their bargain, was hoping unfettered proximity to Rose would spur James's lusty instincts so he'd seduce her even though he'd decided he wouldn't.

Stanley had completely manipulated James yet again, and James could never understand why he succumbed to Stanley's exploitation. James viewed himself as a very obstinate person. Only Stanley got his way with James.

Lucas and Rose were in the line—Lucas flirting, Rose smiling—and James couldn't bear to watch them.

He slid through the verandah doors and had just moved into the shadows when Veronica hustled in from the garden. She didn't notice him, but dashed up the stairs to join the festivities.

As she passed, he nearly called out to her. She and Oscar hadn't been invited to the party, so she must have sneaked out of the rectory after Oscar went to bed, and James was conflicted over what his role should be in the situation.

She shouldn't be creeping around in the dark, but he was fully aware of what a nightmare it must be to live under Oscar's pious thumb. James would have fled too.

At the same juncture, James was in charge while Stanley was away, and he was sort of an older brother to Veronica. Should he say something to her? Should he have a servant take her home?

He would never cause a scene or act like an enraged father figure, and Veronica wouldn't appreciate any lectures. She received too many of them from Oscar.

In the end, he simply kept on into the garden. He'd tell Stanley when Stanley was back. Stanley could decide what should be done.

He strolled to the pond, the noises of the party dimming, but he could see the house lit from all the candles that were burning.

He'd always loved the spot. From his vantage point, the residence looked like a fairy's castle. As a boy, he'd stared at the mansion and invented stories about it, that it was enchanted, that he was a lost prince released from a wicked spell and brought home to where he belonged. It was an orphan's fantasy, but that didn't make it any less potent.

He dawdled forever, until finally, the dancing stopped, the buffet being served. Shortly, Lucas was pounding away on the harpsichord, singing a bawdy song. James smiled on hearing him.

Despite his friend's lazy insouciance, he was an accomplished keyboardist and had somehow managed to focus long enough for someone to teach him how to play really, really well. Plus, he relished being the center of attention and sitting at the bench while others cheered him on.

Suddenly, Rose came out onto the verandah, having snuck away from Lucas's performance. She leaned against the balustrade, cooling her face with a painted fan.

She was wearing another new dress, a blue one this time, with a matching blue feather in her hair. The fan was blue too, as if it had been specifically selected to complement the gown.

Stanley must have bought the clothes for her. There was no other explanation, and James was bothered by the purchases because the transformation disturbed him. Each time he saw her, she was more attractive, and he was more smitten.

She gazed at the pond, as if she'd missed him and knew exactly where he'd be. Like a besotted swain, his pulse raced, and he started toward her. At the same moment, she walked into the garden, proceeding directly to him. He halted, waiting for her to round a corner.

"I'm here," he murmured as her footsteps approached.

"James?" she said.

"Yes."

For an instant, she froze, as if uncertain of her welcome, then he reached for her and she flew into his arms. He captured her lips in a torrid kiss, being thrilled to find that he hadn't miscalculated. When she'd realized he'd left the house, she'd had to learn why. They were alarmingly close in their sentiments.

The kiss went on and on, and she joyfully participated until he tried to let down her hair. It was only then that she clasped his wrists to stop him.

"You can't take down my hair," she scolded. "My poor maid wasted an hour pinning it up. If you tug on any of the combs, the entire thing will fall, and I won't be able to return to the party."

"To hell with the party."

"James! Cursing! My goodness."

"Let's sneak up to your room."

"Absolutely not. It's probably already been noticed that we're both missing. We can't encourage gossip."

"No, we shouldn't."

She was snuggled to his chest, her shapely breasts flattened to his chest. The position rattled him, goaded him to misbehave.

"Why haven't you danced with me?" she asked.

"I couldn't. I was afraid I'd stare at you like a love-sick boy."

She scoffed. "You're being absurd."

"Yes, I am. I can't deny it."

"Why did you leave the party? I looked around and you weren't there."

"I couldn't stay inside. I was wild with jealousy, watching you with everyone else."

"You were not."

"You locked your door," he grumpily accused.

"When?"

"Last night."

"Yes."

"Why?"

She paused for an eternity, finally answering with, "What is your relationship to Veronica?"

"Veronica!"

"Yes. She's quite smitten by you. Do you return her affection?"

"Gad, no."

She studied his eyes. "I don't know you well enough to decide if you're being honest with me."

"Is that why you locked me out? You saw me talking to her on the verandah and you assumed we were involved?"

"She's expecting you to propose."

"Propose! The girl is insane."

"So I barred my door, but it wasn't actually over Veronica."

"What then?"

"You can't continue visiting me. I'm not even sure why I'm out here. It's so wrong, but I can't help myself."

"I can't either."

"It's like there's a madness brewing in me."

He completely agreed, but didn't admit it. He kissed her again, more slowly, letting the passion build. She aroused him in incalculable ways, and it wasn't healthy to be so titillated.

A man's lust had to be assuaged, but there was no chance of it happening with her, so why torment himself? Their flirtation simply made matters worse.

"Come inside," she said when he pulled away.

"Only if you promise to permit me to stop by later."

"James..."

He grabbed her shoulders and shook her. "We have to spend more time together."

"Why?" She scowled. "Did Mr. Oswald tell you to say that?"

"Bugger Stanley! This isn't about him. It's about you and me."

"But it's pointless for us to fraternize, James, isn't it? It can't lead anywhere. You haven't the desire or the means to marry, and you've been very clear with me. We're courting disaster."

"I don't care."

"Well, I do. I can't become embroiled in a scandal with you. I just want to finish out my thirty days and go away."

"If I'm in your room, no one will know."

"You can't be certain of that."

"I'll use the secret stairs—the ones that enter into your dressing room."

He laid the tip of his finger on her neck and traced it down to the bodice of her gown. He dipped into her cleavage, but ventured no further.

"Let me," he demanded.

She gazed at him, and he could practically see the dozen remarks she was ready to hurl as to why she should say *no*. In fact, she'd just said *no*, so he was braced for her refusal. But to his surprise, she nodded—as she grumbled with disgust.

"I can't stay away from you. I order myself to shun you, but I can't. I think I came out here so you'd convince me to proceed."

"You'll be at the estate for a month. It's silly for us to avoid each other."

"You're correct. The guests are heading home at eleven."

"I'll be there at midnight."

They stared and stared, recognizing that a profound bridge had been crossed. James had no idea where it would take them. He predicted it would be somewhere marvelous, but dangerous too.

"Once we're inside," she firmly commanded, "you have to dance with me."

"As you wish, my lady."

He gave a courtly bow, as if they were at a London cotillion.

She snorted, then spun and hurried away.

The floor creaked, and Rose jumped.

She was in her sitting room, and it was almost twelve-thirty.

After she'd shooed people out to their carriages, she'd rushed upstairs.

A cheery fire burned in the grate, two chairs positioned in front of it. She'd poured some wine, then sat down to wait, but James hadn't arrived.

She wondered if she wasn't losing her mind. She'd had so little joy in her life, had had few opportunities to feel special, and her despondency was pushing her into bad choices, but she didn't care. James made her happy. Was it wrong to sample a bit more of the elation he induced?

Yes. She kept conveniently forgetting how he'd schemed with Mr. Oswald. And she didn't know what she believed about Veronica. Yet she was breathlessly waiting for him anyway.

"What am I doing?" she murmured, appalled by her weakness.

If she'd truly yearned to socialize with him, she could have lingered in the parlor after the guests had gone. But she didn't want the public room and longing glances and separate sofas.

She wanted him all to herself and behind closed doors.

Was she a trollop at heart? She couldn't bear to ask the question because she was so sure of the answer.

Suddenly, he was standing in the doorway, and she laughed at her foolishness. Despite her impatience, he'd entered when she wasn't looking.

"Hello," he said, grinning.

"I had begun to think you weren't coming."

"Me? Not come? Are you mad?" He strolled in, all loose limbs and masculine swagger. He dropped into the chair opposite. "Lucas cornered me in the foyer. I couldn't get him to shut up."

"He is a talker."

"An annoying talker."

She chuckled. "Yes."

"Are you liking him any better? He feels he's ingratiated himself."

It was on the tip of her tongue to explain her relationship to Lucas, to spill the whole sordid story, but she simply couldn't reveal the sad tale.

Though it had all occurred before she was born, in a peculiar way, it seemed her fault somehow, that she was to blame for her parents' lapses of judgment.

James Talbot was worldly and smart and sophisticated, and she was anxious to retain his good opinion. Why tell him about Lucas or any of the rest? It would only leave her diminished in his eyes.

"I'm not wild about Lucas Drake," she said, "and I never will be."

"What is it about him that rankles?"

"He's lazy and entitled, and I can't abide how he's squandered his fortunes and talents."

He considered, then nodded. "A valid assessment."

"How is it that you're connected to him?"

"He befriended me in school when I was a boy. Because of my lowly status, I was frequently bullied, and he fought off the scoundrels who picked on me."

"Mr. Drake did that?"

"He was actually quite a gallant champion."

"I can't picture it."

"It's difficult, I know. I helped him on occasion too, as his antics began to enrage his father. When he wasn't welcome at home, Stanley let me bring him here."

"I can't imagine Mr. Oswald acting that way. You're painting a strange portrait of both men."

"Lucas grows on you after awhile."

"And Mr. Oswald?"

James shrugged. "I suppose he grows on you too. After you move past the bluster, he's displayed an incredible capacity for generosity. Toward me, anyway. I can't guess how you feel about it."

"He's been very generous." She waved at her dress. "He bought me clothes."

"I was wondering. The color is very fetching on you."

She blushed furiously, being inordinately pleased by the compliment. "He said I shouldn't gad about the estate looking like a pauper."

"He's got a point."

"I think he hopes—if he showers me with gifts—I'll agree to his scheme."

"There are worse fates than to live out your life as mistress of Summerfield."

"Spoken like a man who is free to trot off and do whatever he likes."

They were quiet then, and there was the most exhilarating sense of expectation in the air, as if any remarkable thing could transpire.

He stood and offered his hand for her to grab hold.

"What?" she asked.

"Come with me."

"Where?"

"Into your bedchamber."

"We shouldn't go in there."

"Why not?"

"We're fine right where we are."

"I hate chatting."

"You do not."

"I want to spend our time in more interesting pursuits."

"I don't."

"Liar. Are you scared of what might happen?"

"Not...scared, precisely." She thought about it, then laughed. "Well, maybe I'm a bit scared."

"I need to show you something. You'll like it. I promise."

"That's what I'm afraid of."

"Why, Miss Ralston," he mocked, "have you a naughty side?"

"Yes. I didn't realize I had a capacity for misbehavior, but you lure it to the fore."

"I'm so delighted to hear it."

He clasped her wrist and drew her to her feet. The swift motion pulled her against him, so in an instant, their bodies were forged fast. Sparks ignited, and she stared up at him, liking how he towered over her, feeling almost dizzy with glee at their intimate positioning.

"First, you have to tell me more about Veronica," she insisted.

"There's nothing to tell."

"She says you confided to Lucas that you're enamored."

"Lucas was just stirring trouble. He told her I was sweet on her, but I'm not."

"I can't decide if that's the truth."

"It absolutely is. She's like an annoying little sister. I could never have affectionate feelings for her."

"Swear it to me," she urged.

"I swear."

She scoffed with derision. "I have asked for your vow, but I have no means of judging if your word is any good."

"It's usually not, but in this case, I'm being candid."

She studied him, seeking a veracity she couldn't locate, and she had to admit that she was desperate to believe him.

It occurred to her that this was how unsuspecting females got themselves into jams. A cad could voice any falsehood, and Rose was disgusted over how rapidly she'd arrived at such an untenable spot.

He could fabricate or trick or conceal, and she'd merrily look the other way. Hadn't they originally crossed paths because of his devil's bargain with Mr. Oswald? Why was she able to ignore such an enormous flaw in his character? Why didn't it matter anymore?

She shouldn't have let him within a hundred yards of her, but in her recklessly smitten state, she was eager to disregard the obvious.

"I guess I don't want to talk about Veronica," she said.

"I *never* wanted to talk about her."

"What is this grand secret you have in store? Let's see if you can amaze me."

"Oh, I can amaze you all right."

"Shall we wager over it."

"Don't ever wager with me. You'll only lose."

She spun away, suddenly in a hurry to go exactly where she shouldn't. She rushed into her bedchamber, and he swooped up behind and lifted her off the floor. In a flurry of petticoat and tangled legs, he tumbled them onto the bed. He came out on top, his large body holding her down in a manner that was unexpected, but particularly thrilling.

"How much wine have you had, Rose?" he asked.

"Not nearly enough."

"If I could coax you in here so easily, I'm betting you've had plenty."

"Drinking has added an entirely new dimension to my personality."

"Are you becoming a doxy?"

"I'm worried I might be."

"Lucky me to have stumbled on you just when you've discovered your first vice."

"I have many vices."

"Name one."

"Cursing. Indecent conduct. Immoral thoughts. If I were a Catholic, I'd have to spend the next week on my knees in the confessional."

"Good thing you're not a Catholic then."

"Yes, a very good thing," she agreed, then mumbled, "I'm happy."

"So am I."

"I'm glad I met you."

"So am I," he said again, and they laughed.

Then they were quiet, staring, and he dipped in and kissed her. Immediately, she was sucked into the swirl of desire. Each time they jumped in the fray, the passion ignited quicker and burned hotter. If they kept on through her month's visit, what would it be like in another thirty days? She couldn't imagine.

He rolled and turned her, bit and licked her. His hands were everywhere, as he pinched and nibbled and massaged, until she could hardly breathe from the excitement he generated. Somehow, without her realizing it, he'd unbuttoned her dress, had bared her breasts and was sucking on her nipple.

"Here is your surprise," he told her.

Like a virgin about to be sacrificed on an altar, she lie on her back, limbs splayed. "I think I'll like it. I think there's no question I will."

He was tugging up her skirt, his fingers wandering up her thigh.

"Have you ever touched yourself here, Rose?"

"Where?" she inquired, not understanding his destination.

"This special spot."

To her astonishment, he caressed her—at the woman's sheath between her legs!

Instantly, she seemed to shatter, seemed to break into a thousand pieces. She was soaring to the heavens, and someone called out a wild, feral sound, and it took her a moment to recognize that the howl had emerged from her own throat.

The tumult went on and on until finally, blessedly, she reached an apex and began to tumble down. Eventually, she landed safely in his arms. He was grinning, preening, nuzzling a trail up her cleavage and neck.

"Gad, but you are so fine," he murmured.

"What was that?" she gasped when she could speak.

"*That* was sexual pleasure."

"It's normal for it to happen?"

"Yes, it's very, very normal."

"Am I still a...virgin?"

"Yes, you're still a virgin."

"So I couldn't be...with child?"

"No. There's quite a bit more to it."

"Show me."

"Just relax, Rose." He chuckled and kissed her again. "Relax for a minute."

She gaped at the ceiling, trying to figure out how such marvelous bliss could have lurked out on the horizon, but she hadn't known.

"Have I amazed you?" he inquired.

"Yes, you bounder."

"Aren't you glad I insisted on visiting?"

"Now that you've so competently demonstrated your devious tricks, I might never leave this bed."

"We'll wallow here for all eternity?"

"That depends. Can you make it happen more than once?"

He laughed, then sobered. "Yes, it can happen every time—if we work at it. I always forget how dissolute my life has been. I forget there are women like you in the world."

"Women like *me?* What does that mean?"

"You're so sweet and innocent. I'm almost sorry I corrupted you."

"I'm not!"

He laughed again, and he shifted onto his back with her draped across his chest. He caressed a lazy hand up and down her arm.

She let out a huge, unladylike yawn.

"All of a sudden, I'm so tired."

"Carnal conduct can exhaust a person."

"I need a nap."

"Feel free to rest. Get your strength up so we can start again."

She was swiftly fading away. "Don't go anywhere."

"I won't."

She didn't want to sleep, but couldn't stop the creeping lethargy. As she dozed off, she thought he was smiling, and vaguely, it occurred to her that he hardly ever smiled. *She* made him smile.

She snuggled closer, slumber encroaching. She simply couldn't prevent it.

When she opened her eyes, it was morning, sun shining in the window. She groaned and stretched, her head pounding from the wine she'd drunk.

Slowly, memory returned, and she recollected the prior evening with James. She glanced over, terrified that he might still be next to her, but he wasn't.

To her eternal delight, he'd left a single rose on his pillow—with a note: *A rose for Rose.*

She sighed, wondering what would ever become of her now.

CHAPTER TWELVE

"Let's walk in the garden."

"No."

James flashed a tight smile at Veronica.

She was at the house again, invited to supper this time so she had every right to be in the parlor. The meal was ended, and there were a dozen ways she could entertain herself, but she was stuck to James like glue. Ever since he'd learned of Lucas's shenanigans, his interactions with her had been incredibly awkward.

He wanted to say, *Look, I'm not about to propose,* but that would make the situation even more awkward.

Obviously, she'd believed Lucas. Whenever she and James were together, she'd grin at him as if they were friendlier than they actually were, and he was particularly careful to not be caught alone with her.

There was a sneaky facet to her character that he'd never liked, and he wouldn't put it past her to engineer mischief.

"Then would you escort me to the buffet table?" she asked. "I'm starving."

"I already promised I'd eat with Miss Ralston."

"Miss Ralston! Miss Ralston!" she snapped. "It's the only name I ever hear."

"Well, she is Stanley's guest, and everyone is talking about her."

"Do you think she's pretty?"

James peered across the room where Rose was chatting with a group of young ladies. His expression blank, he said, "Yes, she's pretty."

Veronica frowned. "Prettier than me?"

"How can a man answer that question without getting himself into trouble?"

"It's not difficult to choose. You think I'm prettier or you think she is."

"I think it's a tie," James judiciously responded.

"You can't mean it."

"You're both marvelous." He tipped his head. "Now then, if you'll pardon me, I'd like some fresh air."

"Are you going out to the verandah? I'll come with you."

"No. I'm tired of the socializing. I need a few minutes to myself."

He hurried off, and as he stepped outside, he could barely keep from glancing back to see if she'd followed him. He leaned on the balustrade, and to his great relief, she wasn't there. But she was watching him through the open doors. She was pretending she wasn't, but she couldn't hide her keen interest in his whereabouts.

He sighed and slid further into the shadows so he wasn't visible to her.

He could wring Lucas's neck. The entire fiasco proved that he should proceed to London—sooner rather than later—but he wouldn't. He was beginning to suspect he *couldn't* go.

Rose had intrigued him to the point where he didn't know up from down. Their forays into passion had left him disturbed in ways he hadn't thought possible. She was just so refreshing, so pure and unsullied, and her innocence enchanted him.

He'd been in the army too long, he realized. Trollops went with the territory, so he was used to women who were rough and tumble, who viewed sexual conduct as a business transaction: money paid for services rendered.

He never crossed paths with virtuous females, and even on those rare occasions when he did, it would have been the height of impropriety to seduce any of them.

Rose shouldn't have let him, either, and he shouldn't have tried, but where she was concerned his common sense had fled.

He was struggling to figure out his plan. How far would he take his flirtation? Would he ultimately relieve her of her virginity? She craved that ending, but she didn't understand what she was truly requesting, so she couldn't be the one to decide.

If he pushed the issue, if he deflowered her, she could wind up with child, which was the conclusion Stanley had sought. Would James give it to him?

He had no intention of carrying out his bargain with Stanley. At least, he didn't expect he would. But whenever he looked at Rose, his masculine instincts flared, and he couldn't convince himself that discipline should be exercised.

Over by the doors, a group of guests surged onto the verandah. Rose was with them. She espied him in his hiding spot and waved him over.

"It's such a warm night," she said. "We're walking to the pond to cool down. Will you join us?"

"Yes, certainly."

People were laughing, pairing up, and they promenaded down the stairs and into the garden, with Lucas leading the way. Rose very shrewdly arranged herself so she and James were the last down, so she could slip her arm into his. It was all very proper, very correct.

"Whose idea was this moonlight stroll?" he asked.

"Mine. I needed to get outside."

"What if I'd refused to accompany you?"

"I'd have had to pick another fellow to escort me."

He snorted. "If you require *escorting,* I am at your service."

"Of course you are. That's why I came to fetch you."

They slowed, the others farther and farther ahead. No one noticed their sluggish pace. No one glanced back to learn why they weren't keeping up.

"Is there always so much socializing here at Summerfield?" she inquired.

"No, there's never any."

"So it's all for my benefit."

"Yes."

"I hate to sound rude, but I'm weary of meeting the neighbors."

"They all like you."

"I'm a likeable person."

He chuckled, his torrid gaze wandering down her body. "You definitely are. I like you more than anyone."

"Would you be serious? And don't look at me like that."

"Like what?"

"Like you want to gobble me up."

He leaned nearer and whispered, "I *do* want to gobble you up."

"Well, don't let the others see you. They might wonder about us."

"Heaven forbid."

"Yes, heaven forbid. I'm determined to get through this escapade with no damage to my reputation."

"Good luck."

"Luck isn't involved. Moral behavior is necessary, but I'm suffering from an enormous lack of it."

"I don't mind."

She grinned impishly. "I wish I could tell them all to go home so I can have you all to myself."

"I wish you could too."

"Instead, I'm reduced to organizing innocent strolls in the garden."

"It's not so bad, is it?"

"No, but when Mr. Oswald returns, if I asked him to stop throwing all these soirees, would he be offended?"

"No. He doesn't like entertaining any more than you."

"Since I'm leaving in a few weeks, it seems so pointless."

He gestured to the couples up ahead. "They're happy you're here. They like the excuse it's furnished for them to make merry. It can be a dreary place most of the time."

"So I'm providing a community benefit?"

"Absolutely. The younger people are especially grateful. Occasionally, months drag by with no amusement at all."

"I'm a blessing in disguise."

"Yes."

James peeked over his shoulder, saw no one behind them. They were passing a dark stretch of bushes, and he clasped her wrist and stepped off the path.

"What are you doing?" she hissed.

"What do you think?"

"We can't disappear."

"We already have."

"They're bound to notice."

"I doubt it."

"They will! We can't—"

He laid a finger on her lips, silencing her. "Rose?"

"Yes?"

"Did you enjoy yourself last night?"

"Yes, you wretched libertine."

"Will we get to do it again?"

"Perhaps." She tormented him by saying, "I'm still deciding if I like you enough."

"Vixen," he muttered.

"Me? Am I?"

"Yes. You're too damned fetching for your own good. I can't stand it."

"How fascinating. I've always viewed myself as being very plain and ordinary. I never believed I had any loose tendencies at all."

"Trust me: You're a natural at this."

Very quickly, she was learning the skills of a coquette. She looked pretty and flirtatious, displaying a refreshing and humorous mix of bravado and charm that made him yearn to throw her down and have his way with her in the grass.

He settled for sliding an arm around her waist, and he kissed her thoroughly, keeping on and on until she was leaned against him, her knees weak, her balance affected.

As he drew away, she was smiling, her beauty rattling him,

annoying him.

He didn't like her to be so marvelous. He wished she was a tad more average as she deemed herself to be. He wished *he* wasn't quite so enchanted by her. It couldn't lead to any beneficial conclusion.

"We'd better catch up with the guests," she murmured, but she didn't move.

"Do you suppose they've noted we're missing?"

"No. I'm sure Mr. Drake has entertained them with his chatter. Their entire focus will be on him and his antics."

"We can only hope."

He stole another kiss, then he guided her onto the path. They started off, sauntering along as if they hadn't a care in the world.

"James!" a female suddenly called.

He glanced over to see Veronica hurrying up.

"There you are!" she said. "I've been searching everywhere."

"Why?"

"When everyone left for the pond, I knew you'd want to go. I tried to find you."

She stopped, and while it was dark and a bit difficult to discern her expression, it was clear she was evaluating them in a manner James didn't like.

"Where were you?" She was acting as if she had the right to question him.

Rose saved him. "I stumbled on him just as we all came outside. He was on the verandah."

"Oh," Veronica slowly mumbled.

"We fell behind the others," Rose said.

"Did you?" Veronica mused, and James could almost hear her thinking, *How convenient.*

"Will you walk with us the rest of the way?" Rose asked her.

Veronica paused forever, studying Rose, studying James. Then she forced a grin. "I'd be delighted to walk with you. Thank you for inviting me."

Rose dropped James's arm and took Veronica's instead. In a smooth move, she steered Veronica past James and kept on down the path.

"You're a liar."

"Am I?"

Veronica glared at Lucas and fumed, "James hasn't said a word to me."

"About what?"

"About anything! You claimed he was smitten, but he's

behaving no differently than he's ever behaved."

"Perhaps he's waiting to surprise you."

Lucas smirked, silently wishing the unpleasant girl would leave, but he didn't have the energy to toss her out.

They were in a rear parlor, and it was very late. The guests had left an hour earlier, and James had gone to bed, so Lucas was sitting and drinking by himself.

Veronica had departed with everyone else, but she'd crept back.

She was dangerous and reckless, and heaven help the oaf who was with her when her bad end arrived. The vicar would marry her off to the first fellow who was snared in her web, and it wouldn't be Lucas.

"Do you know what I think?" she jeered.

"No, but I suppose you're about to tell me."

"He's sweet on Miss Ralston."

"Miss Ralston? What gave you that idea?"

"He's always watching her—when he believes no one is looking."

"Is he? I hadn't noticed."

"That's because you're a man. Men never focus on what really matters."

"I'm sure that's true."

"What should we do about it?"

"About what?" he asked again. She was so annoying he could barely listen to her prattle.

"About James and Miss Ralston."

"What about them?"

"Should I mention it to Stanley? After all, he brought her to Summerfield so he could marry her himself. I don't imagine he'd be too keen on James snatching her up."

"Trust me, Veronica. James isn't in the process of snatching up Miss Ralston. They're scarcely acquainted."

"What do you know? You weren't even aware that he stares at her all the time."

"So he stares at her. So what? She's very pretty. Every man stares at a pretty woman. *I* stare at her. It's not unusual."

"When people were busy at the pond, they sneaked off into the bushes. I saw them with my own two eyes."

He scowled. "You were following James?"

"I wasn't following him," she indignantly huffed. "I was simply trying to catch up with the rest of the group, and they appeared right in front of me."

"What is your point?"

"He can't be sweet on Miss Ralston! She belongs to Stanley,

and James belongs to *me.*"

"Maybe you shouldn't count on it." He was sincerely regretting the idiotic lie. He hadn't realized she'd take it so seriously.

"I am counting on it," she replied. "I'm absolutely counting on it."

He'd finished his drink, so he went over to the sideboard and poured himself another. He returned to the sofa and had plopped down when she ludicrously said, "May I have a brandy too?"

"No."

"Why not?"

"Because you're a child. Because you shouldn't be drinking with a man like me."

"I'm not a child. I showed you the other day."

Defying his edict, she marched over and helped herself, neatly ignoring his command that she not. Lucas's sympathy for Vicar Oswald soared. What must it be like to live with such an unruly, recalcitrant female?

Lucas would slit his wrists rather than endure such agony. How did the vicar stand it?

She blatantly sipped the liquor, coming over and sitting in the chair across. From her ease with the strong liquid, it was obvious she imbibed often, that this wasn't a new experience for her.

He was fairly certain the vicar didn't keep spirits at the vicarage, so she probably skulked around, peeking into peoples' liquor closets and stealing bottles for herself.

What a menace!

"Why are you here, Veronica?"

"I had to ask you about James and Miss Ralston. I couldn't wait until tomorrow."

"You're being ridiculous, and it's very late. You need to go home before your stepfather discovers you're not there. I can't have him storming over and demanding to know where you are."

"I can't go until you tell me how we should handle this. Should I speak to Stanley?"

"About James and Miss Ralston?"

"Yes. I have to get her out of my way. As long as she's distracting him, he'll never pay attention to me."

Lucas sighed. "Veronica, let me be very clear. James is not infatuated with Miss Ralston, nor is he infatuated with *you.*"

"That's not what you told me the other day."

"You were correct: I was lying."

"So? It doesn't mean he couldn't become smitten."

Lucas sighed again. Where James was concerned, the stupid girl seemed deaf and blind. How could he make her listen?

"James and I only stopped by for a brief visit at Summerfield before we travel on to London," he tersely said. "The minute Stanley returns, we're leaving."

"James can't leave! Not until affairs between him and me are settled."

He studied her, wondering if she wasn't a tiny bit mad.

Her obsession had him worrying about James. It wasn't a good idea for James to remain at the estate. With her so adamantly plotting, she might instigate any kind of mischief, and Lucas liked James too much to let him be trapped by her. He liked *any* man in the world too much to let it occur.

He wondered too about James and Miss Ralston. Was James flirting with Miss Ralston? Were they dashing off into the bushes when no one was looking?

If so, it was another recipe for disaster, and Lucas was determined that nothing bad happen to his friend. At the earliest opportunity, Lucas would hightail it to London—and he'd force James to accompany him.

He pushed himself to his feet and placed his glass on a nearby table.

"You have to go home," he firmly stated. "Now."

"You're not my father, Lucas. You can't order me around."

"No, I'm not your father, but I'd be happy to take a switch to you."

"Horse's ass," she muttered.

"Yes, it's my best quality."

He gestured to the door, but she didn't move. She simply sipped her brandy, her expression mulishly insolent.

He stomped over, seized her drink, and tossed it on the floor. The glass landed on the rug with a muted thud, the amber liquid spilling everywhere.

"You can't just take it from me like that," she seethed.

"I already have."

He yanked her up and dragged her to the French windows, shoving her out onto the verandah.

He probably should have offered to drive her to the rectory, but the stable boys were in bed, and he wasn't about to rattle about in the barn, trying to find a harness and a horse. Nor would he walk with her, for he wasn't about to be caught alone with her in the dark.

She'd gotten to Summerfield on her own. She could slither to the vicarage the same way.

"If you show up over here again like this," he warned, "I'll speak to your stepfather. I'm sure he'd be curious about your antics."

"If you say anything, I'll make you so sorry."

"Sticks and stones, Veronica. Sticks and stones."

He closed the door in her face, and he stood, arms crossed, stoically barring any reentrance. He watched her as she fumed and fussed and glared.

She wasn't quite so pretty when she was angry, and Lord help the poor fellow who ended up shackled to her. Her temper was exhausting.

They engaged in a staring match she could never win, and finally, she spat, "Bastard."

"I'll take that as a compliment."

She stormed away.

For a long while, he stayed where he was, on guard in case she came back. Eventually, when it seemed she'd truly gone, he spun away.

He might have had another drink, but he was so aggravated by the encounter that he'd lost interest. He blew out the lamp, and as he proceeded to his own bed, he was assessing the arguments he'd use to persuade James that they had to leave immediately.

Stanley gazed through the peephole in the secret stairwell outside Miss Ralston's bedchamber. It was very late, and no one knew he'd returned home. He'd ridden in quietly, without announcing his presence.

He'd been away for several days, having run out of ideas as to how he could cajole James into remaining at Summerfield.

The boy was very stubborn. Once he made up his mind, it was incredibly difficult to change it. He'd backed out of his bargain with Stanley, had planned to head for London, and Stanley would have employed any ruse to prevent his departure.

After Miss Ralston's virginity was squandered, after she was increasing with Stanley's heir, James could do whatever he liked. But until that situation was achieved, Stanley would have his way. He always did.

As he'd hoped, his absence had brought about the precise conclusion he'd sought. James and Miss Ralston were lying on her bed. Obviously, some type of limited sexual act had occurred, but Stanley had missed it.

They were talking, and Miss Ralston's gown was unbuttoned, her breasts bared, but Stanley's view was blocked so he'd only managed a quick glimpse.

He pressed a hand to his crotch, desperate for his cock to stir, but it was flaccid, dead as a piece of rotten meat.

When he wed her, he would make her disrobe for him, would

make her strut about without her clothes. He would suckle her taut nipples and touch her between her legs. Even though he couldn't be physically aroused by her, he could and would enjoy looking and feeling.

Ultimately, he would sample every gift she could possibly bestow.

On the bed, she and James were murmuring their goodbyes. They were kissing, smiling. James rose, and she did too. She accompanied him to the dressing room, the rear door leading directly to the spot where Stanley was lurking. He crept away, his salacious spying over for the evening.

But there would be other nights. Other opportunities.

He grinned and gleefully rubbed his palms together. The entire affair was working out exactly as he'd intended, and it was just a matter of time before he received everything he'd ever wanted.

James would give it to him. In the end, James wouldn't be able to resist.

CHAPTER THIRTEEN

"Let's head for London in the morning."

"What?"

James was in the front parlor, staring out the window and completely distracted by the sight of Rose out in the driveway. They'd had another supper party, a smaller one, and she was waving goodbye to a female acquaintance.

They'd passed a day filled with so many entertainments that he was starting to feel like a rich, indolent dandy. With his having spent the prior decade in the army, he couldn't remember when he'd ever had so much free time. He could definitely get used to such idleness and frivolity—if Rose was present.

He thought he might be in deep, deep trouble. He thought he should run away and never look back.

"James!"

"What?"

"Are you listening?"

James yanked his gaze from the window and glared at Lucas.

"Yes, I'm listening."

"What did I say?"

He tried to recollect, but couldn't. "I have no idea. You prattle on constantly. How is a man to keep track?"

"I want to leave tomorrow."

"Why? There's no hurry. You said yourself you'd be hounded by creditors in town."

Lucas stood and came over to the sofa where James was meticulously watching Rose. As he saw what had James so transfixed, he snorted with disgust.

"Veronica was right," he chided as he stomped back to his chair.

"Right about what?" James asked. "What are you talking about?"

"She told me you were having an affair with Miss Ralston."

James's heart literally skipped a beat. "And you believed her?"

"No, but obviously, I should have."

"Veronica isn't smart enough to guess my business."

Lucas was undeterred. "What the hell are you doing?"

"Nothing. Veronica is a nuisance, and I'm aggravated that you'd chat about me with her."

"James, how long have I known you?"

"Twenty years or so. Why?"

"Don't lie to me! You can't. You shouldn't even try."

"I'm not lying."

"Oh, please," Lucas jeered. "Shut up. You're embarrassing yourself."

"Miss Ralston is here to marry Stanley."

"Yes, she is—as you seem to be conveniently forgetting."

"If you imagine I would actually—"

"Are you fucking her?" Lucas crudely hissed.

"No."

"Do you think I'm stupid or what?"

"Of course not."

"Then tell me what's happening. Tell me this instant and don't omit any pertinent details."

James scoffed. "For a moment there, you sounded just like your father."

"Leave the old codger out of it."

"You're not in any position to lecture me, Lucas."

"Somebody should."

"Well, it won't be you, so bugger off."

An angry silence festered, when suddenly, Stanley bustled in.

He'd ridden in late the previous evening, had been sitting at the breakfast table when James had come down that morning. On seeing him, James had bristled with irritation. If Stanley had returned, there was no reason for James to tarry.

He and Lucas should depart at once, but the notion disturbed James in ways he couldn't bear to contemplate.

"The last carriage has pulled away," Stanley said as he marched over to the sideboard and poured himself a brandy. "I'll be glad when all these introductions are over." He paused, waiting for one of them to chime in. When they didn't, he muttered, "I hate socializing."

Still, James and Lucas didn't retort.

"What's wrong?" Stanley asked. "Are you two fighting?"

"No," James said as Lucas said, "Yes."

Stanley had always believed Lucas over James, and he honed in on Lucas. "What's the matter?"

"I want to leave for London," Lucas explained. "James doesn't."

"Why rush off?" Stanley pasted on a magnanimous smile. "I'm delighted to have you boys home. Stay as long as you like. I don't mind. Really."

He shifted his gaze to James, his eyes gleaming with an almost religious zeal that left James uneasy.

"I'm not ready to go," James informed him.

"Wonderful," Stanley beamed. "So it's settled. Let's put your quarrel aside and enjoy our drinks."

But Lucas couldn't let it rest. "I'm worried about Veronica."

Stanley smirked. "Aren't we all?"

"She's obsessed with James."

"Obsessed over what?" Stanley inquired.

"She's convinced he's about to propose."

James snapped, "Only because *you* told her I was smitten."

"You what?" Stanley barked. "Lucas, why must you behave like such an idiot?"

"It was a joke," Lucas contended, "but joke or not, she insists she's meant to wed James—as if it's some sort of destiny."

"The only *destiny* she has," Stanley sneered, "is to get herself in trouble with some farmer. When she does, her stepfather will teach her a few life lessons—such as how horrid it is to be a farmer's wife."

"You're underestimating her," Lucas persisted. "She can be so devious. I could see her ensnaring James with some ruse."

"Oh, for pity's sake," James protested. "I told you she's not smart enough."

"What if you're mistaken?" Lucas pressed. "What if she traps you?"

"She won't," James grumbled. "She couldn't. I'd never place myself in a dangerous situation with her. I know better—as opposed to some people I could name."

James glowered, and Lucas ignored him.

"I don't necessarily suppose *you* would have to do anything," Lucas pointed out. "She could spew any lie to the vicar, and you'd be ruined."

Stanley waved a hand, cutting off Lucas's complaints.

"There's no reason to fret over Veronica," Stanley declared. "I won't invite her to my suppers. If she's not here, she can't engage in mischief."

"She sneaks over anyway," Lucas said.

"Then if she dares," Stanley replied, "I'll throw her in a carriage and drive her to the rectory myself. I'll share some choice words with my brother, and he'll put an end to it."

"She's deranged," Lucas asserted. "It won't help to speak with the vicar."

"It *will*," Stanley countered as he gulped down his brandy. "I've had a long week, and I'm for bed. How about you boys? Don't sit down here fighting."

"We won't," James agreed, but he suspected they would. Lucas had never been so worked up over any topic.

"Goodnight then," Stanley said, and he left.

Lucas and James listened as his footsteps faded down the hall, then Lucas went over and closed the door.

"Last chance," he warned as he seated himself again.

"Last chance to what?" James asked.

"To tell me the truth. If I don't understand what's occurring, I can't guard your back. I can't protect you when it all crashes down."

"Nothing will *crash* down. Stop worrying."

Lucas sipped his drink, staring, staring. Finally, he mused, "There's a curious aspect I've never fathomed about Miss Ralston's betrothal to Stanley."

"What's that?"

"You and I used to laugh over the rumor that Stanley is impotent."

"We did," James cautiously responded.

"Yet you don't seem to find it odd that he's about to marry so he can sire an heir."

"No, I don't find it odd. He's very vain, and he views himself as some sort of god. If he's had difficulty fornicating in the past, he's probably persuaded himself that he can order his body to perform as required."

"You loathe him. You loathe Summerfield. Veronica is nipping at your heels, desperate to draw you into a mess, but wild horses can't drag you away."

"Give me another week or two. I'll be ready then."

"Why aren't you ready now?"

"I'm just not."

There was a deadly silence, then very quietly, Lucas said, "Has he asked you to seduce her? Is that it? Is he paying you? Is he blackmailing you? What?"

James's shoulders sagged, his irritation waning. Lucas was the brother he'd never had, the brother he'd always wanted. He hated to bicker with him and had never been able to lie to him.

"It's not what you're thinking," James claimed.

"What is it then?"

"I simply like her."

"Miss Ralston."

"Yes."

"As a friend."

"Yes."

"So…what is your plan? Are you some kind of troubadour from

the Middle Ages? Will you pull out your lute and begin composing love ballads? Somehow, I can't picture you behaving that way."

"I have no plan. I'd merely like to spend a bit more time with her."

"Well, you don't get to," Lucas fumed. "Have you any idea how wrong this is? You're flirting with her, luring her away from Stanley. Then what? When her emotions are fully engaged, you'll jump on your horse and ride away? Is that how you intend to treat her?"

"Why are you concerned about this? It's none of your affair."

Lucas looked perplexed, his fury uncharacteristically peculiar. "I like her very much too, and she's all alone in the world. She's been at Stanley's mercy, and now, she's at your mercy. I won't let you two harm her."

"Harm her!" James huffed. "Stanley is eager to make her his bride, to make her mistress of Summerfield. Where is the bloody *harm* in that?"

Lucas rose to his feet, appearing imperious and irate and very grand. "You and I are leaving in the morning."

"Don't boss me, Lucas. You can't."

"If you don't agree to accompany me, I'll speak with Miss Ralston. I'll tell her you're about to become betrothed to Veronica, that you're a renowned cad and you deliberately seduced her while Veronica is on pins and needles, expecting your proposal. I'll destroy you in her eyes."

"Why would you?"

"It's bad enough that she has to wed Stanley when this is through. I won't have her heart broken too, because she assumes your affection is real."

"Maybe my affection *is* real."

"So what? Will you steal her away from Stanley? Will you wed her yourself? And then what?"

"You know I haven't the desire or money to marry."

"But apparently, you have the time to deceive and ruin." Lucas walked to the door and yanked it open. "In the morning, we're getting on our horses and riding away. Don't force me to talk to Miss Ralston. Don't force me to hurt her."

Lucas stormed out, and James muttered, "Asshole."

Lucas was correct that they should depart, but James couldn't imagine it. Yet why would he remain? There was no benefit.

Lucas wasn't aware that—at the end of the month—Rose would be gone, that she'd refused to be Stanley's bride. James couldn't confide in Lucas, because then he'd have to explain about his original bargain with Stanley, how Rose wouldn't proceed, how James had backed out.

It was a secret James would take to the grave. If he owed Stanley anything, he owed him that.

He downed his drink and wandered out onto the verandah. A cool wind was blowing, the trees in the park swishing their branches, making an eerie sound that set him on edge.

Suddenly, he couldn't bear the house or Stanley or Lucas or his choices. Why couldn't he be happy? Why couldn't he have what he wanted for a change? If he committed a few sins, who cared? If no one ever learned of them, were they actually sins at all?

He hurried to the stables, saddled a horse, and galloped down the road.

Rose impatiently paced her sitting room, waiting for James to arrive. But he hadn't come, and she wasn't sure what his absence portended.

As she'd said goodnight to everyone after supper, he'd whispered that he'd visit her shortly, but he hadn't.

She worried that perhaps—with Stanley at home—James had finally recognized that their liaison couldn't continue. Rose understood too, that it had to end, but she couldn't stop. With each passing minute, she grew more attached to James.

Having always viewed herself as being very pragmatic, she couldn't believe she'd landed in such a horrid predicament. She blamed it on the fact that she'd been so isolated at Miss Peabody's school. Her social experiences, particularly with men, had been limited, so she hadn't realized how fast a woman could dig herself into a hole.

She'd never been in love before, so she wasn't certain how a person felt when it occurred, but she suspected she was madly, desperately in love with James. Her obsession had risen to a dangerous degree, and she didn't know how she'd leave Summerfield in a few weeks. Could she go away and never see him again?

She didn't think so.

She went to the window and stared out at the stars, and she made a wish that Amelia and Evangeline would have a better conclusion than Rose had had, that Rose would find a stable conclusion too.

Life was so unfair. Why couldn't she marry James? Why couldn't her dreams come true?

She'd never asked for special favors, had never reached for more than had been provided. Why couldn't she—just one blasted time—have what she craved?

She wondered about James and thought he might be falling in

love too. She was exasperated by his insistence that they couldn't be together. He had no interest in matrimony, and with there being so many veterans searching for jobs in London, he wasn't optimistic about his prospects, but *she* was. They were both smart and competent. Why blithely accept that they had to separate?

A flare of hope ignited, and it burned hotter and hotter.

Why not? Why not? The words seared her mind.

Why not speak up? Why not tell him her opinion?

They could find a way to support themselves; she was convinced of it. She wasn't some highborn aristocrat, didn't need a fancy house full of servants and baubles. She simply needed James, the two of them united as husband and wife forever.

Resolve swept through her. For once she'd grab for what she wanted, and why shouldn't she? The worst that could happen was that he'd refuse, but after he heard her arguments, she didn't imagine he would. She was positive she could persuade him to share her vision of the future.

She paced a bit more, pondered and planned, until a clock chimed the hour of three. A wave of exhaustion crept up on her, and she stumbled to her bed and lie down.

Very quickly, she fell into a deep slumber, and her dream turned erotic. She was in a field of blue flowers, the sun shining down, and James was stretched out on top of her. He was kissing her and kissing her.

"Wake up, sleepyhead," he murmured.

She frowned. His voice seemed so real.

As if drugged, she pulled herself out of her reverie and opened her eyes. He was with her and definitely not a hallucination.

"James!" she said, smiling.

"Hello."

"When did you arrive?"

"Ages ago. I was watching you."

"How embarrassing. Was I snoring?"

"Only a little."

"Oh, you beast. You were supposed to say *absolutely not.*"

"You didn't snore," he admitted, his expression warm and affectionate. "I was teasing."

"Where have you been? I gave up waiting for you."

"I went for a ride."

"You were out on the road in the dark?"

"Yes."

"I'm glad I didn't know. I'd have been worried sick. Why did you go?"

"I was...quarreling with Lucas."

"What about?"

He stared and stared, then claimed, "It was nothing."

Obviously, he was lying.

"Tell me."

"It wasn't important. He and I have been friends for a long time. We bicker occasionally like an old married couple."

She rested a hand on his cheek. "Did your ride calm you?"

"A bit."

He sighed and rolled onto his back, and he seemed very tired, as if he had the weight of the world on his shoulders.

"Are you still going to London with him?"

"He's insisting I should. That's why we were arguing."

"You don't want to depart?"

"No, but I probably should."

Her pulse raced. This was the spot where she had to speak up or lose her chance.

"Would you take me with you?" she inquired.

"To do what?"

Her cheeks flushed. When she'd been alone and plotting, she'd thought this conversation would be easy, but she'd been wrong. The *man* tendered the proposal. The woman wasn't allowed to propose herself. It upset the natural order of the universe.

"We've…grown so close," she tepidly stated.

"We have."

"I can't bear to consider our parting."

"It's hard, isn't it? But it had to come eventually."

"Could you really trot off and never see me again?"

"I don't know."

"Well, *I* know what you should choose."

"What is that?"

She felt as if she were on a cliff, that she was running toward it and about to leap off.

"I think we should travel to London together," she said. "I think we should marry and live happily ever after."

"You do, do you?"

"Yes."

He stared for another lengthy interval, her optimism sinking with each second that ticked by.

"We could be happy," she pressed. "I'm certain of it."

He chuckled, but dejectedly. "I'd be an awful husband, Rose."

"I disagree. I'm positive you'd be wonderful."

He shook his head. "You've never engaged in an affair before, so you don't grasp how physical amour can make things more potent. It's confusing you."

"Don't denigrate my feelings. I'm not some naïve schoolgirl with a crush."

She attempted to climb off the mattress, but he slipped an arm across her waist and held her tight so she couldn't escape.

"Let me go," she fumed.

"No."

"I've sufficiently embarrassed myself for one night. Please leave so I can begin reclaiming my dignity."

"I'd love to wed you," he insisted.

"Don't throw me any bones. They're not necessary. I'm an adult. I took a risk, I completely humiliated myself, and I'd like to be alone."

"A match between us would be difficult. I don't have money or place or family, so I have naught to offer. You could do so much better than me."

"Yes, I'm sure I could."

"Don't be angry."

"I'm not angry. I'm...resigned. I figured this would be your answer, but I had to try."

Her heart was breaking, as if he'd yanked it out of her chest and stomped on it, but it was ridiculous to be sad. She should have known Fate wouldn't be on her side. It never had been.

Perhaps he was right. Perhaps there was no viable ending for them. But just as she'd given up, he mumbled, "I'll ponder the situation."

"Don't raise my hopes merely to dash them."

She squirmed away and sat on the edge of the mattress, her back to him.

"I'm sorry," he muttered from behind her.

"So am I." There was an awkward pause, where she could sense him hovering. "Would you go? Please?"

There was another uncomfortable pause, then he said, "Rose."

"What?"

"Would you look at me?"

"No. Just go away."

He slid to the floor and rounded the bed so he was standing in front of her.

"If I stay at Summerfield," he said, "we could have two more weeks together. Why can't that be enough for you?"

"Because I want more than that. Despite what you suppose, I believe you're worth having."

"You're wrong."

"Then I guess we're at an impasse, aren't we?"

"I guess we are."

He whipped away and stormed off.

She didn't watch him depart, but it was on the tip of her tongue to call to him, to agree that two weeks was fine, that she'd be delighted to settle for so little.

But she'd *settled* her entire life, and she was quite weary of it.

CHAPTER FOURTEEN

James reached the door, prepared to brazenly depart her room directly into the hall. He was too enraged to care if anyone saw him.

But better sense prevailed.

He stopped, steadied his breathing, tried to understand why he was so incensed. Rose had boldly asked him to marry, but he didn't wish to marry, so why be angry?

He was using Rose—and with despicable motives too. He was lonely and bored and chafing over the same old issues that constantly plagued him at Summerfield. Who was he? What was his past? Where did he belong?

It had never seemed to be Summerfield, but then, it had always seemed to be Summerfield. Rose had filled a void, had been caught up in his peculiar, disordered world. With his army career being over, he was at loose ends, and she was a pretty, intriguing distraction.

He had to head to London and start the next phase of his life. He was considering a move to India, an acquaintance having offered him a position there. Such a gigantic undertaking would be expensive. He'd have to buy his share in the venture, then travel across the globe.

It would mean begging Stanley for money. It would mean relying on Stanley yet again to settle James's future.

What James actually needed was to meet and wed an heiress. A rich bride would cure his problems, but it seemed so mercenary. And since he'd only contemplate matrimony to gain a fortune, Rose was the very last person he'd select as a wife. She was poorer than he was.

He was very attracted to her and worried he might be falling in love, but so what? Marriage was off the table, so how could it matter if he left immediately or in two weeks?

If he stayed at Summerfield, they'd simply grow more attached, and while James could walk away without a backward glance, Rose couldn't. She would suffer and mourn their parting, so James shouldn't behave more contemptibly than he already had.

Why not leave in the morning?

He knew what was best, yet he whirled around and marched to the bedchamber. She was still on the bed where she'd been minutes earlier. She stood and turned to face him.

"I asked you to go," she said.

"I can't."

"We'll hash it out tomorrow. I don't have the energy to quarrel with you right now."

"We're not quarreling."

"Fine. We're not quarreling, but there's no reason for you to remain."

"There's every reason."

She shook her head. "We want different things in our lives, James. I want to wed. I hadn't thought I did, but I've changed my mind. I could be happy on that path, but it doesn't appeal to you at all. From the beginning, you've been very clear. It's ridiculous to continue."

Oddly, James's pulse was racing. He was overcome by the burning need to propose. Despite his pitiful fiscal condition, despite his dim view of matrimony, he could barely keep from dropping to his knees and begging her to have him.

The notion of their separating was suddenly quite terrifying. He couldn't imagine it, but as quickly as the panic arose, he tamped it down.

His infatuation was driving him wild with desire, but that's all it was: inappropriate desire.

She was like a disease in his blood. He ceaselessly pondered her, yearned to be with her every second, but no viable conclusion could be gleaned from fraternization.

He *had* to leave the next day, and the decision swept over him with a cold resolve.

He was never ruled by emotion. For the moment, he was obsessed with her, but time and distance would cause his fascination to wane. The sooner he departed, the sooner he would recover his sanity.

But before he left, he would treat them both, would satisfy them both, would give them both a more suitable ending than an abrupt goodbye.

"We share a blatant physical attraction," he told her.

"So what?"

"It's pointless to ignore it."

"No, it's pointless to pursue it."

"Why deny ourselves?"

"Because it's wrong for us to dally. It lures us farther into an impossible relationship."

"As you said: So what?"

"There's more to life than hedonistic indulgence," she claimed.

"I disagree. If you don't have anything to call your own, hedonism is the only pleasure available."

"We're not animals. We don't have to succumb to our base drives."

"There's nothing *base* about what I feel for you."

He bent down and kissed her, his lips capturing hers in the sort of torrid embrace they'd come to relish. She didn't protest or attempt to escape. They jumped into the fire together, overwhelmed by the need to be closer.

For a brief instant, she wrenched away and murmured, "You're mad."

"Yes, mad for you."

"You're a sorcerer. I'm under a wicked spell, and I can't resist you."

"You shouldn't resist me. It's ludicrous to try."

He drew her nearer and tumbled them onto the mattress. His cock was hard as stone, demanding release. He couldn't stand that they were still dressed, that he'd never had the chance to press his bare skin to hers.

Gradually, he unbuttoned buttons and tugged at fabric as he nibbled and bit, keeping her distracted, pushing the passion higher and higher, so she wouldn't stop him, so she wouldn't object.

Finally, she was naked, and he gazed down her body. She was mortified by her nude condition, and she snuggled against him, her face burrowed to his chest.

"Let me look at you," he said.

"No. You're embarrassing me."

"Don't be embarrassed. When we're alone like this, every behavior is allowed."

"It's too much."

"You're so beautiful, Rose."

"Don't say that."

"Why shouldn't I?"

"Because you make me forget myself."

"Good."

"You spew your pretty compliments, and I'm eager to do whatever you ask. I can't tell you *no*."

"You shouldn't tell me *no*. Not ever."

He dipped to her breasts, sucking on one, then the other, until she was writhing and pleading for mercy.

He abandoned her nipples and traveled down, kissing her chest, her stomach, and eventually arriving at the vee between her thighs. She arched up and tried to pull away.

"What are you doing?" she inquired.

"I want to taste you."

"No."

She was on her elbows, glaring down at him.

"Lie back," he urged.

"This is so unseemly. It has to be a sin."

"I'm sure it is."

He licked across her sheath, flicking his tongue inside.

"Oh, my Lord!" she muttered, and she flopped down, swiftly losing the energy required for complaint.

It only took a few seconds for her ardor to crest, for him to throw her over the edge. She went joyfully, blissfully, and as he nuzzled a trail up her torso, she was smiling, laughing, looking so ecstatic that his heart raced with his own burst of joy. She was staring at him as if he were a god, as if he walked on water, and it was heady stuff, making her happy. He didn't know if he'd ever again stumble on any other endeavor that would prove quite so satisfying.

"You're the worst." She was chuckling, sighing.

"I certainly am."

"I can't believe I have such loose tendencies."

"You like carnal activity. Admit it."

She groaned with dismay. "What will become of me? I'm thoroughly corrupted."

"It will be hard to go back to being the prim, proper spinster you were before."

"That's what I'm afraid of. After this, I'll never be the same."

"No, I don't suppose you ever will."

He couldn't bear to have her mention the future, couldn't bear to have her mention the time—very soon—when they would be parted forever.

A gnawing sadness welled up, but he ignored it. He wasn't a maudlin person. He didn't rue and regret his choices. He picked a path and forged ahead.

He and Rose had a fine sexual attraction, and that's all it was! He had to stop his ridiculous moping.

Still, he was inundated by the realization that they were at the end of all that would ever be between them. It seemed so wrong for this to be their finale. They'd already crossed so many ethical boundaries. How could it hurt if they took a few more steps down the road to perdition?

He'd never been so aroused, and his body was intent on having her in the only way that counted. What purpose was served by her keeping her virginity? She claimed that—after she left Summerfield—she would return to teaching, so what benefit was her chastity? Or would she save it for later to squander on some elderly oaf like Stanley?

There was no reason for James to deny himself, no reason for Rose to delay.

It was the desire talking. He was thinking with his phallus, convincing himself to proceed when he was fully aware of why he shouldn't. But unlike most every other occasion in his life, he couldn't behave rationally.

Where she was concerned, proper conduct was impossible.

"I want you to do something for me," he murmured.

"Anything, James. I will do anything for you."

"That's what I was hoping you would say."

Rose gazed into his blue, blue eyes.

She didn't imagine she'd ever grow tired of looking at him. Not if she had another hundred years. She didn't need a hundred, though. She'd be content with another forty or fifty—if only she could have him until her dying day.

He insisted they were having a brief fling, but he was a fool. She'd brazenly asked him to marry, and he'd crushed her by refusing, but he couldn't have meant it.

The fact that he'd tried to storm out, but hadn't, told her all she needed to know. He had feelings for her—*deep* feelings—but didn't realize it and couldn't tell her.

She wasn't precisely sure what boon he was about to request, but she had a fairly good idea. His manly lusts were inflamed, and he was eager to assuage them.

She should have said *absolutely not*, but if she agreed, she was positive he'd recognize his heightened sentiment. When they were finished, he'd *have* to wed her. Honor and decency required it. The law and morals required it.

She wasn't tricking him into a leg-shackle. No. She was simply helping him clarify his position. She was simply helping him to acknowledge that they should be husband and wife.

They'd spent their lives alone. Wasn't it time to form a permanent connection? Wasn't it time to bond and unite? Wasn't it time to be happy?

He drew back onto his haunches and tugged off his shirt, baring his chest. She'd never seen a man's chest before and hadn't grasped that the sight would be so riveting. Her belly tickled.

There was a matting of hair across the top, then it thinned

down his flat belly to disappear into the waistband of his trousers. Her eyes traced that line, wondering where it ended, wondering what was hidden beneath the fabric. She'd heard that men and women were built differently in their private parts.

What was different? Why was the difference necessary?

He kissed her, easing her down onto the mattress, and his skin was warm and smooth against her breasts.

"I'm sorry we were fighting," he said.

"I am too."

"I was being an ass."

"I surprised you."

"You're so brave," he absurdly stated.

"*I* am brave?"

"Yes. I'm constantly amazed by you. You're not afraid to grab for what you want."

"I wouldn't pin any medals on me," she scoffed.

"I would. I've *never* grabbed for what I want." He paused and frowned. "Or maybe it's more correct to say I've never known what to grab *for*."

Wasn't that exactly what she'd just been thinking? Given sufficient opportunity, he'd figure out that he loved her. He merely needed to adjust his attitude so he'd comprehend that his path and hers were the same.

"I'm so glad we met," he said.

"So am I."

"It's the best thing that ever happened to me."

"Really?"

"Yes." He seemed stunned by the admission.

"How sweet of you to tell me."

He'd embarrassed himself, apparently having gone as far as he could in professing any elevated sentiment.

He started kissing her in earnest, swiftly leading them into the spiral of passion, and it occurred to her that this was where he was more comfortable. This was where he thrived, where he could show her with his hands and body what he couldn't share with words.

He dipped to her breasts, his fingers slipping down her belly and into her sheath. He toyed and played, quickly bringing her to the cliff of desire and pitching her over the edge.

She flew merrily, and he held her during the tumult. As it waned, there was a new resolve in his gaze. He widened her thighs, wedging in his torso. Down below, he was fumbling with his trousers, unbuttoning the flap.

A flare of nerves shot through her, and she panicked. Should she let him proceed? Or should she stop him?

As rapidly as the anxious thoughts arose, she shoved them away. She was right to persist. They would complete the marital act, and his reservations about matrimony would vanish.

"I'm desperate to carry on precisely as we shouldn't," he told her.

"We're far past that point."

"But there's no retreat from this."

"I understand"

"I don't think you actually do." He studied her, appearing conflicted. "I'm using you horridly."

"No, you're not. I want this. I want *you*."

"You'll never be a maiden again. We can't repair your body or turn back the clock so that you're a virgin."

"I know, James. I know."

"Are you certain?"

"Yes."

"I shouldn't pressure you, but I want this so much."

"So do I. And you're not pressuring me."

He evaluated her, and she stared back, her expression serene and untroubled.

Evidently, he saw what he needed to see, and he nodded.

"Promise me one thing," he said.

"Anything."

"Promise me you'll never be sorry. No matter what happens in the future, you can't ever regret this."

"I'll never be sorry, you silly man. I asked you for this, remember? I practically demanded it."

"I'm so lucky. Luckier than I deserve to be."

"I'm lucky too," she quietly murmured.

A charged moment sizzled where she thought he might declare himself, but he didn't. The interval passed, and he fell to her breasts again, as he worked his fingers between her legs. Then something bigger was there, something she hadn't expected. He was pushing it into her, and she tensed.

"Just relax," he advised.

"It feels odd."

"The first time is awkward."

"Are you sure this is the proper way?"

"Very sure. You trust me, don't you?"

"No."

He chuckled. "Take a deep breath." She did, and he said, "Take another."

She settled a bit, but not as much as he was hoping. The encounter was escalating much quicker than she'd anticipated, and she was more disturbed than she'd assumed she'd be. More confused too.

He was kissing her again, his hands massaging her nipples, as he flexed and flexed. Finally, her passion crested and she cried out. As her body shattered, he gave a hard shove with his hips. There was a tear and a sharp pain, then...he halted.

He was trembling, and he gazed down at her.

"Are you all right?" he asked.

"Is that it? Is it over?"

"No. There's a tad more."

"Show me."

"Let's hold still for a minute while you acclimate."

She struggled to calm herself, and gradually, the ache waned. She sagged into the mattress, realizing that the strange coupling wasn't so strange after all. It was actually quite...interesting, like nothing she could have imagined or described.

He began to move, pulling out of her, then pushing in again. He started slowly, but the tempo increased until it grew shockingly wild, and he was slamming into her in a perfect rhythm as if they'd cavorted a thousand times previous.

She seemed to instinctually know what to do. She met him thrust for thrust, her questing hands stroking his shoulders and back, even dipping down to brazenly clasp his buttocks.

She simply couldn't bring him close enough, couldn't feel him near enough, and she was curious as to how long it would continue. He was able to manage the pace, as if he was an expert at controlling the pleasure.

Fleetingly, she speculated over just *how* he'd become an expert, the notion crossing her mind that it could only have been from experience with many partners. If she hadn't been so in love with him, she might have focused on the question of his heightened skill, but apparently, he'd reached the end.

He froze and tensed, and while at the last second, he twisted his torso as if he might withdraw from her, for some reason, he didn't. He growled with satisfaction and collapsed on top of her.

For an eternity, they lay together, pulses slowing, perspiration cooling. Ultimately, he pulled away. She winced, figuring she'd be very sore in the morning. He'd torn her on the inside. Would the injury heal? Or would she always carry this small memento of what they'd perpetrated?

He smiled, looking young and handsome and somewhat abashed.

"Did you survive?" he asked.

She grinned, not wanting him to discover how undone she was by the event.

"Hale and hearty," she replied. "I'm not a virgin anymore, am

I?"

"No."

"Good. I didn't need that silly old chastity anyway."

"I'm delighted you gave it to me."

"So am I."

He rolled her onto her side and spooned himself to her back. The room was quiet, and she reveled in the silence. She hadn't known it would be so intimate afterwards, hadn't known it would be so spectacularly charged with emotion. Tears swarmed to her eyes, but she couldn't fathom why.

She wasn't sad. She was very, very happy. Perhaps they were tears of joy.

"I have a confession," he whispered in her ear.

"What is it?"

"You arouse me beyond my limit."

"I'm a vixen, am I?"

"Yes. There at the end, I should have pulled out."

She frowned. "I don't understand what that means."

"A man spills a seed in the woman's womb. That's how a babe is created. But if he pulls out..."

His voice trailed off, and she completed his sentence for him. "He won't sire a child."

"Yes. I shouldn't have finished that way."

"Could I be...with child now?" The possibility left her absolutely breathless. If she was increasing, he'd have to marry her. He'd have no choice.

"No, no," he hastily responded. "It can't happen from just one time. Well, it *can,* but it's very rare."

He reached over her shoulder, took her hand, and kissed her palm.

"You're wonderful," he said, almost as if he was surprised.

"If you continue complimenting me, I'll get a big head."

"We can't have that, can we? I'd better keep my flattery to myself."

She elbowed him in the ribs. "Don't you dare stop. I'm a glutton for your adulation."

"Then, Miss Ralston, I shall persist until you're sick of hearing my praise."

She'd never grow tired of it. Never.

Behind her, he yawned. She sighed with contentment, visualizing their future, where they would fall asleep in each other's arms every night for the rest of their lives.

"You wore me out," he claimed. "I need a nap."

"I do too." She yawned, as well. "You can only doze, though. The maids can't catch you in here in the morning."

"They won't. I'll go in a bit."

She wished she was shameless enough to have him stay, to let the maids catch him. It would be one more nail in his coffin toward a leg-shackle, but Rose wouldn't flaunt their relationship in front of Stanley for she didn't want to ever have to admit how they'd misbehaved under his roof.

She wanted to travel to London with James, to wed him there where they would be far away from Stanley and their union accomplished long before he ever learned of it.

"Everything will be all right now, won't it?" she inquired.

"Yes," he promised.

"We'll always be together?"

"Yes," he mumbled.

"And we'll have to work out our differences with Stanley, so he's not hurt or angry."

A snore sounded, and he didn't reply.

Sighing again, she lay very still, listening to him breathe, feeling his large, warm presence curled around her. She was ecstatic and wistful and blissfully in love, and she couldn't imagine she'd ever suffer a more perfect moment.

She must have slumbered, for when she opened her eyes, dawn was breaking. Birds were chirping, the sky lightening.

Without glancing over her shoulder, she knew he was gone, but she looked anyway. He wasn't there.

Though she'd hoped and expected it, there was no rose on her pillow.

CHAPTER FIFTEEN

Veronica tiptoed into her bedchamber without making a sound.

It was very late, and the vicarage was a creaky old house. The slightest weight on the wrong floorboard would produce a screech like a banshee. But she was an expert at sneaking out and sneaking in, could come and go without a trace.

"Where have you been?" a voice suddenly hissed behind her.

A candle flared to light, and she whipped around to find her stepfather seated in the chair in the corner.

"Papa Oscar!" Her mind whirred frantically as she sorted through the ramifications of discovery.

"Where have you been?" he repeated as he rose to his feet.

"Why are you up?" she replied, stalling. "I know how you hate to miss your sleep."

"I will not ask you again." He approached, the flickering candle enhancing his features so he looked utterly demonic.

"I was hungry. I went downstairs to get a glass of milk."

"Don't lie to me!" he bellowed.

He raised his hand, and she only had an instant to see that he was clutching his riding crop. He slapped her with it, across the arm and shoulder—not the face—so there'd be no visible marks.

"I'm not lying."

"You would stand here, in my home, under my roof, and blatantly tell untruths? You would dare?"

"I would never be untruthful. I'm a good daughter. I am!"

"I watched you leave!"

Damn! She'd been positive he was asleep. His snoring had rattled the rafters. What had awakened him? Why had he bothered to glance out the window?

He hit her over and over, and briefly, she considered grabbing the whip and turning the tables on him. She'd like to give him a hard whack so he'd realize what it felt like to be struck.

But she didn't. For all her bluster, he thoroughly intimidated her, and she hadn't a clue how to openly defy him. In that regard, she was very much like her poor, beleaguered mother who'd never stood up to him either.

He seized her by the scruff of the neck, his fat fingers squeezing tight. He was bent over her, his disgusting lips pressed to her ear.

"You will apologize at once!" he ordered.

"Yes, yes, I'm sorry."

"You will beg my forgiveness."

"Of course. Please forgive me."

He tightened his grip, pushing her down and down until her forehead was touching the floor. Her knees were already screaming in agony, her back too, and she wondered how long he'd hold her before his rage was spent. Sometimes, he could continue for hours.

"I ask you again," he seethed. "Where were you?"

She'd been at the spot by the pond that she'd shown to Lucas Drake. Several young people from the village had met there for a party. One boy's father owned the tavern in the village, and he'd stolen some ale, but only a small amount so they'd each been able to have just a few sips.

The entire affair had been so boring that she should have stayed home. It certainly hadn't been worth this trouble. Oscar's temper and penchant for punishment was legendary, so she'd never hear the end of it.

Mentally, she reviewed her choices. What should she confess? She wasn't a tattle, so she'd never mention the party or the pond or the people who'd attended.

He was ranting from Scripture about the sins of Eve, the wickedness of women, but she was barely listening. As he droned on and on, the most marvelous idea occurred to her. It was the answer to all her prayers and would bring about the perfect conclusion.

"Who were you with?" he shouted.

"James."

There was a thrilling, exhilarating pause, then he demanded, "Who?"

"I was with James Talbot."

He shoved her away as if she was unclean, as if she had a fatal disease that might be catching. She crumpled to the rug, but didn't attempt to rise. With the state he was in, movement would encourage another lash of his riding crop.

"What were you doing with him?"

She peeked up, trying her best to appear shy and maidenly.

"We were...kissing and...other things."

"What other things?"

"I really can't say it aloud. Don't make me."

She stared at the floor, a veritable model of contrition and remorse, but actually, she was hiding a grin.

"You were with James Talbot," he muttered.

"Yes."

"Shaming yourself. Disgracing yourself. Dishonoring my good name."

"I'm sorry. When he asks me to go off with him, I'm afraid to refuse."

He gasped. "It's happened before?"

"Yes."

"How many times."

"Three?"

"Harlot!" he charged. "Daughter of Eve! Spawn of the devil!"

He grabbed Veronica's hair and yanked her up so she was kneeling in front of him. He slapped her once, and again and again.

"One time for each ignominy," he explained. "One blow for each of your adventures, but trust me, there will be much more castigation before you and I are through."

If three firm clouts were all it took to get a proposal from James, it was a very tiny price to pay.

"What about James?" she inquired. "What will you do? I hate to cause him any difficulty."

"That shall be your greatest punishment of all. You shall have the reprehensible libertine as your husband, and it will be a penalty to make you recall—for the rest of your days—that the wages of sin are very high indeed.

"I don't believe James wishes to marry me," she tentatively said.

"After this humiliation, he has no choice."

"What do you mean?" She pretended to be confused, but she simply wanted to be very clear as to Oscar's intent.

"I will speak to Stanley first thing in the morning. I will apprise him of all that's transpired, then we will send a messenger to London to obtain a Special License. You and James will be wed at once."

"At once!" She tried to look shocked, but could barely conceal her glee.

"There will be no delay. I will see to it. In my congregation, no man is permitted to salaciously fornicate. It will not stand!" he thundered. "Now say your prayers."

"What should I pray about?"

"Pray for forgiveness. Pray for guidance. Pray for the strength you will need to be James Talbot's bride, for there is no heavier burden a woman could assume than to be his wife."

Veronica folded her hands, bent her head, and began.

The ordeal might last for hours, until dawn, or he might make her keep on until he left to talk to Stanley.

For once, she didn't mind a bit.

"Where have you been?"

"Have you become my nanny?"

"I asked you a question. What is your answer?"

Stanley glared at James, not surprised in the least by James's sharp tone. James had never liked to be interrogated as to his whereabouts or any other topic. His attitude hadn't mellowed with age.

They were in James's bedroom suite, and he'd just slinked in from a clandestine visit to Miss Ralston. James wanted Stanley to think their bargain terminated, but Miss Ralston was very pretty and very lonely, and James never had been able to resist a conquest.

Stanley's only regret was that he couldn't watch them together awhile longer. Their carnal escapades were extremely erotic, yet all good things came to an end. Some sooner rather than later.

"I ask you again," Stanley said, "and I don't have time for lies or evasions."

"Oh, for pity's sake, Stanley, it's nearly dawn. I can't see why we must quarrel when I've been up all night and I'm exhausted."

James went over to the sideboard and poured himself a whiskey. He glowered at Stanley—as if he could force Stanley out with a mere scowl—and Stanley simply sighed and relaxed in his chair.

James stomped over and slouched into the chair across. He was sipping his drink, studying Stanley with what had to be an incredible amount of distaste, perhaps even hatred. Stanley supposed he deserved it.

He'd never been kind to James, but then, Stanley firmly believed that hefty doses of discipline and disdain made a man out of a boy. Stanley's own father had raised Stanley in similar fashion, and Stanley was shrewd and tough because of it. There'd been no reason to coddle James, and Stanley never would have. And look at the man James had grown to be!

When James was older, when Stanley was dead and buried, James would be grateful for his stern upbringing. Stanley was convinced of it.

"I'm not here to pester you, James," Stanley said, "and I won't beat around the bush."

"Praise be. Maybe I'll get some sleep before this night is through."

"I doubt it."

"Why?"

Stanley rose and poured his own drink, then sat back down. He assessed James, pondering the future and how it would unfold. As he'd initially plotted over having James deflower Miss Ralston, he hadn't peered down the road to the end. He hadn't fully considered the ramifications.

He'd simply thought to pay James for his assistance, then set him free. But he hadn't counted on James's affection for Miss Ralston.

One fact was clear: James couldn't stay at Summerfield.

Miss Ralston had developed her own infatuation, which had to be quashed. Otherwise, she might start hoping she could wed James, but she belonged to Stanley, and James couldn't have her.

During the past few days, Stanley had been fretting over how to crush their flirtation, and this conclusion was for the best. He really didn't have to do anything at all. Fate had already determined the finale. Stanley only had to guide the players on their proper paths.

"I will ask you once, James, and you can't dilly-dally or falsify."

"Yes, yes. What is it? What's wrong?"

"Were you with Veronica this evening?"

James couldn't completely stifle a gasp. "Veronica?"

"Yes. Were you with her in ways you shouldn't have been? I'm certain you're smarter than that. Tell me the truth."

James scoffed, appearing disgusted at the very idea. "No, I wasn't with Veronica. What an absurd notion."

"I expected that as your reply, but I had to inquire."

"Why?"

"Because she's accusing you of misconduct."

"The little trollop." Two red slashes colored James's cheeks.

"My feeling exactly," Stanley concurred. "I won't ask you where you actually were, but I assume you were with a woman?" James hemmed and hawed, and Stanley said, "I don't have to know her identity."

"Yes, I was with a woman," James carefully admitted.

Stanley nodded. "So we can't use the truth as your defense. It would bring Oscar's wrath down on an innocent party. Here is what we will do instead."

James raised a hand, motioning Stanley to stop. "Wait, wait. What's happening?"

"My brother caught Veronica sneaking into the rectory a few hours ago. She's named you as the culprit who lured her out."

"She's a liar. I never did!"

"I was sure you hadn't, but I've been informed by a well-placed servant at the vicarage that—once the sun is up—my brother will barge in and demand you marry her."

"Dammit! I won't!"

"No, I would never let you, and I guess Lucas was correct in his warning that you were in danger. We should have heeded him."

"Yes, we should have."

"If she spins an involved tale about you, it will be the very devil to refute it." Stanley paused, realizing this moment was key. "You have to leave. Immediately."

"To where?"

"To London. Right now. I'll tell everyone—but especially my brother the vicar—that you left last night after supper and that I rode with you part of the way. You couldn't have cavorted with her because you weren't here."

James froze, seeming to hold his breath, his mind racing as he struggled to figure out how to refuse without mentioning Miss Ralston or his affair with her.

Stanley pressed his advantage. "I have your horse saddled and a bag packed. It has to be now before the house begins to awaken. The servants are loyal, but I don't want anyone to see you who could contradict my claim."

"I don't know, Stanley," he finally said. "I hadn't planned to go so soon."

"There's no other choice, James. You understand what Oscar is like. You can't be eager to embroil yourself in a conflict with him."

"No." James studied the floor, thinking, thinking. "I should say…goodbye to some people, though. I should explain—maybe to Lucas."

"I'll speak with Lucas in the morning, and he can corroborate our account as to the time of your departure."

"Yes, I'm certain he would."

"And what about the paramour with whom you spent the evening? Will she remain silent? I trust she wouldn't incur Oscar's fury by announcing your tryst. She'd never come forward with a story that differs from mine, would she?"

"No, she wouldn't."

Stanley stood and approached James. Disaster was about to strike, and James needed to hurry. Stanley would never permit Oscar to harm James, but it was easiest to accomplish Stanley's goal with James spirited away. If James wasn't on the premises, if he didn't return, the whole incident would die down without too much of a mess.

With James having cancelled their deal regarding Miss Ralston, Stanley hadn't expected to pay up on their arrangement, but to coerce James into leaving, he decided to tender his prior bribe as an added inducement.

Besides, though James wasn't aware that Stanley knew the truth, James had carried out his part of the bargain. Stanley only had to wait to learn if James's seed had caught. James deserved to be remunerated for his efforts, and Stanley handed him an envelope.

"What this?" James asked.

"It's a bank draft for the money I promised you earlier—when we were haggling about Miss Ralston."

"There's no agreement between us. You don't owe me for anything."

"It contains the other details too. About the orphanage."

"I see." James stared at the envelope, running his thumb over and over the front.

He might have passed up the money, but he wouldn't forego the information about his parents. He couldn't. He'd wanted it forever.

"Let's go, James," Stanley urged. "I saddled the horse myself so I wouldn't have to involve any of the stable boys. It's behind the barn. You can use the back road."

James peered up at Stanley, and he looked so torn. Did he realize he was in love with Miss Ralston? Had the notion occurred to him?

It was the most important reason why James had to leave.

"This is so sudden," James said. "It doesn't seem right."

"Get yourself to London. Oscar's temper will calm, and I'll have Veronica married off somewhere else. Then you can come home."

"That might be awhile in the future."

Stanley shrugged. "It shouldn't be that long. Just until matters have resolved. I'll be quick about it."

Actually, he wouldn't work toward a resolution. While he'd certainly deal with Oscar and rid himself of Veronica, he wouldn't allow James to return. Miss Ralston had to wed Stanley, and he almost hated to hurt James so terribly, but some behaviors couldn't be helped. Some endings couldn't be avoided.

"Let's go!" Stanley snapped.

He gestured impatiently to the door, but James didn't move.

"Time's wasting, James," Stanley said. "Each minute that ticks by, we're closer to Oscar arriving. Will you remain here and be trapped in Veronica's web? Is that the conclusion you envision for yourself."

"No." James stared at the floor again. Ultimately, he said, "If anyone inquires about me, tell them why I left, would you? Make sure people know I didn't seduce Veronica—and that I will be back very soon. Take Miss Ralston, for instance. I've really grown to like her. I wouldn't want this nonsense to ruin her good opinion of my character."

"I will tell her. In fact, I will shout from the rooftops that you are much too smart to involve yourself with Veronica and that she is a bald-faced liar."

"Thank you."

James couldn't say more than that—he'd have to admit his affair—and Stanley wouldn't listen to more. While he understood James's attachment to Miss Ralston, it didn't signify. It couldn't.

James had to *go*.

"Come," Stanley said. "I'll walk you out."

"All right."

James thoroughly assessed the room, clearly concerned over when he'd return, which was a valid worry. After Stanley wed Miss Ralston, James would *never* return.

"I'll send the rest of your things," Stanley told him.

"I appreciate it."

"Write me so I'll know where you're staying."

"I was thinking...ah...I might head to India. I have a friend from the army who asked me to join him in a business venture."

"A grand idea." Stanley forced a smile, the enormity of James's departure gradually sinking in. "I can assist with your travel arrangements, and if you have fees or commissions to pay, I'll gladly buy them for you."

"I have no idea how much it will be."

"The amount doesn't matter."

Then there was nothing else to say.

Stanley went to the door and pulled it open, peeked out to ensure the hall was empty. They tiptoed down the rear stairs, and Stanley led him to the spot where his horse was tethered to the fence.

Neither of them spoke, Stanley stoically watching as James checked the saddle, his pack, as he swung himself onto the animal.

"You've been good to me," James said. "I'm grateful for your many kindnesses."

"You're welcome."

"This seems so final." James glanced around. "I wonder if I'll ever be back."

"It's your home, James. I'll always be happy to have you."

They shared a lengthy visual exchange, and Stanley was

disturbed by how emotional it was. He'd thought he could push James off into the night, that he could coerce James away without consequence, but evidently, their separation would be much more difficult than Stanley had imagined.

He was an old man—without friends and only Oscar as family. He'd assumed he was beyond sentiment, but apparently, he wasn't. Apparently, he possessed a long-buried and completely unnecessary pebble of affection for James.

"Be safe," Stanley said.

"I always am."

"Write to me," Stanley said again, suddenly desperate to hear that James would.

"Once I'm settled," James said.

He tugged on the reins and was gone, swiftly swallowed up by the dark.

CHAPTER SIXTEEN

"You'll pay for this!"

"I already have—just by you showing your face over here. It's never pleasant when you visit."

"I won't be mocked!"

Rose was coming down the main stairs when angry voices drifted up from down below. She halted on the landing and peeked over the banister to see Stanley and Oscar Oswald, toe-to-toe, their fury evident.

"She's a tart and always has been," Mr. Oswald was saying. "You're the only one who didn't know it."

"My daughter will not be shamed like this. Neither will I."

"She needs to marry."

"On that point, we agree."

"I'll find her the husband she deserves," Mr. Oswald fumed, "but it won't be *him*."

"He will do right by her! If I have to sue him in the courts to make him behave properly, then I shall."

"I'm weary of your melodrama, and I've had enough. It's time for you to leave."

The butler was standing by the front door. As if on cue, he whipped it open.

The vicar was so incensed he was shaking, and Mr. Oswald watched him with a bored expression.

"You haven't heard the last of this," Vicar Oswald hurled like a threat.

"I'm sure that's true," Mr. Oswald stoically retorted. "You never did know when to shut up."

"A moral crime has been committed, and a moral price must be paid." The vicar wagged a finger at Mr. Oswald. "We'll see who is victorious in the end."

"Yes, we will." Mr. Oswald batted the finger away.

"Tell him what I said! Tell him he's in my sights, and I won't stop until he makes the appropriate amends."

"He'll be delighted to receive your message." Mr. Oswald

motioned to the door. "Now drag your ass home to that little trollop and inform her it will be a cold day in Hades before anyone believes her lies."

The vicar stormed out, and the butler closed the door after him. Then he and Mr. Oswald tarried, frozen in place until they were certain the vicar had left.

When it became clear that he had, Mr. Oswald spun to the stairs and peered up at Rose, having realized she was eavesdropping. She should have guessed he would. He was incredibly astute.

"Good morning, Miss Ralston."

"Hello."

"Come down, would you? We need to talk."

"I was...ah...on my way to breakfast."

"I'll have the servants deliver a tray for you." He gestured down the hall toward his library. "If you'll join me...?"

As always in her interactions with him, she couldn't refuse. She was a respectful person in general, and he was elderly. Plus, with his promise to return her dowry after her month's sojourn was concluded, she didn't want to upset him. She simply wanted him to follow through and give her the money.

Upon awakening, Rose's first thought had been about that money. She had no idea how much it was, but she and James could use it to live on until they found new positions in London.

She was so happy! With matters resolved between them, she'd raced downstairs, anxious to see him at the breakfast table. She was excited to spend the day making plans and couldn't bear to waste time in a private chat with Mr. Oswald. But apparently, it couldn't be avoided.

Forcing a smile, she started down.

"Yes, of course, I'll join you," she cheerily agreed.

"Thank you."

He waited for her, offering his arm as he escorted her to his library.

He went around and sat behind his massive desk, and as she seated herself in the chair across, she said, "I couldn't help but overhear you in the foyer with Vicar Oswald. He seemed very angry."

"He was."

"I hope it's nothing serious."

"Actually, I need to discuss his visit with you. There are some issues of which you must be apprised."

The comment surprised her. "My goodness. What are they?"

He sighed, looking horridly aggravated. "I'm embarrassed to tell you, but I must. The gossip will spread like wildfire."

"Gossip about what?"

"James has landed himself in a jam, and I'm not sure I'll be able to get him out of it."

"What sort of...jam?"

"He's always flirted with Veronica. You're aware of how it is with forbidden fruit, and the vicar's daughter is the most forbidden of all."

Rose's pulse began to gallop. "What are you talking about?"

"He finally went too far." More to himself than to her, he muttered, "I warned him about her, but he never would listen to me."

"What happened?"

What, what, what? It seemed the only word she knew.

"There's no polite way to explain it," Mr. Oswald replied, "so I'll just blurt it out. Forgive me for being blunt."

"Yes, please be candid. I prefer it."

"He was with her last night, doing what he shouldn't have."

Rose gasped. She couldn't hold it in. "He was with Veronica in an improper situation?"

"Yes."

"When?"

"I'm not certain exactly. My brother caught her sneaking into the rectory about two o'clock, and she's confessed her transgressions."

Rose was so shocked, she was amazed she didn't slide off her chair and collapse on the floor in a stunned heap. At two, she'd been pacing her bedchamber, wondering where James was and starting to suspect he wasn't coming.

He'd been with Veronica? Rose couldn't believe it. He wouldn't betray her like that, wouldn't treat her so badly. She and James were in love. They were moving to London to marry and live happily ever after.

Rose inhaled a deep breath to calm herself, then said, "I wouldn't necessarily take Veronica's word for it."

"I feel the same."

"Have you spoken to Mr. Talbot?"

"Yes, I have. Can you keep a secret for me, Miss Ralston?"

"Absolutely."

Mr. Oswald sighed again, appearing as if he had the weight of the world on his shoulders. "Unfortunately, he's verified her account."

"He admitted it?"

"Yes. The little tart has him boxed into a corner, and I'll have to work like the dickens to save him from her marital noose."

"Mr. Talbot and Veronica." She pronounced the names slowly,

as if her mouth couldn't articulate them.

"It's pitiful, isn't it? But I'm afraid I have to ask for more discretion from you. For all my quarrels with James, I really like the boy. I can't punish him by having him wed to Veronica."

"I imagine it would be awful," Rose mumbled.

"So while you and I know the truth, I am denying Veronica's claim. I've told my brother that James departed for London directly after supper, that he couldn't have trifled with her because he was gone. You didn't see him after supper, did you? If you did, I need you to keep that information to yourself."

Rose stared down at her hands where they were folded in her lap. Her fingers were interlaced, and she was squeezing them together so tightly that her knuckles were white.

"No...ah...I didn't see him," she ultimately said.

"Good, so you don't have to lie about it." He chuckled. "I'll lie for both of us."

"Where is Mr. Talbot?"

"He left for London just before dawn."

At the news, her heart lurched in her chest, suddenly aching so painfully that she worried it might quit beating.

"He left?"

"There wasn't any reason for him to stay, was there?"

"Well..."

"Not that I could discern anyway." Mr. Oswald paused, then said, "And with our situation concluded, it didn't seem appropriate for him to remain."

"What do you mean?"

"I'll be blunt again, Miss Ralston."

"Yes, please."

"You remember the bargain he and I had with regard to you."

"Your bargain?"

"Yes, that he would help me with my problem. Before he rode off, he confided that he'd taken care of things with you. I can't tell you how grateful I am that you decided to proceed."

Rose was shocked again, to her very core. James had revealed their affair to Mr. Oswald? James had admitted to Mr. Oswald that he and Rose had fornicated? He'd divulged the private, personal encounter?

"Mr. Talbot talked to you about me?"

"Yes. He told me all the details."

"He wouldn't have," she breathed.

"He was most concerned about this nonsense with Veronica. He claimed he was very friendly with you now and didn't want you to have a bad opinion. He wished you'd never find out."

"Find out?"

"I advised him that I couldn't keep it from you. The entire mess will cause quite a stir, and Summerfield is a small place. There's no way I could have prevented you from hearing about it."

If Mr. Oswald had beaten her with a stick, she couldn't have felt anymore pummeled. He stared at her—coldly, dispassionately—and she returned his stare, her mind so chaotically confused that she was dizzy with dismay.

She'd assumed she knew and understood James Talbot, but if Mr. Oswald's tale was accurate, she hadn't known James at all.

What was true? What wasn't? How was she supposed to glean the difference?

"Will...ah...Mr. Talbot ever come back to Summerfield?"

"I don't expect he will," he killed her by saying. "I had promised him several boons for his assistance with you—mainly some information about his parents—and I've given him a substantial amount of money too, as a reward for services rendered. He'll use it to sail to India."

"India!"

"It's for the best, Miss Ralston. You have to realize that it is."

"Why?"

"If he'd stayed on at Summerfield, it would have made matters between you and myself extremely awkward."

"Matters between us?" She was too befuddled to concentrate.

"Yes, after we wed and you have the child, I couldn't have James loitering and interfering. He and I never intended that he'd remain. It was always the plan that he would leave after he finished with you."

The way Mr. Oswald pronounced the word *finished* was a slap in the face to Rose. She could have been a brood mare out in the stable.

"Well, *my* plan," Rose forced out, "is that I will depart in another ten days or so. I'm no longer interested in marrying you."

He scoffed. "Of course you'll marry me. You can't be trotting around the countryside, with child and without husband."

A wave of nausea gurgled in her stomach, and she was afraid she might wretch all over the expensive carpet.

"Would you excuse me?" She pushed herself to her feet.

"I will for now, but we must confer later. Once we've determined your condition, we'll send for a Special License and begin planning the wedding. I have to invite many of the neighbors, but the final guest list will be up to you."

"Yes, yes..." Rose didn't mean to agree. She just wanted to escape, to lie down so the world would stop spinning.

As she turned to go, her nausea increased, her dizziness too. She stumbled as if she might faint, and she had to grab onto the chair to keep from falling.

He was around the desk in a flash, and he clasped her elbow to steady her.

"Are you all right?" he asked. "I'm a tad...dizzy."

He called for a housemaid to escort Rose to her room. Rose was too disoriented to walk on her own, and she clutched the maid's arm and staggered up the stairs to collapse on her bed. The girl covered her with a blanket, then pulled the drapes to shut out the bright morning sunlight.

He left! Rose mourned. *He left without a goodbye! I could be having his baby, and he left me here with Mr. Oswald!*

Impatiently, she shooed the maid out, and once she was alone, she started to cry.

"May I speak with you?"

"Certainly."

Lucas gestured to Miss Ralston, urging her over.

She'd found him in the music room, dabbling on the harpsichord. It had been an odd day and an even odder evening. There had been no company for supper. He and Stanley had dined in the small parlor, huddled together and discussing Veronica. They were grand conspirators, and as they'd gotten their stories straight, Lucas had been delighted to find that Stanley's devious brain worked much like Lucas's.

Trouble had been brewing with Veronica—he'd predicted it— and he regretted that he hadn't dragged James away when they'd initially quarreled over her. And he'd be eternally grateful to Stanley for saving James from the terrible fate of being Veronica's husband.

He hadn't seen Miss Ralston all day, and he wondered what she thought of the drama. Had she been apprised?

He was seated on the bench at the harpsichord, and he ran his fingers over the keys with a flourish.

"Aren't I remarkable?" He grinned up at her. "My ability to play is my only skill. Please tell me I'm marvelous. I won't be able to stand it if you don't."

"I'm not feeling very well," was her quiet reply. "Could we not joke and jest?"

At her solemn tone, he noticed she was wretched and pale as a ghost, as if she'd been ill.

"I apologize. I never know when to be serious. Actually, I'm *never* serious. My father would insist it's my worst flaw."

She didn't respond, and he pointed to a nearby sofa.

"You look awful," he said. "Sit down before you fall down."

She sidled over and eased herself onto the cushion. He slid from the bench and sat in the chair across. There was a lamp on the table, and it highlighted her face, starkly enhancing her misery.

Was this woe because of James? Had she been that attached? Or was it something else? Had Stanley hurt her? If so, Lucas was hardly the one to fix any problem.

"What's wrong?" he asked.

"I've kept a secret from you."

"A secret! Then you must spill all, my dear." She couldn't begin, and he waved her on. "Go ahead. I'm a good listener."

She dithered forever, as if her next comment would be extremely difficult to voice. Ultimately, she said, "We have a personal connection I haven't revealed."

"What connection?"

"We're cousins."

"Cousins?"

"Yes."

"Through which kin?"

"Your father and my mother were siblings."

"First cousins? Really?"

"Yes."

"All this time, and you were silent about it." He frowned. "You're sure? You're not making it up?"

She snorted with disgust. "Trust me: I wouldn't invent a relationship with you."

"What's that supposed to mean?"

She shrugged. "The Drake family never claimed me, and in return, *I* haven't claimed them."

"But all of a sudden, you're eager. Why?"

"I need your help."

He was a treacherous ass and the very last kind of man a woman should rely on for anything, but he was so intrigued by her. She didn't like him! She didn't like his family! He couldn't decide what to think.

"Where have you been all these years?" he inquired, then raised a hand to stop her. "Obviously, you were at Miss Peabody's school."

"Yes. When my mother died, I was four. Your grandfather was named my guardian, but he was so angry with my mother that he refused to assist me."

"You were only four," he indignantly huffed.

"Yes."

"Why was he so angry?"

"My mother had sought his permission to marry my father,

and when it was denied, they eloped. She was disowned and forgotten."

"And never forgiven. How typical of the Drakes."

"I always thought so."

"Your parents died in Egypt, right? It's all coming back to me."

"Yes, we were in Egypt, and some people there—I don't remember who—contacted your grandfather so he could bring me to Sidwell."

"But he wouldn't?"

"He sent me to Miss Peabody instead. After he passed away, your father kept me there."

"You never visited. You never wrote."

"Don't be a dunce, Mr. Drake," she snapped. "Of course I didn't write or visit. Your father and grandfather were quite clear. I wasn't *welcome* at Sidwell."

"Oh."

He could certainly understand it. The two men had always been pompous and ridiculous. It was entirely predictable that they would have tormented a little girl.

"I'm sorry." The apology was inadequate, but he offered it anyway. "We can be friends now, can't we? We don't have to labor under their idiotic rules."

"I hope we *can* be friends. That's why I asked to speak with you."

"Would you call me Lucas? It's ludicrous for us to be so formal."

"I'd rather not, Mr. Drake."

"Fine," he sighed. "Please continue. What do you want of me?"

"I'm alone in the world, and you're a male family member. I'm begging for your help."

"With what?" He scowled. "And don't beg. I hate that sort of heightened sentiment."

"I have to leave Summerfield." Tears filled her eyes, making them glitter like diamonds. "Would you take me away from here?"

"To where?"

"London? Or Sidwell Manor? Your father is very wealthy. He must own a dozen houses. Could I stay in one of them? Just until I can figure out what to do."

"What happened that you can't stay at Summerfield? Is it James? Is it the fact that he left?"

"I won't discuss Mr. Talbot."

"Is it Mr. Oswald then? Has he been awful to you?"

She growled with exasperation. "I simply need to leave, Mr. Drake, and I'm a female cousin in grave distress. Must I furnish a reason beyond that?"

Lucas stared at her, irked by the realization that she viewed him as a possible savior. Which he wasn't and never had been.

How precisely did she suppose he could aid her?

He couldn't bring her to Sidwell. He was barely allowed there himself, and with his latest imbroglio with his creditors, he was even more of a pariah. If he waltzed in with her, his father would chase them both out with a broom. The exalted Lord Sidwell was that much of a caustic boor.

As to London, Lucas had no money, no apartment, and no decent companions he could prevail upon to give her shelter. His life had been a long pursuit of decadence, with James being the sole individual who had even the slightest hint of good character.

So...while he wished he could act the role of champion, he hadn't the means, and it wasn't in his nature to behave honorably.

"We couldn't go to Sidwell, and I don't have my own home, so there's no place I could provide to you in London."

"Perhaps you have an acquaintance you could recommend."

"Not really. Not anyone you should meet anyway. James is the only one who's the least bit reputable."

"I see."

"I'm not even sure I'll remain in London myself. I'm traveling there tomorrow to find James, and I believe he and I might sail for India."

"He's truly considering it?" she murmured.

"Most definitely. We resigned our commissions in the army, but we don't have any prospects in England. India could be a new start for us."

She pushed herself to her feet. "Thank you for your time. I appreciate your speaking with me."

"Rose," he grumbled, standing too. "Don't be upset."

"I'm not upset. I was merely searching for fairy dust."

"Fairy dust?"

"It's something that doesn't exist—just like the aid I'd foolishly thought you might supply."

"I'm sorry." Two apologies in a single afternoon!

"Don't be. I've had a long history with the men in your family, Mr. Drake. I'm not surprised by your answer at all."

He felt vile, like the cad he was, and for once, he was disgusted with himself. He'd never had a woman plead for his assistance before. The females in his world knew what he was like. Nary a one would ever have lowered herself.

"Why don't you stay at Summerfield?" he said. "Isn't it still an option for you to marry Mr. Oswald?"

"Yes, Mr. Drake, it's an option."

He clasped her hand. She didn't pull away, but didn't exhibit a cordial response, either.

"Don't you have friends of your own who could take you in?" he inquired.

"Only the other teachers from my old school, and they're going off to wed—as I went off. I hardly think they'd be in a position to impose on their husbands by asking if I could move in."

"Then isn't it best to remain here? Mr. Oswald isn't the greatest person—he can be difficult and annoying—but he's generous occasionally. He's willing to have you as his wife, so you'd be mistress of Summerfield. Most women in your situation would deem it a huge blessing to be offered so much."

"I'm sure they would," she muttered.

"You'll realize it too, eventually. You'll be safe here. You'll be rich and settled and protected by Mr. Oswald's name and fortune. At the moment, you're distraught, but once you calm, you'll see that I'm right. You'll see that this is the only viable solution." He paused, wondering if he'd gotten through, if he'd made his case. "It's not such a bad choice, is it, Rose?"

"It's Miss Ralston to you." She yanked away and stomped out.

"Well?"

"My brother called you a liar. He claims it never happened."

"He what?" Veronica raged.

She'd been on pins and needles, waiting for her stepfather to return with the news that she and James would marry. She'd expected to be his bride in the next day or two.

"What did James say?" she asked.

"He's gone to London."

"He can't have," she wailed.

"He has," her stepfather tersely stated. "He slithered away like the snake he's always been."

"Bring him back!"

"How would I?" Oscar bellowed. "How would I make James Talbot do anything? How would I make Stanley Oswald do anything?"

"You're an adult, and you're my father. You're supposed to know how."

"They have shamed and emasculated me. Both of them! Both of them have emasculated me."

It was typical of Oscar to view the incident as to how it had affected *him*. But *she* was the one who'd been damaged. She'd been reminiscing about James so intently that she'd practically convinced herself that a seduction had actually occurred.

"Who cares about you?" she scoffed. "*I* am the ruined party. I told the housemaid this morning. The gossip will have spread around the village."

"You little harlot. Why would you tell others?"

"I wanted people to hear about it. I thought it would help me to snag James."

"Oh, you fool! You idiot!"

"If I don't wed James, what will become of me?"

"My brother will find you a husband—but it won't be James Talbot."

"Stanley will find me a husband? No, no, absolutely not. I won't have any man he'd pick for me."

"You don't think so? You think you could sit in this rectory—dishonored and disgraced—with the whole town snickering? You think you could refuse a husband who is provided to you?"

"I'll have James or I'll have no one."

"Then you will have no one. And you'll be living in a ditch—because you won't be living here with me."

He stormed up the stairs to his room.

CHAPTER SEVENTEEN

"Are you happy, Miss Ralston?"

Rose glanced over her shoulder to see Veronica marching up. She grimaced, then hid her reaction.

She'd packed her bag and sneaked away from Summerfield, having left all the pretty dresses and baubles Mr. Oswald had provided. She was carrying just the pitiful pile of belongings she'd brought with her when she'd arrived.

She was on the lane, walking to the village and not exactly sure what she'd do once she was there. She'd stooped to thievery, having stolen a few pounds from Mr. Oswald's desk. There had been a huge stack of money, but she'd only taken a bit, figuring he wouldn't discover the petty larceny.

She supposed she should have been aghast at her behavior, but so far, there'd been nary a ripple in her conscience. He'd inflicted plenty of misery, and she viewed the money as a small down payment on what she felt she was due for the trouble she'd suffered since she'd come to Summerfield.

A mail coach traveled through, and she intended to purchase a fare and return to Miss Peabody's school. She was praying Evangeline or Amelia would still be in residence. Attorney Thumberton had given them numerous tasks to complete as they shuttered the place and prepared it for the new owner.

If they were present, they could advise her as to how she should proceed. If they'd already gone, at least Rose would be back in a spot that was familiar. She'd lived in the area for twenty-one years and was desperately hoping to receive assistance from people in her past life—for it was glaringly evident she would receive no help from those in what should have been her new life.

"Hello, Miss Oswald."

Veronica stomped up and waved a scolding finger at Rose.

"You're the greediest, most selfish person I've ever met."

Rose scowled. "I'm sorry. What?"

"You blustered in here to marry Stanley. You'll get his entire fortune, so Oscar and I won't get anything. But was that enough for you? No."

"What are you talking about?"

"You had to take James too."

"Mr. Talbot?" Rose was so disordered that she felt dizzy again. She couldn't concentrate, couldn't focus on why Veronica was complaining.

"He and I were to be husband and wife," Veronica claimed. "Everyone knows it."

"How grand for you."

"You flirted with him constantly. You turned him against me."

"You're mad, and I'm busy."

Rose tried to continue on, but Veronica blocked her path.

"He wouldn't wed me because of you!" Veronica said. "You had him so besotted, he didn't notice me anymore."

"I have no idea why you'd think so. I'm barely acquainted with Mr. Talbot, and I have no influence or control over him."

"Liar. Just so you know"—Veronica leaned in, sneering—"he showed me *everything* a boy and girl can do together."

Rose was positive Veronica was lying, but she couldn't begin to tabulate all the ways Veronica's words hurt her. She was crushed by James's betrayal and departure, crushed by Mr. Drake's refusal to aid her, crushed by Mr. Oswald's demented belief that she was still willing to marry him.

Why was life so hard? Why were people so cruel?

Rose calmly responded, "How marvelous for you that Mr. Talbot has taken such a special interest."

"He always liked me. *Me!* Not you."

"I'm sure when he returns, the two of you will be blissfully happy."

"I'm sure we will be too."

"He's proposed, has he?"

"He hasn't, but he will. Stanley told my stepfather that he'll make James marry me."

The boast was an outright falsehood. Stanley had said so himself.

"Good for you," Rose replied. "I'm certain you'll end up with the future you truly deserve."

Rose scooted by her, humored to catch Veronica's confused expression as she tried to figure out if she'd been insulted. Rose smirked. One benefit of fleeing was that she'd never have to see the horrid child ever again.

"Where do you think you're going?" Veronica seethed from behind her.

Rose should have ignored the question and kept on, but she

was exhausted, beaten down by events, and not behaving rationally.

She whipped around and said, "You'll be delighted to learn that I'm leaving Summerfield."

"Are you?"

"Yes, so you needn't fret. You and your stepfather can inherit all of Mr. Oswald's assets. *You* can wed Mr. Talbot. As for myself, I don't have to stay and watch any of it unfold."

Rose was carrying her faded, worn satchel, and Veronica studied it with a great deal of scorn.

"Have you sneaked away? Or has Stanley realized how unlikeable you are? Did he kick you out?"

Rose shook her head, wondering how Miss Peabody could have arranged such a hideous fate for Rose. Clearly, her old friend and mentor couldn't have ever visited Summerfield. Clearly, she hadn't understood the snake pit into which Rose had been tossed.

At least Rose would tell herself that Miss Peabody hadn't understood.

It would be too painful to imagine that Miss Peabody hadn't actually liked Rose, that she'd suspected how awful it would be, but had orchestrated the intolerable conclusion anyway.

"Good day, Miss Oswald." Rose used her most stern schoolteacher voice. "If I'm lucky—and I haven't usually been—we won't ever cross paths again."

"I certainly hope not."

"I certainly hope not too."

"When my situation with James is settled," Veronica said, "I'll send you a wedding invitation. You can eat your heart out."

"Yes," Rose sarcastically jeered, "I will constantly regret that I couldn't latch on to such a decent, moral specimen."

Veronica gasped. "Are you insulting my fiancé?"

Rose whirled away and continued on, muttering, "The girl is mad as a hatter."

Veronica called out several times, trying to get Rose to re-engage in their juvenile spat, but Rose pretended she couldn't hear the summons.

"She what?"

"I believe she's left the property."

Stanley glowered at the butler. "You believe she has? Or she has?"

"I spoke with her maid. It appears her belongings and satchel are missing, and no one's seen her since breakfast."

"Dammit," Stanley mumbled.

"Also," the butler added, "we just had a delivery from the village. She was observed walking on the road into town."

"Bloody hell."

He'd been eating and had ordered Rose down to join him so he could probe her health.

The prior afternoon, she'd been dizzy and nauseous. Had a babe caught already? She had to be increasing. Stanley could feel it in his bones, so he couldn't let her escape.

He threw his napkin on the table and shot to his feet.

"Have the carriage brought round," he grumbled. "Fetch my coat."

The butler hurried off to issue commands, and Stanley went to his library. As he reached into his desk to pull out his purse, he instantly noticed that someone had riffled through his money. He always had a large amount in the drawer, but never worried about being robbed.

The servants were aware that the money was present and also aware that he kept close track of the quantity. They wouldn't dare steal from him, so apparently, Miss Ralston had helped herself, and in light of what he knew about her character, he noted that she'd taken only a small sum.

He didn't begrudge her the theft. Desperate people often did desperate things, and she was frantic.

The main flaw in Stanley's plan to sire an heir was that he hadn't foreseen Miss Ralston falling in love with James, hadn't foreseen the havoc James's departure would wreak on the poor woman's emotional state. Stanley had to tamp out the fires he'd started, first and foremost by guaranteeing that she couldn't flee with Stanley's son in her belly.

The precious cargo was *his*. He'd bought and paid for it.

He walked outside as the coach was rolling into the drive. He climbed in without waiting for the footmen to lower the step.

Miss Ralston might be desperate, but Stanley was desperate too. Desperate to keep her at Summerfield. Desperate to have what he'd coveted for decades. A child. Hopefully a boy with James's blood in its veins. No, Miss Ralston was a fool if she thought he'd allow her to make off with such a valuable prize.

It didn't take long to find her. She was nearing the outskirts of the village, and as his vehicle approached, she didn't realize it was Stanley. She moved to the side of the road, but the driver maneuvered the team to cut off her path.

Frowning furiously, she peered over as Stanley opened the door and hopped down.

"Hello, Miss Ralston."

She was calm and poised, not providing a hint of evidence that she was running away. She nodded her greeting. "Mr. Oswald."

"I expected you to join me for my noon meal."

"Sorry," she said, offering no explanation for her absence.

"It's a beautiful day for a stroll, but I have to insist you come back to the manor with me."

"No, thank you."

"I insist!" he stated more vehemently.

"I'm leaving Mr. Oswald."

"To what destination, Miss Ralston?"

"I can't see how it's any of your affair."

He scowled. "Not my affair? You are my fiancée. I can hardly have you traipsing across the countryside. If something happened, I'd never forgive myself." A footman was behind him, lowering the step, and Stanley gestured to the coach. "Please get in."

"No."

"I understand that you're upset, and I've always found that it's not wise to make decisions when you're distraught. It leads to bad choices."

"Yes, well, they'll be my *own* bad choices."

"Let's go home. You can rest, then we'll discuss a better solution that doesn't involve you walking down the road with your suitcase in your hand."

She sighed, looking tired and heartbroken and very, very pretty. Oh, how he wished he was younger and could have her as his bride in truth.

"I really need to return to my friends," she said. "For some time now, I've felt that it was a mistake for me to come."

"Nonsense. You're safe here, and I'm so happy to have you. You can't leave."

"I have to."

As lord and master of Summerfield, he was never contradicted, never denied, and he hated to be countermanded. He most especially hated it when a *woman* countermanded him. It couldn't be tolerated.

She was overwhelmed by events, but he was in a worse condition. Though he couldn't admit it to anyone, he was reeling from James's departure too. He'd thought he could finally let the boy go, had even provided the funds with a bank draft, but the notion of James's traveling to India was too much to bear.

Stanley had fretted all night, ultimately realizing that he couldn't permit James to move so far away. He'd sent a message to his bank, delivered by a rider on a fast horse, to cancel the draft, to tell James—when he tried to cash it—that the document wouldn't be honored.

James would be furious, but he wouldn't have the means to leave England. Not until Stanley could figure out a different conclusion.

Stanley was an old man, and he didn't feel well—as if things in his body weren't working as they should. He's always been stern and unbending, had always been sure that his way was the only way, that those who'd sinned deserved their fates, but he was starting to rue and regret.

Now, he wasn't certain about his opinions. His first wife, Edwina, had argued against his severe views, but he'd refused to listen and had been determined to prove her wrong. But she'd been dead for decades, so what was the point of any of it?

James couldn't go to India! Stanley wouldn't let him, and as to Miss Ralston, who was probably carrying James's child, *she* couldn't go, either. The silly girl, assuming she had a say in the matter.

He leaned in and whispered, "If you don't come with me, I will accuse you of theft and have you arrested."

Her blanched with consternation. "Theft of what?"

"You took money from my desk, Miss Ralston. Shall I have you searched?"

"I didn't take any money," she claimed.

"I keep track of exactly how much is in the drawer. Why am I positive it is the same amount we will find in your bag?" He gestured to the coach again. "Don't force me to bring the law down on you. Just come home—as I've asked."

She stared and stared, then her shoulders sagged with defeat. "All right."

"Thank you. I hate to quarrel."

"I stole your stupid money," she confessed, "and I'm not sorry."

"I don't blame you. As I mentioned, you're distraught. You're not making good choices."

"I've never previously stolen anything in my entire life."

"I know that about you."

"This is the level to which I've descended since we met. This is how low I've had to stoop. I hope you're happy."

She trudged to the coach, and Stanley followed. He offered her his hand as she climbed in, but she clasped the footman's instead.

Stanley sighed, wondering how to calm her, how to salvage any benefit from the burgeoning calamity.

"James! There you are. I've been looking everywhere."

James whipped around to see Lucas hustling up.

They were on a sidewalk in London, and James had just exited Stanley's bank, having suffered through the humiliation of having the draft refused.

The embarrassment was heaped on top of his recent visit to the orphanage where Stanley had supposedly found him when he was a toddler. It had burned down some ten years prior, with all records lost, and he'd only been able to locate a handful of people who recalled that an orphanage had ever been there.

Stanley must have known about the fire at the orphanage. Most likely, it wasn't even the place where he'd stumbled on James. It was simply another dead end, another way for Stanley to demonstrate his cruel streak, to show James that he'd never learn about his past.

On many previous occasions in their long and strange relationship, Stanley had tricked and deceived James, so James shouldn't have been surprised. But he was in the worst mood and extremely upset over many issues: fleeing Summerfield as he had without a goodbye to Rose, slinking off from a confrontation with Oscar, letting Veronica spread her lies unchallenged.

Rose had to have heard by now. What must she have thought?

The hectic moment of his departure seemed surreal, as if he'd dreamed it, and he was disturbed by how Stanley had manipulated him into sneaking away. In such a hurry too.

His rapid flight made him appear guilty, as if he was running from Veronica and her false story. Stanley had practically tossed James on his horse and sent him packing. James wasn't sure what it was all about and—with Rose involved—he couldn't decide how he should be behaving.

"What are you doing here, Lucas?"

"I told you I'd join you in the city."

"I didn't expect you for a few days."

"It was too boring at Summerfield with you gone."

"How were things when you left?"

"Veronica was squawking, and Oscar was fuming. That's about it. Stanley was quite dynamic in defending you."

"Were rumors circulating about me and Veronica?"

"The stupid girl spread them herself."

"Has she been believed?"

"I didn't poll the masses. I don't know."

"How is Miss Ralston weathering the storm?"

James could barely stand to speak of her. He'd relieved her of her chastity, then—not an hour later—had trotted away without a backward glance.

What was wrong with him?

He'd never been the most moral person, and the army had definitely roughened the edges, but he possessed an incredible fondness for her that hadn't faded, and he doubted it ever would.

Yes, he'd said he didn't wish to marry, that he didn't have the means to support a wife, but what if he'd been mistaken in sticking to that view?

Fate had shoved her into his path. Would he abandon her to Stanley? Was he prepared—for the rest of his life—to recollect that he could have had her for his own, but he'd been too much of a coward? Was that the biography he intended to write for himself?

He was so confused! If he'd been poor before, without the funds to wed, he was in even worse shape now. There was no money to travel to India or for any other purpose.

The city was full of starving, crippled veterans, but James couldn't imagine his own destiny would end so badly. He had many acquaintances and a distinguished service record, so he'd likely find a position without too much bother, but right that moment, he seemed adrift and endangered.

"You won't believe what I learned," Lucas said. "It's about Miss Ralston. Guess what?"

"What?"

"She's my cousin."

"Your cousin?"

"Yes. Remember that day you and I were talking, and I mentioned that I'd had a cousin whose parents died in a foreign country?"

"Yes, I remember."

"It was her! She'd been at Summerfield all this time and didn't breathe a word to me."

"Did she say why not?"

"She doesn't like me or my family."

James shrugged. "I always thought she was smart as a whip."

"And guess what else?"

"Just tell me, Lucas," James snapped, in no mood for games.

"She asked me to take her away from Summerfield, to Sidwell Manor or one of our other houses."

"Why?"

"She was extremely distressed and didn't want to stay at Summerfield. I don't suppose you'd have any details to share about that, would you?"

James sighed. "I behaved horridly toward her."

"Well, I wasn't much better. I told her that my father would never welcome her. My advice was that she remain at Summerfield with Stanley."

"What was her answer?"

"She thinks I'm an ass."

"She's correct. You are."

"I feel awful about the whole thing. I let her down."

"So did I."

James gnawed on his cheek, pondering, wondering what was best.

If he went to the estate and rode off with her, what precisely was his plan? He had no idea, but he muttered, "I'm going back to Summerfield."

"To do what?"

"To do what I should have done all along. To keep Rose for myself. She and I should elope to Gretna Green."

"Elope! Isn't that a bit drastic?"

"Probably, but I'm making decisions on the fly. I'm worrying about Rose for a change rather than myself. I want her to be happy."

"She let's you call her *Rose*, does she?"

"Yes."

"That must mean you've seduced her—as I suspected."

"Yes, and I can't leave her there. This entire business with Stanley is fishy. He pushed me away in the middle of the night. It was all so strange, and I was gutless in not standing up for myself."

"What about India? Is that still in the cards or what?"

"The bank draft was fake. There's no money."

"Stanley gave you a fake bank draft?"

"Yes."

"The prick."

"My feeling exactly."

James started off, and Lucas hurried to catch up.

"Are you heading back right now?" Lucas asked.

"Yes. Everything about this smells to high heaven."

"What about Vicar Oswald and Veronica?"

"Bugger Oscar and Veronica. I'm not afraid of them, and I can't let Stanley have Rose."

"You'll actually marry her yourself?"

"If I can. If she'll have me."

Lucas snorted with amusement. "I'd better come with you. If you're about to propose, it's a sight I have to see. And just so you know…"

"What?"

"She doesn't allow *me* to call her Rose. With me, it's Miss Ralston all the way."

"As I said earlier: She's very smart, and clearly, she's possessed of a fine amount of common sense too."

CHAPTER EIGHTEEN

James tiptoed up the secret stairwell to Rose's bedchamber.

He and Lucas had ridden hard all day, and it was very late, the house abed, which he considered a blessing.

He wasn't about to strut into the front parlor with the servants watching and Rose glaring. He had a ton of explaining to do, and he planned to do it quietly and in private. He wasn't the most eloquent man and wasn't sure he could obtain her forgiveness.

If she gave him a tongue-lashing and sent him on his way, he didn't want any witnesses. But if he was successful, and she was glad he'd returned, he wanted no witnesses for that moment either. He simply wanted to pack her things and slip out the back with her. They'd be gone before anyone knew he'd arrived.

Yet as he reached the landing outside her hidden door, he stumbled to a halt, his mind not able to process what was occurring.

Stanley was there, his eye pressed to the wall, clearly looking into Rose's suite through a peephole.

The perverted ass!

How long had he spied on her? What had he seen? Had he observed her dalliances with James? The notion didn't bear contemplating.

A wave of rage swept over James, the likes of which he'd never previously experienced.

"What the bloody hell...?" he seethed.

Stanley was confused by James's voice. He frowned and began to turn, but before he could, James grabbed him by his coat and tossed him toward the stairs. He stumbled down them, cursing as he descended, but James wasn't sorry for the rough treatment.

Stanley was much shorter than James, so James had to lean down to stare through the peephole. Rose was pacing in her bedchamber. Attired in just her robe, the belt was loose, the front flopping open to give him glimpses of her cleavage and private parts.

She must have heard Stanley's fall, because she froze, obviously wondering what had happened.

James was sick with disgust.

He lurched away and raced down to grab Stanley again. He lifted the smaller man by his coat, seams popping, as they exited into the hall on the lower floor, then James marched them down to Stanley's own bedchamber. James dragged Stanley inside, flung him away, then slammed the door behind them.

Stanley pulled himself up, deviously scrambling to formulate the lies and evasions that would cool James's temper, that would paint a better picture of Stanley so he wouldn't look like such a lecher.

"James"—his smile was fake, cajoling—"I wasn't expecting you. When did you get home?"

"You have one minute to explain yourself."

Stanley scowled as if he couldn't remember where they'd just been, then he laughed as if it had been a harmless prank. "Oh, you mean up in the stairwell?"

"Rose and I are leaving, Stanley, and I swear to God, this is the very last time you and I will ever speak. So tell me what you wish me to know, for I am never—*never!*—coming back."

"James, James, calm yourself. Let's have a brandy, hmm?"

"One minute, Stanley, starting now."

Apparently, Stanley thought he could bluff James as he constantly had in the past. He went over to the sideboard and poured them both a drink. He held out the glass to James like a peace offering, and James batted it away, liquor splashing everywhere.

"Spying on her, Stanley," James fumed, "when she's alone and undressed?"

"It's not what you think," Stanley claimed.

"It's exactly what I think!" James bellowed. "You ghastly wretch! Is this the sort of person you are? Spying on an innocent woman who is a guest in your home? All these years, I've wondered what drove you, and I guess I have my answer."

James yanked the door open, ready to storm out, when Stanley murmured, "Don't go."

But James ignored him. He was too incensed for conversation. His mind whirred with images of how he'd respected Stanley, feared Stanley, loathed Stanley, been grateful to Stanley. The odd cord binding them had been severed, and James was floating free, untethered to Stanley or to Summerfield.

"James!" Stanley beseeched.

James whipped around, desperately eager to beat Stanley to a pulp, but Stanley appeared elderly, contrite, and diminished in a way he never had before.

"What?" James barked.

Stanley gestured to his room. "Talk to me. Humor an old man."

"Screw you."

"I'm embarrassed, James. I'm ashamed. Please talk to me."

James knew he should have kept on, but Stanley had never previously admitted to having emotional flaws. Not ever, so James was exasperated to find himself insisting again, "You have one minute. That's it. Then I'm done with you."

Calling himself an idiot and a fool, he swept into the bedchamber. He poured himself the drink Stanley had initially offered, then seated himself in a chair. Stanley closed the door and eased himself into the chair opposite. He stared at the floor, unable to begin.

"How long has it been going on?" James demanded.

"Since she first arrived."

"For pity's sake, Stanley. You're reprehensible."

Stanley's gaze was furious. "You don't understand what it's like to be me, to have my physical...problem."

"Don't try to justify your behavior. You can't."

"All right, I won't."

"When did you drill your peephole? Has it always been there? Or was it created just for her?"

"I've had it there for years." He studied his hands. "I like to watch women, especially now."

"You are *never* to tell her," James warned. "Do you hear me?"

"I won't, and don't you tell her, either. I really like her. She's a fine girl."

"Shut up, Stanley." James downed his drink and stood. "Will that be all? I'm sick to death of you. I have to get out of here."

"But...I don't want you to leave. I want you to stay with me at Summerfield. I couldn't bear for you to go away."

"Are you mad? You presume I would stay after this...infamy? You're worried about losing Rose's good opinion. Well, what about mine? Oh, that's right. It never mattered to you."

"It always mattered!" Stanley hotly asserted.

"You couldn't prove it by me."

James had the fake bank draft in his coat pocket. He pulled it out and tossed it at Stanley. It drifted to the floor.

"I'm returning your bank draft," James spat. "You remember it, don't you?"

"Yes, I remember it."

"Have you any idea how stupid I felt when I was informed that it wouldn't be honored? Have you even the slightest clue of how I detest you?"

"Don't say that." Stanley was rubbing his forehead, seeming bewildered and befuddled, his age showing more and more with each passing second.

"And thank you for the directions to the orphanage. Of course I'm sure you knew that it burned down a decade ago."

"Yes, I knew. I wish I'd torched the place myself."

"Why didn't you? Why not hurt a few street urchins? Who cares? You're rich and powerful. You can act however you please."

"I deserved that I suppose," Stanley quietly said.

"Yes, you did," James scoffed.

"Sit down." Stanley sounded as if he was begging. "Sit—and I'll tell you all of it."

"All of *what?*"

"Your past. Your history."

"After all this, you think I'd believe you?"

"It'll be the truth. I swear."

James laughed miserably. "That will make it true? Because you *swear*? You're the biggest liar who ever lived."

"I'm your grandfather," Stanley suddenly announced.

At the words being so casually hurled, James was glad his chair was behind him. His knees buckled and he slid into it.

"You're my grandfather? You admit it now, after all these years?"

"Yes."

"Not my father. My grandfather."

"Yes."

"You let the rumors percolate, let people gossip and titter over me like dogs at a bone. You couldn't have confided in me? You couldn't have given me peace of mind? Would that have been so hard?"

"I thought it was for the best." Stanley rubbed his forehead again, his bewilderment increasing.

James threw up his hands. "I don't even know what to say."

"I had a son. Charles. You're aware of that."

"He was killed in an accident."

"No, not in an accident. He was...ah...killed in a duel. In London."

"A duel over what?"

"Over his mistress. Her husband shot him dead. My son, Charles. My one and only son. Shot dead over a woman."

"The woman...was my mother?"

"Yes. Her husband killed her too, after the duel, then killed himself. It was a revolting scandal, but we managed to cover it up without too much difficulty." There was a charged silence, then Stanley choked out, "She wasn't fit to shine Charles's shoes, and he was murdered because of her."

"That's why you always hated me? Because of my mother?"

"Yes. I told Charles and told Charles he had to give her up. I arranged a marriage for him—to a good girl, a proper girl—but he wouldn't even consider it. He claimed there could never be anyone for him but your mother."

"Yet she was married."

"Yes, and he was a blind fool. His name was never spoken in this house again."

James was reeling, a thousand questions on the tip of his tongue, but he didn't voice any of them. He was an educated, traveled man who'd spent a decade in the army, and he'd learned that the world wasn't black and white.

He wouldn't listen to Stanley denigrating his parents, wouldn't allow Stanley to paint a bad picture of them. James would form his own opinion and come to his own conclusions, without Stanley insisting his parents were immoral and horrid.

"What was my mother's name?" he asked.

"Mrs. Susan Talbot. She was an actress of some renown and viewed herself as being quite remarkable, but she was simply a money-grubbing doxy."

"Have you a portrait of her?"

Stanley snorted with disgust. "As if I'd have permitted a portrait of that mercenary trollop in my home."

"And my father? How about him?"

"We burned them when he died."

"I see."

James could just imagine how those dark days would have unfolded. Stanley had been defied by his only child, and he would never have forgiven his son, would never have set aside his pointless fury. These many years later, he was still raging.

"What about me?" James said. "Was I really in an orphanage?"

"Yes. I had warned Charles that we wouldn't clear up any mess he made with that woman, and you were the biggest mess of all."

"Well, that certainly explains a lot."

"You have to know how it was back then, James."

"Oh, I know how it *was,* Stanley. You were proud and angry, and you took it out on a little boy." James shoved himself to his feet. He went over to the liquor decanter and drank straight from the bottle. "How did I end up here?"

"Once Edwina realized she was dying, she had a change of heart."

"But not you."

"No, but I'm glad that she forced me into it. I was surprised by you! You're better than both your parents put together."

"High praise indeed."

They endured another fraught silence. James was so overwhelmed that he felt numb and besieged, weighted down by a burden that seemed too heavy to bear.

He could have railed at Stanley, but Stanley looked small and defeated. Why berate him?

"I can't let you go to India," Stanley said. "It's why I cancelled the bank draft. If you were so far away, I might not ever see you again"

"You seriously expect me to believe you were worried about that?"

"I want you with me. I want you home. You've learned the truth, and now, we can have the relationship we never had before. I don't care about your tainted bloodlines. Summerfield can be yours—I'll change my will and make you my heir. I should have done it years ago, but pride was stopping me."

"Pride! You blame this on your blasted pride?"

"I'll meet with my attorney tomorrow. I'll rewrite the terms so it will all be yours eventually. Just promise me you'll stay."

"After what I witnessed upstairs with Rose, you assume I'd remain?"

"We've quarreled often in the past, and we've always moved beyond it."

"I don't think we will this time, Stanley. I don't think so."

"I need you with me. Please. Don't leave me here—old and alone."

"You've pushed everyone away your entire life. Maybe you deserve to be alone. Maybe this is the exact fate you've engineered for yourself."

"But I was wrong! I shouldn't have carried on like this. Things can be better now. They can be different."

James stared and stared, struggling to muster some affection for the pompous, obstinate ass, but he couldn't. He attempted to discern some resemblance in their features, some proof that they were kin and that Stanley wasn't simply manipulating James with another deceit. Yet there was no resemblance and never had been.

"I don't know if I can forgive you, Stanley. Perhaps it will happen someday in the future, but it won't be today."

He started out, and Stanley moaned and dropped to his knees.

"James, I'm not well!"

"Goodbye. We'll talk later—if I decide I can stomach it."

James whirled away, and when Stanley called to him again, James kept going.

Rose emerged from her dressing room, having put her clothes back on. She'd gotten ready for bed, but had been too incensed to climb under the blankets.

She'd been pacing for hours, trying to figure out what to do.

When Mr. Oswald had caught up with her in the village, he'd threatened her with legal action over her stealing his stupid money. He'd frightened her, so she'd reluctantly agreed to return to Summerfield with him.

She'd been in her room, taking a nap, and she'd awakened to discover that the deranged ass had locked her in! She'd knocked and fumed and bellowed, but no one had come to her aid.

Stanley Oswald was insane. The servants abetting him in her confinement were insane. Every single person she'd met since her arrival was insane.

She'd retrieved the poker from the fireplace, and it was on the floor by the door. The moment a key was inserted in the lock, she would grab the poker and brace for battle. She hoped it would be Mr. Oswald, for she'd be delighted to beat him to a pulp. She was that angry.

She marched to the dressing room again and lifted the tapestry that concealed the secret door. She pressed her ear to the wood, listening, listening. A bit earlier, she was certain she'd heard someone fall down the stairs, as if there'd been a scuffle in the stairwell, but all was silent.

No matter what, she had to escape the madhouse before she was infected by whatever illness had sickened everyone else to the point of lunacy.

Suddenly, booted strides pounded down the hall outside her suite. She raced to the sitting room and picked up the poker.

The knob was spun, then rattled. Then a fist hammered on the wood, and a male voice—that definitely seemed to belong to James Talbot—called to her.

"Rose? It's James. Let me in."

For the briefest second, she seriously considered ignoring him, but better sense quickly prevailed.

"I can't open it!" she fiercely replied. "He's locked me in!"

"Who? Stanley?"

"Yes, and he won't let me out."

"Oh, that is the very limit!" There was some huffing and puffing, then he said, "I'll have to kick it in. Stand back."

She stepped away, watching as the doorknob flew off, the latch smashed to pieces. James stormed through the wreckage, proceeding directly toward her as if he would sweep her into his arms and all would be instantly forgiven and forgotten. But he couldn't miss her visible fury, the iron poker in her hand.

He stumbled to a halt.

"Are you all right?" he asked.

"Yes, just fit to be tied. The man is deranged."

"I agree."

"And I've had enough. Of him. Of you. Of Veronica Oswald. Of Vicar Oswald. Of Lucas Drake. Of Miss Peabody and her meddling in my life and my future. I'm leaving this asylum and don't you dare try to stop me."

She tossed the poker at his feet, and it landed with a clang, as she spun away and went into the bedchamber to retrieve her portmanteau. She stomped back to the sitting room and was headed for the hall when she noticed he was stomping along with her.

She whipped around.

"What are you doing?" she demanded.

"I'm coming with you. We're leaving together."

"*We* are not leaving together. In case you weren't paying attention, I just named the people who have tormented me and abused my good nature. You were at the top of the list."

She kept on, when from behind her, he absurdly said, "Would you wait a minute? I need to ask you something."

She whipped around again. "What is it?"

"Will you marry me?"

The question was so absurd that it rammed into her like a hard blow. She had to rest her palm on the wall to steady herself.

He wanted to marry her? He had the gall to propose?

Rose was the thickest woman ever. She'd gleefully participated as he'd flirted, seduced, then deflowered her. Though he'd vociferously claimed to have reneged on his devil's bargain with Mr. Oswald, he'd deftly performed his role and had been remunerated for his efforts.

The moment he'd accomplished Mr. Oswald's goal, he'd left for London. He hadn't even told her goodbye.

Rose was naïve and foolish, was lonely and alone. She'd dawdled in her bed with him, had listened while he'd spewed lie after lie about how they'd live happily ever after, and the whole time he'd been catching his breath from his dalliance with Veronica a few hours earlier.

Had any man in all of history ever behaved more egregiously? Had any man ever been more cruel and callous? Had any man ever broken a heart as painfully and completely as he'd broken hers?

She shook her head, banged her palm on her ear as if it was plugged. "I must be hearing things. I could have sworn you just asked me to marry you."

"I did ask, and I'm asking again. Will you have me?"

"Not if you were the last man on Earth."

She raced down the stairs and stormed out into the cold, dark night.

Lucas was exiting the stables when he saw Rose approaching.

She looked mad as a hornet. Shoulders hunched, portmanteau in hand, she hadn't noticed him yet.

He and James had arrived so late that Lucas had taken care of the horses so they wouldn't have to awaken any of the stable boys. James had been too impatient to speak with Rose, so he hadn't stayed to help. He'd hurried inside, supposedly to smooth over their difficulties, but evidently, he'd failed miserably.

"Rose," Lucas murmured, not wanting to scare her. Then he remembered himself and said, "Miss Ralston, it's Lucas Drake."

He emerged from the shadows as she halted and glared.

"Hello, Mr. Drake."

"Call me Lucas."

"No."

He sighed. "Where are you going? Are you leaving? That can't be your plan."

"It is."

"Well, I feel I must counsel against it."

"Well, I feel you have no right to lecture me about anything."

He wouldn't bother to argue with an irate female, and he dipped his head. "I stand corrected."

"I begged your assistance once before, but you refused to give it. My condition is now more dire, so I ask again: Might I prevail on you?"

"Ah..."

"When last I saw you, you convinced me to remain at Summerfield, where you insisted I would be *safe*. I took your ridiculous advice, and since then, I have been locked in and held captive by Mr. Oswald."

"Locked in!" Lucas couldn't believe it. Stanley had always possessed the potential to be a brute, but even for him, the conduct seemed a tad excessive.

"Yes, Mr. Drake, locked in like a slave, and I am fleeing this madhouse. I will not tarry another second. Will you escort me so I am not forced to ride off in the dark by myself?"

"Have you spoken to James? He went in to talk to you."

"I have spoken to Mr. Talbot, and *he* has spoken to me. Now then, will you escort me or not?"

"Let's slow down a bit. James wanted to—"

"Do not mention Mr. Talbot to me!"

"But...but..."

"Oh, never mind. If there is a human being on this planet more worthless than you, I can't imagine who it might be."

She pushed by him and huffed into the stable, as he dithered and debated.

Should he aid her as she was demanding? Should he fetch James and let James deal with her? Should he ignore her and go inside to bed? That probably wasn't a very honorable choice.

Behind him, she lit a lantern, and he turned to find her struggling with a saddle, lugging it to one of the stalls.

"You're leaving now, Miss Ralston?"

"Yes, Mr. Drake. I'm leaving now."

"To go where?"

"Back to Miss Peabody's school where I lived all my life, where I had friends who care about me, where I was safe until I came to this asylum of lunatics."

Lucas had always been just as worthless as she'd accused him of being, but he felt awful about his previous refusal to assist her. If she trotted off and suffered a mishap, he'd never forgive himself.

He was useless, but he liked to think he had occasional tendencies toward chivalry. It wouldn't kill him to be kind.

He wrenched the saddle away from her and dropped it on the ground.

"I'll help you," he said. "I'll take you home."

"Don't break a sweat over it."

"I'll rouse the stable hands and have them saddle our horses. You wait here."

"Why?"

"I need to run to the house to tell James what's happening."

"I'll give you fifteen minutes. If you're not back by then, I'm departing without you."

"I'll hurry. I promise."

"Do you travel with a pistol, Mr. Drake?" she asked as he started out.

"Not usually, but I can bring one if you like. Why?"

"Bring it then, but don't bring James Talbot. Don't let him come out here, for if I ever see him again, I will shoot him right between the eyes."

CHAPTER NINETEEN

"There's a horse tied out front."

"Could it be the new owner?"

"I hope not."

Evangeline smiled over at Rose. They were in no hurry for the proprietor to appear, for then there would be no reason to linger at their beloved school.

It was a cool, blustery day. The wind whipped at their cloaks and bonnets, angry clouds flying overhead, hinting that rain might blow in later. They'd walked to the village and were slowly strolling back, reminiscing over their years as students, then as teachers.

It had been a good life, a satisfying life.

Amelia had left already, having sallied forth to meet her father-in-law, which seemed odd to Rose. Why wasn't she on her way to meet her fiancé? Rose crossed her fingers that it wouldn't be another catastrophe orchestrated by Miss Peabody.

Evangeline, the gardener, the cook, and a housemaid were the only ones still on the property. The servants were anxiously waiting to be offered jobs in the new household, while Evangeline was simply delaying the inevitable, staying in what she viewed as her childhood home for as long as she could manage it.

Rose was staying, too—for as long as she could.

She'd been back for a month, her useless, degenerate cousin escorting her as he'd promised he would. Their trip had been uneventful, and Lucas had actually proved to be a humorous and interesting traveling companion. Rose had spent the entire journey reminding herself not to like him.

Once they'd arrived, she'd shooed him away, not wanting to introduce him to Evangeline, not wanting to have any further contact with him for it forced her to remember Summerfield and James Talbot.

Rose was determined to move on from that horrid episode.

She wasn't prone to regret or remorse, didn't like to rue her decisions or lament her choices. By behaving so foolishly with Mr.

Talbot, she understood the debacle was her own fault. She knew how to conduct herself in an honorable and moral way, but she wouldn't chastise herself over her lapses in judgment. It was a waste of energy.

She had to focus on the future and start over. Since her return, she'd been writing letters of introduction, visiting neighbors to inquire about job possibilities, to beg for references, for help.

So far, no leads had magically presented themselves, but she wouldn't give up. She couldn't.

A particularly strong gust of wind hammered them, and Rose glanced up at the clouds. They were drifting by so fast that they made her dizzy. Ever since she'd departed Summerfield, she'd been having the strangest episodes of vertigo, and she stumbled slightly and grabbed Evangeline's arm.

"Are you all right?" Evangeline asked.

"Just a tad dizzy."

"That's the third time this week you've told me that."

"Is it? I hadn't realized it was happening so often."

"You're not ill, are you?"

"No, merely tired, but with all I've been through, who wouldn't be exhausted?"

"Too true." They reached the front door, and as they stepped inside, Evangeline asked, "Do you suppose Miss Peabody knew that Mr. Oswald was insane?"

"He hid it well," Rose said. "She might not have."

"I would hate to think she knew he was mad and arranged the match anyway."

"I can only hope she didn't. I always assumed she liked me. I couldn't bear to admit that she'd hurt me deliberately."

She and Evangeline had been debating the issue, and Rose's dreadful experience had certainly rattled Evangeline. She was packing her bags, preparing to leave to join the young vicar Miss Peabody had picked for her.

Evangeline had a vivacious and flamboyant personality that Miss Peabody had constantly sought to tamp down. She'd felt a staid and quiet life as a country vicar's wife would be just the ticket for reining in Evangeline's cheerful tendencies.

Rose reveled in Evangeline's high spirits, and the notion of Evangeline tethered to a fussy, grumpy vicar was disturbing. Rose prayed he wasn't fussy or grumpy, that he was handsome and fun and kind, but after Rose's awful ordeal, they were both unnerved.

The vestibule was empty, the servants off to parts unknown. Rose peeked into the main parlor, but there was no one in it. Whoever's horse was tethered in the drive, the individual wasn't waiting for Rose and Evangeline.

They were removing their bonnets when Evangeline saw the mail laid out on the table. She riffled through it, grinning with excitement to find a letter from Amelia.

Rose watched as she flicked open the seal and scanned the words. But her grin swiftly turned to a frown.

"What is it?" Rose asked. "Don't tell me she's already having difficulty."

"She's at Sidwell Manor."

Rose gasped. "Sidwell?"

"Isn't that your uncle's estate?"

"Yes. Who is her fiancé?"

"Lucas Drake. That's your cousin, isn't it?"

Rose jerked the letter from Evangeline and read it herself. Her jaw dropped. "Oh, no. This can't be right."

"Isn't he a libertine and wastrel?"

"You have no idea."

"What should we do?"

"Well, for starters, she's absolutely *not* marrying him." Rose hung her cloak on a hook by the door, then dashed up the stairs. "I'll write immediately to warn her."

"Then what? By the time you contact her, we won't be here. If she refuses him, where would she go?"

"I don't know—as I don't know for myself—but I have to at least try to stop her."

Rose hurried on, her temper spiking as she thought about Miss Peabody and her interference in their lives. How dare Miss Peabody play God! How dare she endanger Rose and Amelia! And what was Rose to think about Evangeline? She couldn't possibly be riding off to a good ending.

Disgusted, incensed, she was muttering to herself as she marched into her room.

It bore no resemblance to her lavish suite at Summerfield. There was no inner bedchamber with a huge bed, no dressing room beyond, filled with plush towels and a silver bathing tub.

There was just the one room—it could have been a nun's lonely cell—a narrow cot along the wall, a writing desk in the corner. The sole window looked out at the rolling hills that led to the village.

Yet even with her entering such a tiny space, she wasn't paying attention.

"Hello, Rose," a male voice said. "Fancy meeting you here."

She whipped around to see Mr. Talbot seated in the chair at her desk. Apparently, he'd brazenly sneaked in as he used to at Summerfield.

If she suffered a race in her pulse, if she suffered a giddy moment of joy at realizing that he'd come for her, she ignored it and gave free rein to her unbridled fury.

He was slouched down, his fingers folded over his flat stomach, his long legs stretched out and crossed at the ankles. He appeared handsome and lazy and pompously exasperating—as if he had every right to show his face, to bluster in without notice or permission.

This wasn't Stanley Oswald's house of decadent disrepute. This was a renowned, respectable girl's school, and she was a renowned, respectable teacher.

"What are you doing in my room?" she raged.

"I thought we should chat."

"Chat?" She was so angry, she worried she might faint.

"Yes, you were in such a rush to leave Summerfield. We didn't finish our conversation."

"Oh, we finished plenty."

"I beg to disagree."

"Get out!" She yanked open the door and made a shooing motion toward the hall, but of course, he didn't budge.

He was an obstinate, annoying man who behaved however he pleased and bedamned to everyone else.

"Get out!" she repeated.

"No."

She hollered for Evangeline, but no footsteps hastened in her direction. She called for the gardener, for the maid, the cook, Evangeline again.

"This place is deserted." He was very smug. "No servant will run to your rescue."

"I don't need any help. I'm completely capable of stamping out vermin on my own."

"Vermin!" He pushed himself to his feet, rising slowly to his full height. She'd forgotten how tall he was, and in an instant, he towered over her. He laid a palm on the wood of the door and shoved it closed.

It had a lock, and the key was in it. Before she saw what he meant to do, he spun the key and dropped it in his pocket.

"Give me that."

"No."

"Give it to me!" she bellowed, and it occurred to her that she probably sounded like a lunatic. But when she was around James Talbot, such demonstrations of madness couldn't be avoided. He inspired that sort of derangement.

She pounded on the door and kept on pounding until her fist grew sore, but no one arrived to assist her.

"Where is everyone?" she fumed. "Did you bribe them to disappear?"

"Yes, actually." He grinned and waved to the chair. "Sit down, Rose."

"No."

"I insist."

"As do I. I don't want you in here, and I won't blithely submit to any of your ridiculous orders."

"I won't let you out until you calm yourself and listen to me."

"You might as well choke on a crow as persuade me to listen."

"When you were at Summerfield, I occasionally witnessed this side of you. Have you always had a temper?"

"I've never had an irate moment in my life—until I met you."

"I'm sure that's true. I've frequently been told that I can be vexing."

"You don't know the half of it."

"Would you like to hear how I've occupied my time since you left Summerfield?"

"No."

"I'm going to tell you anyway."

"Is there some reason you think I care?" She gestured to the locked door. "Shouldn't you head home? Won't your darling Veronica be wondering where you are?"

"See?" He wagged a scolding finger in her face. "That's exactly the type of idiotic comment that proves why we need to have a long, frank talk."

"What? You don't like me mentioning your beloved? Aren't there wedding bells in your future? Have you come to stick in the knife? To twist it a bit?"

She was exhibiting an enormous amount of rage, but deep down, she wasn't incensed. She was heartbroken.

The past few weeks, she'd been able to rationally appraise her situation, admit to her mistakes, and begin to move on. It hadn't been easy, but it had had to be done. Yet now, with him blustering into her small bedroom, she couldn't breathe. Regret was devouring her like a sea monster.

She wanted to grab him by the lapels of his coat, to shake him and say, *How could you hurt me?* But she didn't know how to have that discussion.

"First of all," he said, "she was never more to me than Vicar Oswald's spoiled, fussy stepdaughter."

"A likely story! After you slinked away to London, Mr. Oswald told me everything."

"He did, did he?"

"Yes."

"Well, guess what?"

"What?"

"Your cousin, Lucas Drake, told me a few things too. Interesting how you never revealed a kinship with him."

"Why would I confess a relationship with a complete wretch?"

"Point taken, Miss Ralston, but be that as it may, Lucas shared some tidbits that he learned while *you* were slinking off to this decrepit old school."

"Me! Slinking off!" She grumbled low in her throat. "I promised my cousin if I ever saw you again, I'd shoot you. Too bad for me that he took his pistol with him."

"But not too bad for me—for I refuse to be blamed for sins I didn't commit."

"You're the innocent party, are you?"

"Absolutely." He motioned crossly to the chair. "Sit down, Miss Ralston!"

"I prefer to stand."

"Are you always this obstinate?"

"Are you?"

He reached into his coat and pulled out a letter. He waved it under her nose. "Since you're so thoroughly convinced you know all, read this, then—if you still wish to ride your high horse—you can harangue at me a tad more."

She tore the letter from his hand and scanned it, assuming she'd quickly peruse it, then toss it back, but as the meaning dawned, she slowed to a halt.

"This was written by Veronica Oswald," she mumbled.

"Yes. To her stepfather."

"She's run off with a traveling peddler," she muttered like a dunce.

"Yes."

"She says she's blissfully happy, and he shouldn't try to find her."

"And I might add, it's precisely the sort of end Stanley and I predicted for her. I wouldn't have touched that girl with a ten-foot pole."

She scowled, her mind whirring as she struggled to decipher what she was supposed to glean from the information.

"Mr. Oswald told me," she hesitantly started, "that you were sweet on her. He told me you'd seduced her."

"I don't fault you for believing him. He's an accomplished liar."

"He begged me to be quiet about when you'd left the manor so he could thwart the vicar on your behalf."

"Yes. He was also desperately anxious for me to leave Summerfield, and like the silliest fool in the world, I let him pressure me into going."

"Why would he want you to leave?"

"For *some* reason, he got the idea that I was sweet on *you*. Not Veronica. You."

"Where would he get an idea like that?"

"How would I know? But he was afraid you might elope with me and refuse to give him what he's craved forever."

Her scowl deepened, her confusion growing. Mr. Oswald yearned for a child, an heir, but in order for him to obtain his heart's desire, Rose would have to be increasing.

"How are you feeling, Rose?" James inquired.

"Fine."

"That's not what I heard."

"What do you mean?"

"I mean your cousin spent several days traveling with you."

"What's your point?"

"He claims you suffered dizzy spells the whole trip."

"So...?"

"I'm not an expert on female bodily conditions, but I am aware that one of the first signs to appear when a woman is carrying a child is for said woman to be constantly overcome by dizziness."

"I've just been tired," she insisted, a horrid inkling creeping over her.

It was more than the vertigo. Her breasts ached, she was frequently nauseous—especially in the mornings—and she felt different, as if she possessed a new and exciting secret.

"Tired? Really?" he smirked. "Is that what you presume is happening?"

"Yes. I'm exhausted by you and Mr. Oswald. Who wouldn't be worn down by what I've endured?"

"Who wouldn't indeed?"

She glared up at him, hating his smug expression, his handsome face.

She'd loved him so much that there had been days she couldn't breathe with being so happy. She'd pinned her hopes on him, had staked her future, had ruined herself with the foolish belief they'd be together forever.

All of that jumbled sentiment was still roiling her, and she kept trying to convince herself that time was the cure she required, yet she hadn't been granted any *time*. She'd barely left Summerfield, and he was already here, destroying her equanimity, stirring up every raw, bald emotion that had to remain buried.

The dizziness he'd mentioned raised its ugly head. It always came on so suddenly. She swayed to one side, then the other, and he clasped her arm and eased her down into the chair.

"You claim you don't need anything from me, Rose, but there seems to be one thing you need very, very much."

"What is that?"

"A husband." He grinned. "I'm available."

She gasped. "You think I'm having a baby?"

"No, I think *we* are having a baby. You and me, Rose"—he gestured from her to himself—"having a baby."

"You said it couldn't occur from only doing it once!"

"No, I said it didn't usually occur. I didn't say it couldn't."

She gaped at him, wishing the floor would open and swallow her whole. What on Earth was she to do now? Her plight had been bad enough when she was simply penniless and unemployed. With a baby on the way, her problems would grow and grow until they became insurmountable.

"I should have made Mr. Drake leave that pistol." She shook her head with disgust, as tears flooded her eyes.

"Oh, Rose, don't cry."

"I will if I want to."

"You're not playing fair. You know I can't bear to see you sad."

"Then go away. I didn't invite you here."

"No, you didn't, but how could I stay away?"

He was standing much too close, their feet entwined, the tips of his boots slipped under the hem of her skirt.

She didn't understand why he'd journeyed so far just to speak with her, didn't understand what he sought or why he'd come. He wasn't a chivalrous person, had no desire to be leg-shackled, and it was ridiculous to suppose he'd wed her merely because she was in a jam and he was the culprit.

She simply needed to be alone, needed to ponder and plan and accept her situation. Her woe was visible. Why didn't he have mercy on her and depart?

"Back at Summerfield," he said, "I asked you a question."

She could hardly remember that last, revolting night. Was that to when he referred?

"What question?"

"I asked you to marry me."

"And I said *no*."

"Well, I'm asking again."

"Please don't."

"Why shouldn't I? In case it hasn't dawned on you, you're having a baby, and you have to wed. Right away, Rose. There's no time for dithering."

"But...you don't want to ever marry, and you most especially don't want to marry me. You told me so over and over."

"Can't a fellow change his mind?"

"Not you. If you tried, I wouldn't believe you. You insisted you were poor and hadn't the funds to support a wife."

"What if I was wrong?"

She was still seated, and he was still standing. She stared up at him, and his expression was warm and affectionate. It perplexed and rattled her as she recollected those bliss-filled weeks at Summerfield when she'd been so happy, when she'd felt so vibrant and alive.

"You left Summerfield so fast," he stated, "that I didn't have a chance to explain a few things to you."

"What things?" she inquired.

"I've now had several heart-to-heart chats with Stanley."

"What about?"

"It seems, my dear Rose Ralston, that Stanley Oswald is my grandfather."

"Your grandfather?"

"Yes, and like the ass you and I know him to be, he kept it a secret."

"But...why?"

"Simply to torment me—and to prove a point."

"To you?"

"No, to my parents, who've been dead for over two decades."

Rose rubbed her forehead. "That makes no sense."

"You're correct, but when has Stanley ever made sense?"

"Why did he finally break down and tell you?"

"He's old and alone and he's regretting his choices."

"He should regret them."

"My feeling exactly," James said. "Guess what else."

"I can't imagine."

"I'm Stanley's heir. He's rewritten his will and publically claimed me."

"You're joking."

"He's having trouble with his health, which is why I didn't come for you sooner."

"What trouble?"

"He's had a collapse. His doctor has diagnosed a minor apoplexy."

"He's incapacitated?"

"Bedridden for now anyway." James shrugged. "So I'm in charge at Summerfield, and my first act was to convince the vicar to retire and move."

"Vicar Oswald is gone?"

"Yes. The estate will be mine once Stanley passes, so Oscar realized there was no reason for him to stay. I saved the community from him, so at the moment, I'm very popular. I am also being lauded as Stanley's grandson and heir—with people insisting they'd suspected all along. Do you know what this turn of fortune indicates, Rose?"

"No, what?"

"All of a sudden, I'm a rich man."

"You're not," she breathed.

"I am, and I've decided I should bring home a bride to help me rule at Summerfield. Are you acquainted with anyone who might be available? How about a very pretty, very kind woman who is having a baby and needs to wed right away?"

Rose started to tremble, the shuddering increasing until she could barely remain in her chair. He dropped to a knee and clasped her hand.

"Will you marry me, Rose Ralston?" he said again. "I never used to view myself as much of a catch, but my situation has drastically improved. How about yours? Has it changed?"

He reached out and laid a palm on her belly, reminding her of the child that was very likely growing there.

She frowned. "You can't be serious."

"I'm deadly serious."

"If you're truly wealthy, I couldn't possibly be your bride. My father was a penniless missionary."

"At least your parents were lawfully wed. My father was an adulterer, and my mother—his mistress—was a notorious actress."

"How do you know?"

"I told you: Stanley confessed all."

"You should select someone who suits you, someone who could be your equal."

"I agree. I also think I should marry for love. Don't you?"

She scowled. "What?"

"I love you, Rose," he shocked her by declaring. "Tell me you love me too."

"What? You *love* me?"

"More than I can say. Please have me. Please tell me you'll be mine."

He leaned down and kissed the spot where their hands were joined, then he stood, and he was smiling, his affection washing over her like cool rain.

"If you refuse me," he continued, "if you force me to leave without you, the rest of my life won't be worth living."

"Oh, James..." she sighed.

"I couldn't go on without you. Don't make me."

He drew her to her feet, his beautiful blue eyes holding her rapt.

She remembered those wild, ecstatic days at Summerfield, when she'd peek around corners or stare out windows, hoping for a glimpse of him. She remembered those seductive, marvelous nights when he would sneak into her room, when he would cajole and entice her to wicked conduct.

She'd never been happier. She'd never felt more desired.

If she sent him on his way, what would happen to her? Could she cast herself out into the world to face the hard choices of a woman alone, of a woman in peril?

Though she hated to admit it, she wasn't really strong or independent. She'd always yearned for a family, for a place to belong. He was offering her everything she'd ever craved. A child. A husband. A home of her own.

"Swear to me that you mean it," she murmured.

"I swear on all that I am, on all that I will ever be."

"Swear to me that you'll always be glad you picked me."

"Rose, you silly goose. As if I could ever want anyone but you."

Suddenly, a knock sounded on the door. Evangeline called, "Rose, are you in there?"

James raised a questioning brow, and Rose said, "It's my friend, Evangeline."

He went over, unlocked the door, and pulled it open. On seeing that Rose was entertaining a gentleman, Evangeline blanched with astonishment.

"The cook heard you hollering," Evangeline explained to Rose. "She thought you might be having some trouble."

"I am James Talbot," James said to her. "The only trouble she's having is that I'm proposing marriage."

Evangeline gasped. "Marriage!"

"Yes," James replied. "She's having a baby, and I think she should say *yes,* don't you?"

"James," Rose scolded, "be quiet. You're embarrassing me."

"I won't let you wiggle out of this," he responded. "I'll shout the news to the rooftops if that's what it will take to convince you."

Evangeline studied Rose. "You're having a baby? Obviously, there's a large part of the story you didn't share with me."

"Obviously," James concurred.

Evangeline gazed up at him. "Do you love her?"

"More than my life."

"Have you a way to support her?"

"I've recently become a very rich man."

"My favorite kind." Evangeline laughed and peered over at Rose. "Do you love him too?"

"With all my heart."

"Is there some reason you're debating then?"

Rose delayed for a second, then a second more, absorbing every detail, eager to remember it all so—in the distant future—she would never forget any of it.

"No," she ultimately said, "I'm not debating." She smiled at James. "My answer is finally easy."

"And what is it?" he asked.

"Yes, James Talbot, I'll marry you. And considering what you just announced about my condition, I'd better do it as fast as I can."

"You'll never be sorry," he vowed.

"I know," she agreed, "and neither will you."

THE END

**Don't Miss the Second Novel in
Cheryl Holt's "Reluctant Brides"
Trilogy!**

WANTON

**The story of
Amelia Hubbard and Lucas Drake**

Coming in June, 2014!

CHAPTER ONE

"I'm here. I've arrived."

Feeling overwhelmed and a tad lost, Amelia Hubbard called out her announcement to the empty bedchamber. But she was alone, so there was no one to hear or reply.

She'd been given a grand, ostentatious suite—a sitting room, bedroom, and dressing room—located in a drafty, isolated wing of Sidwell Manor. A rented carriage had brought her to the estate, and after being deposited in the front drive, a maid had led her in and wound them through the quiet halls.

Her battered portmanteau was on the bed. It contained all of Amelia's worldly possessions, and it looked terribly shabby and much too threadbare to have been carried inside. The maid had offered to unpack it, but Amelia had declined any assistance.

She hadn't wanted the girl to see the pitiful condition of Amelia's clothes. Then again, with the plain gray dress she was currently wearing, her penury was obvious. The posh décor only highlighted the odd contradiction created by her presence.

At age twenty-five, she'd spent the prior two decades at Miss Peabody's School for Girls, first as a student, then as a teacher. She'd never precisely thought of herself as poor. She'd always had a roof over her head and food to eat. Once she'd become a teacher, she'd earned an income, too. It hadn't been much, but it had furnished a sense of independence and security.

Yet with her surroundings revealed, she couldn't help but be perturbed by her overt poverty. The stark disparity between her circumstances and that of her host unnerved her as nothing else had so far.

Hadn't she been anxious from the start? Hadn't she been disconcerted by the swiftness of events?

After a long and painful decline, Miss Peabody had died. Out of the blue, her attorney had visited to declare that the school would be shut down and sold, the students sent away. Amelia's teaching position had ended as abruptly as a snap of the fingers.

During Miss Peabody's last days, she'd told Amelia and the other two teachers—Rose Ralston and Evangeline Etherton—that she'd provided for them in her will. They'd naively and foolishly assumed they'd receive a monetary bequest, that they could pool their funds and buy the school themselves.

So it had come as a huge shock to learn that their inheritances weren't pecuniary at all. Miss Peabody had dowered them and arranged marriages to men they'd never met. She'd never wed or had children herself, and apparently, she'd regretted that fact and had wanted Amelia, Rose, and Evangeline to have a different option.

Amelia was an orphan with no prospects and no family except for her wayward brother, Chase. She'd never expected to wed, so it had never occurred to her that she'd have the option, but she'd reluctantly agreed to Miss Peabody's scheme.

With the school being closed, if Amelia hadn't accepted the fiancé Miss Peabody had selected, she'd have had no money and nowhere to go. Matrimony had suddenly been a very good choice, and she'd grudgingly journeyed off to her husband's home.

But now that she'd arrived...well...

Every part of the situation seemed wrong—as if there were factors in play of which she hadn't been apprised.

Her betrothed was Lucas Drake, of the Sidwell Drakes. The name hadn't meant anything to her and hadn't concerned her much until the carriage had passed through the gates and rumbled down the orchard-lined lane to the manor.

It was a three-story mansion, perfectly placed on a sloping hill so the occupants could gaze out at the thousands and thousands of acres of their land holdings.

Her prospective father-in-law, George Drake, was *Lord* Sidwell, an earl and peer of the realm. Why would such a lofty person pick lowly, ordinary, and very common Amelia Hubbard to marry one of his sons? How could Miss Peabody have crossed paths with such an eminent individual? How was she able to persuade him that Amelia was a suitable candidate to join the Drake family?

Amelia's mother had been a British actress, her father a French count. Supposedly, they'd been madly in love, but her father had already been married, so they couldn't have wed. When they'd passed away from the influenza, Amelia and Chase had been disavowed by their French relatives who'd promptly shuttled them off to English boarding schools and never taken an interest in them after that.

Amelia had no antecedents that would recommend her to Lord

Sidwell. The entire notion of her being welcomed into the wealthy, aristocratic family was bizarre and impossibly fantastic, like a princess in a fairytale.

None of it made any sense, and if she'd had the financial resources to leave, she'd have hurried back to the village to wait for the first mail coach that went by.

Not that she had a destination in mind. Miss Peabody's school was Amelia's sole connection to her past. Her friend and fellow teacher, Rose Ralston, had left for her own wedding. Her other friend, Evangeline Etherton, was completing the last few chores to prepare the school for the new owner, then she'd depart for her wedding, too.

Amelia was stuck at Sidwell, and she hoped Miss Peabody had arranged a viable conclusion. If it turned out to be awful, if it turned out to be some sort of trick or deception, Amelia didn't know what she'd do.

She'd probably have to travel to London to find her brother, Chase, but he was a shifty, shady character, and she had no idea how she'd locate him.

A clock chimed the half-hour, and Amelia jumped, realizing she'd been daydreaming when the most important interview of her life was about to occur.

For reasons that hadn't been explained, her fiancé was not yet on the premises. Lord Sidwell hadn't been present to greet her, either, but she'd been ordered to attend him promptly at four in his library. She was terrified about the appointment and didn't dare be late.

She rushed to the bed and dumped out the contents of her portmanteau. Briefly, she considered changing clothes, but she only owned three dresses—all of them a conservative gray with white collars and cuffs—so she had nothing more flattering or glamorous.

She went into the dressing room and assessed herself in the mirror. Her mother had been a great beauty, and Amelia had inherited her good looks: dark brunette hair, a slender, shapely figure. It wasn't vanity to admit she was pretty, so she thought Lord Sidwell would be pleased. But still, no amount of beauty could conceal her faded wardrobe or general air of poverty.

The trip to Sidwell had left her pale and weary. Her green eyes—usually so vibrant and merry—appeared haunted and afraid. She pinched her cheeks, trying to add a blush, but it didn't help, and she abandoned the effort.

She walked to the hall and started off.

When the maid had delivered Amelia to her suite, she'd offered to return to escort Amelia down to the library. Amelia had insisted she could manage on her own, but rapidly, she grew disoriented and became lost.

She was approaching a pair of double doors at the end of a hall, that most likely led into another grand suite, when she heard a woman moan—as if she was injured or ill.

Amelia halted, listened, heard the moan again.

She couldn't decide if she should intervene or not. The manor contained hundreds of rooms and several wings, and since Amelia had arrived, she hadn't stumbled on another soul. If someone was hurt, she was the only person available to render aid.

The noises were emanating from the room directly in front of her. If she barged in, it might be a huge *faux pas*, and she was anxious to make a good impression and couldn't commit a foolish act so early in her tenure. Yet if someone was in trouble, she couldn't ignore the situation.

The moan echoed a third time, louder and more desperate by the moment. Without giving herself opportunity to reflect, she spun the knob and peeked inside.

It was a masculine space, decorated with heavy mahogany furniture and dark maroon drapes and carpeting. The sitting room was empty, but there was movement in the bedchamber beyond. The door was ajar, and she caught fleeting glimpses of a man and woman who seemed to be wrestling. Was the woman being ravished?

Amelia's initial sense was to run out and summon assistance, but it would take forever to find a footman. In the interim, the woman could be seriously harmed, which Amelia couldn't allow.

She tiptoed to the fireplace and picked up the poker, worried that she might have to whack a miscreant on the head. Then she continued on to the bedroom door and peered through the crack. Only then did she realize that no assault was occurring

The man and woman were avidly kissing. The moans were coming from the woman, but they weren't cries of distress. They were cries of pleasure. Amelia was embarrassed to the marrow of her bones and weak with relief that she hadn't blustered in and humiliated herself.

The two lovers were so involved they hadn't noticed she was lurking and watching them. She needed to tiptoe out as quietly as she'd entered, and she had to do it quickly before they glanced over and saw her, but she couldn't force herself away.

She'd been enrolled at Miss Peabody's school when she was five, and even though she was now twenty-five, her upbringing had ensured she'd had very limited contact with men or amour.

She'd been kissed exactly three times, the episodes happening as an adolescent at the harvest fair. Those brief encounters had been thrilling, but also fraught with the danger of discovery. The embraces had been awkwardly groping and had proved so unsatisfying that Amelia had emerged from the experiences wondering what all the fuss was about.

As an adult, after she'd attained her position of teacher, she hadn't engaged in any further flirtations, and she hadn't witnessed any other people kissing, so she hadn't understood that it could be so wild and feral.

They were clawing and scratching, laughing and biting, waging a sort of carnal dance that was as exotic as it was fascinating.

She studied their attire, attempting to figure out who they were. The woman appeared to be a housemaid. She was wearing a plain black dress, a starched white apron tied around her waist, but the man made short work of it. He yanked on the apron's bow and tossed it away, then started in on the bodice of her dress, flicking at the buttons and pushing down the sleeves to reveal a spectacularly ample bosom.

"It's nice that some things never change around here," he said.

"I've been keeping them warm for you." The woman grabbed the shapely mounds as if offering them to him.

"You knew I'd be back?" he asked.

"Of course. You never can stay away."

Suddenly, a second female chimed in. "Stop hogging him. It's not fair."

"He always liked me best."

"He did not."

The second woman stepped in behind him, her face not visible, and Amelia could only presume she was observing another housemaid. She'd stripped down to just her petticoat, so her breasts were bared. They were smaller than the first woman's, but still rounded and full, the tips pink and sticking out as if proud to be on display. Amelia was transfixed by the sight.

At Miss Peabody's school, where there had been limited privacy and modesty expected at all times, Amelia had rarely seen her own bosom, let alone anyone else's, and the scene excited and disturbed her. She felt overheated, her pulse racing, her own nipples growing hard.

"You have too many clothes on," the newcomer told the man. "We must discard some of them."

"Gladly." He held out his arms as if he was at his tailor's and being measured for a suit.

Amelia switched her attention to him and was irked to admit that he was incredibly handsome. He had blond hair, the color of golden wheat, and he wore it too long so it brushed his shoulders as if he was a pirate or brigand.

His eyes were very blue, his face aristocratically formed with high forehead, strong nose and chin. His skin was bronzed from the sun as if he toiled out-of-doors to earn his living. Was he a deliveryman? Was he a tradesman from the village? Was Lord Sidwell aware that a man sneaked into the manor to cavort with the maids? Was he aware that his maids were slatterns?

Amelia's spirits flagged. What type of domicile had she entered? What type of family was she marrying into? If the maids could vanish in the middle of the afternoon without being missed, if they could disrobe and disport in an abandoned bedchamber, who was in charge?

It was shocking misbehavior, and now that Amelia had learned of it, what was her duty to her father-in-law? Should she tattle? Should she keep her mouth shut? If she spoke up, what can of worms would she be opening? She'd certainly make enemies of the staff, which could never be a benefit.

Lord Sidwell was a widower, so there was no Lady Sidwell to rule the large residence. Perhaps that was the problem: There was no mistress, so the servants were free to frolic and debauch.

When Amelia wed Lucas Drake, would she be placed in a role of authority over the servants? The notion didn't bear contemplating. With what she was currently witnessing, she had no desire to supervise such loose doxies. She'd have no idea how.

Inside the room, the man's shirt had been removed, and Amelia's consternation increased. She couldn't remember ever seeing a man's naked chest before, and she grew even more unsettled.

There was a matting of hair across the top, a shade darker than the golden hair on his head. It thinned to a straight line that ran down his flat, muscled belly and into his trousers.

As with his face, his torso was bronzed from the sun—as if he constantly strutted about unclad. The prospect was too thrilling to be believed.

She was inundated by an exhilaration she didn't understand. For a wild, crazed instant, she yearned to burst into the room, to demand the chance to rub her hands over all that exposed male flesh.

The two women had him wedged between them. Their upper bodies were bared now, so he had breasts pressed to front and back. He was grinning, preening, delighted by the sordid escapade.

The woman in front reached down and stroked him between his legs.

"My, my," she murmured, "you've missed us, haven't you?"

"Only every minute."

"How long has it been since you had any?"

"Three hours at least."

This statement appeared to be a private joke with them, and they all laughed.

"You always were a randy dog."

"And proud of it," he responded.

"Tell us we're more fun than any of your regular trollops."

"You're much more fun. It's no contest." He smirked. "Why do you think I always come back for more?"

Amelia continued to observe, mesmerized as their fervid kissing kicked up once more. At the same time, he was massaging her breasts, pinching her nipples in a way that had the woman moaning again.

"Hey, love," the other woman scolded, "give me a turn, will you? She can't have you all to herself."

"I apologize if I've been remiss," he said.

He spun and dipped down and—shocking Amelia to her very core—sucked a nipple into his mouth. He licked and bit at it, sending the woman into paroxysms of ecstasy, and she put a hand behind his head and pulled him closer, urging him to feast.

Amelia couldn't breathe, couldn't move.

Did adults truly behave so brazenly? Was it common? She had no idea.

From the strict religious and moral teachings she'd had over the years, she knew they were sinning hideously, yet she was as elated as they seemed to be. She couldn't stop watching, couldn't force herself away.

With each tug of his lips on that nipple, Amelia's own nipples ached and throbbed, her womb clenching, the secretive woman's spot between her legs growing warm and wet until she was shamefully aroused.

The man was becoming more amorous. He tipped his partner backward so she was draped over his arm. At the change of position, her features were finally visible.

It was the housemaid who'd initially escorted Amelia to her room! It was the housemaid who'd offered to unpack her bag! It was the housemaid who'd been assigned to attend Amelia during her stay! But considering what Amelia was witnessing, she couldn't imagine how she'd ever look the woman in the eye again. She'd be too embarrassed to acknowledge her or converse.

She gasped aloud—she couldn't help it—the fireplace poker sliding to the rug with a muted thud.

The ardent trio heard her, and they froze, scowling. Their momentary confusion gave Amelia the split second required to turn and run.

As she sprinted through the door, the man said, "Was there someone out there?"

"If there was," a maid replied, "they definitely got an eyeful."

Hilarious laughter rang out, but Amelia ignored it and kept on, dashing down the hall as if she was a madwoman.

Distractedly, she'd realized that she'd loitered too long and was late for her appointment with the earl, which was alarming.

In light of her disoriented state, how would she sit and chat? How would she pretend she was fine, that she was glad to have arrived? How would she answer questions, drink tea, and smile prettily?

The squalid scene was burned in her mind, and it seemed an ill omen. If this was her beginning, how would the rest of it go?

Amelia & Lucas
WANTON
Coming in June, 2014!

ABOUT THE AUTHOR

CHERYL HOLT is a *New York Times, USA Today,* and Amazon "Top 100" bestselling author of over thirty novels.

She's also a lawyer and mom, and at age forty, with two babies at home, she started a new career as a commercial fiction writer. She'd hoped to be a suspense novelist, but couldn't sell any of her manuscripts, so she ended up taking a detour into romance where she was stunned to discover that she has a knack for writing some of the world's greatest love stories.

Her books have been released to wide acclaim, and she has won or been nominated for many national awards. She has been hailed as "The Queen of Erotic Romance" as well as "The International Queen of Villains." She is particularly proud to have been named "Best Storyteller of the Year" by the trade magazine *Romantic Times* BOOK Reviews.

She lives and writes in Hollywood, California, and she loves to hear from fans. Visit her website at www.cherylholt.com.

Printed in Great Britain
by Amazon.co.uk, Ltd.,
Marston Gate.